The Hammon
and the Beans
and
Other Stories

Américo Paredes

with an introduction by
Ramón Saldívar

Arte Público Press
Houston, Texas
1994

This book is made possible through support from the National Endowment for the Arts (a federal agency), the Lila Wallace-Reader's Digest Fund and the Andrew W. Mellon Foundation.

Recovering the past, creating the future

Arte Público Press
University of Houston
452 Cullen Performance Hall
Houston, Texas 77204-2004

Cover design by Mark Piñón

Paredes, Américo.
   The Hammon and the Beans / by Américo Paredes.
     p.   cm.
   ISBN 1-55885-071-6 : $11.95
   1. Mexican Americans—Fiction. I. Title.
   PS3531.A525H36 1994
   813'.54-dc20   93-45644
                                                CIP
⊛ The paper used in this publication meets the requirements of the American National Standard for Permanence of Paper for Printed Library Materials Z39.48-1984.

2 3 4 5 6 7 8 9 0   10 9 8 7 6 5 4 3 2

Para mis hijos
Américo,
Alan,
Vicente—
Todos tres.

And for Frances Terry, coworker and
friend for a quarter century.

Contents

Introduction

Renowned as an ethnographer, literary critic, and social historian for well over thirty years of magisterial production, Américo Paredes stands today as one of the most respected of contemporary Chicano intellectuals and as the founder and virtually unparalleled practitioner of what has come to be known as Chicano Cultural Studies.[1] Honored in 1989 by the National Endowment for the Humanities as one of the initial recipients of the Charles Frankel Prize for lifelong contributions to the humanities, and in 1990 by the Republic of Mexico as one of the first Mexican American inductees to the Order of the Aztec Eagle, Mexico's highest award to non-citizens for the advancement of Mexican culture, Paredes's historical position is assured.

Paredes's fame rests on his foundational work of the 1950s and 60s on the ballads, legends, and everyday folklife of Mexican Americans and on his subsequent elaboration of that work during the seventies and eighties. His initial scholarly contribution from this early period, *'With His Pistol in His Hand': A Border Ballad and its Hero* (1958), is a masterful work of intellectual intervention decades ahead of its time. In an epoch when the intellectual modes dictated either an old historicism or a restrictive new critical formalism, *'With His Pistol in His Hand'* went emphatically against the grain of the accepted analytical methods of the day. Combining literary, sociological, ethnographic, and historical analysis of traditional border ballads— *corridos*—it offered, as José David Saldívar has claimed, a stinging rebuttal and a devastating "deconstruction of [the] established [white supremacist] authority and hierarchies"[2] that operated as the common wisdom and official histories of the relations between Anglos and Mexicans in Texas and the rest of the West and Southwest. Moreover, Richard Bauman notes in his "Introduction" to a newly published collection of Paredes's essays that Paredes "has produced the most important and influential scholarship of our generation on the folklore of Greater Mexico in general and of the Lower Border in particular."[3] Before Paredes, the cultural politics of Texas and the Southwest were virtually the singular product of the Anglo American imagination, responding exclusively to the hegemony of Anglo American material interests. But as Michel Foucault claims, "Where there is power, there is resistance."[4] After Paredes, with the publication of his exemplary scholarly work, the cultural politics of the region began to be re-cast in the decidedly different mold of transculturalism, reflecting the true, multicultural realities of the American social world.

Among his most recently published works, a novel, *George Washington Gómez* (1990), and a book of poetry, *Between Two Worlds* (1991), have added yet another, literary, dimension to the imposing array of Paredes's contestational work in the historical, ethnographic, and theoretical realms. These imaginative works address the predicaments of contemporary Chicano/a cultural politics, identity formation, and social transformation. Given the contemporaneous nature of their concerns, it is interesting to learn that the literary works are not contemporary pieces at all, nor even products of the fifties and sixties. They are instead works from the thirties and forties, period decades before that of Paredes's groundbreaking scholarly work. As products of an era and of literary formations other than those enjoying current vogue, the literary texts belie their postmodern, post-Chicano Movement thematics and publication dates.

Composed for the most part during the Depression and World War II years in the Texas-Mexican borderlands of deep South Texas, the novel and the poetry anticipate with great imaginative force the sophisticated insight of Paredes's later exemplary trans-disciplinary work of social criticism and cultural intervention. Moreover, they prefigure crucial aspects of the growing body of postmodern Chicano writing and cultural studies from a high modernist, pre-movement historical moment. Paredes's literary texts offer a striking confirmation of Adorno's notion that "Modernity is a qualitative, not a chronological, category."[5]

Together with the later scholarly work, the novel and the poetry can now be seen as a part of larger imaginative project to invent a figural discourse of transnational epic proportions appropriate to the construction of a new narrative of a modern American social and cultural history. For Paredes, this new, pan-American history is not limited by the imaginary geopolitical borderlines and symbolic security checkpoints, or customs and immigration offices, but extends beyond these to include cultures and peoples that traverse national boundaries and inhabit the fluid borderlands of culture.

The new Mexican American consciousness that Paredes decisively underwrites in his novel and poetry, a consciousness that resides in the cognitive, social, and political-economic space "between two worlds" and that speaks a bicultural tongue, also emerges triumphantly in the present collection of short stories. The narrative voices of *The Hammon and the Beans and Other Stories* contest other official discourses for the authority to assign different meanings and different directions to everyday Mexican American reality. And while contesting the unqualified racism of Anglo American representations of that reality, they simultaneously resist the tendencies of both the progressivist modernity of New Deal rhetoric and the assimilative, pluralistic ideology of other Mexican American reformers of the day.[6] Paredes's stories strike out in a singularly different direction, anticipating analytical formations and discursive strategies that lay decades in the future.

Like Antonio Gramsci, a contemporaneous philosopher of working class culture, Paredes already in the thirties and forties had grasped the notion that, in Edward Said's phrase, "culture serves authority, and ultimately the national State, not because it represses and coerces but because it is affirmative, positive, and persuasive."[7] Unlike J. Frank Dobie, Walter Prescott Webb, and other official state intellectuals of the day who in their mythopoeic renderings of the American West and Southwest sought to legitimize one particular vision of American culture, and unlike even oppositional Mexican American writers who sought to

Introduction

pluralize that legitimacy, Paredes sought instead precisely to *de*-legitimize it by showing the production of a modern American "nation-space" in process, *in medias res*, half-made, "caught in the act of 'composing' its powerful image"[8] on a regional and global scale, and whose modernity was liable to a critical reproduction. In another context, Homi Bhabha has noted that:

> The marginal or "minority" is not the space of a celebratory, or utopian, self-marginalization. It is a much more substantial intervention into those justifications of modernity—progress, homogeneity, cultural organicism, the deep nation, the long past—that rationalize the authoritarian, "normalizing" tendencies within cultures in the name of the national interest or ethnic prerogative. In this sense, then, the ambivalent, antagonistic perspective of nation as narration will establish the cultural boundaries of the nation so that they may be acknowledged as "containing" thresholds of meaning that must be crossed, erased, and translated in the process of cultural production.[9]

As we shall now see, it is precisely these cultural boundaries and epistemological crossings, the border checkpoints of cultural production, that Paredes crosses and translates in many of the finest short stories of the present collection. His interventions into the ideological justifications of American modernity make powerful additions to the ongoing critical revision of the heretofore unquestioned prerogatives of the entire narrative of American cultural nationalism.

and Other Stories

Ramón Saldívar

Paredes's first stories are set, significantly, in his home region, the South Texas border country. In that region, by the mid-1930s when Paredes began to write his fictions, many of what had been for generations small, family-owned, or family-tenanted farms and ranches, held and worked in common, were now being taken over by large, corporate, agribusiness interests, organizing production for a newly developing competitive global market.[10] In the process of this shift from family to corporate relations of production, Mexican Americans were increasingly being displaced onto smaller and smaller parcels of land which they worked primarily through contract sharecropping, thus "ensuring the availability of cheap resident labor throughout the year."[11] Already in the late 1910s, however, with the coming of new irrigation and large-scale farming technologies, ranch land bought cheaply from native Texas Mexicans (*Tejanos*) was being "resold dearly as farmland—all on the basis of water."[12] As Anglo investors, speculators, and settlers arrived in large numbers into the South Texas region in a land speculation boom that changed the cultural and ethnic character of the region from Mexican to Anglo American, even sharecropping became increasingly economically unfeasible for white landowners, as they could make more money by hiring Mexicans as wage laborers than by leasing to them. Especially at harvest times, agricultural work now came to be handled by a migratory work force that was itself controlled, as Montejano points out, by various economic and legal means (i.e., wage-fixing, mobility restrictions, vagrancy laws, etc.). These labor controls amounted to a program

The Hammon and the Beans

Introduction

of labor repression and legalized discrimination. In the face of this growing oppression and overt deterritorialization, many *Tejanos* sought ways of expressing their frustration and outrage. James A. Sandos has shown how the anarchist politics that were influencing sectors of the contemporary revolutionary movement in Mexico and were being heard in the U.S. through radical media outlets such as Ricardo Flores Magon's revolutionary newspaper, *Regeneración*, offered for some natives of the South Texas region a strategy of resistance to the unjust displacements and outright oppression to which they were subject.[13] Floresmagonista anarchist thought was disseminated throughout the region and "became progressively more militant about the need for direct action to redress the wrongs done to Mexicans and Tejanos on both sides of the river."[14] The anarchist program of "direct action" (a code phrase for revolutionary praxis) came to mean for some Texas Mexican sympathizers of Mexican anarchist revolutionary thought the reclaiming of the land Mexico lost between 1836 and 1848 by staging an armed uprising against the United States.

By late 1914 conditions seemed ready for this sort of "direct action." In January 1915, a tiny group of Floresmagonistas based in San Diego, Texas, a small, border ranching community in Duval County in South Texas, scripted a plan for action. Following the dictates of this manifesto, the revolutionary Plan of San Diego, a proclamation outlining the structure and strategy for revolutionary direct action in support of social justice, a plot for a full-blown rebellion against American imperial domination of former Mexican territories was set in motion. According to the broadsides announcing the manifesto, Plan supporters, marching under a red banner, would reclaim all of the former Mexican territories now comprising the American West and Southwest and proclaim a multi-ethnic, social revolutionary Border Republic. Its political and social agenda clear, the Plan offered membership only to "the Latin, the Negro, or the Japanese race."[15] Moreover, American Indians were offered a promise that "their ancestral territory would be restored to them in return for their support."[16] In a later revision, the revolutionary cast of the Plan became even more pronounced as it now called for a complete social revolution, "decried the exploitation of land and labor by whites and denounced their racist discrimination against people of color."[17] Finally, the Plan pronounced the establishment of "the Social Republic of Texas."[18]

Following the principles outlined in this anarchist-inspired, ideally conceived blueprint for revolution, armed Mexican irregulars crossed the Rio Grande on July 4, 1915, and attacked Anglo ranches, burned railroad bridges, cut telegrah wires, and killed several Americans. Reprisals followed quickly, and over the next two years Texas Rangers and other law enforcement agenies set out with vigor to obliterate the rebellion by putting into final effect "the long-standing Ranger practice of ridding [the] area of Mexican 'undesirables.'"[19] As one contemporary Anglo Texan observer put it:

A Ranger can shoot a poor peon with impunity, and he is scarcely even asked to put in the usual plea of self-defense, which is as a general rule an untrue one anyway. No race, however ignorant or downtrodden, is going to submit to this for long without feeling an

Introduction

overwhelming sentiment, not only against the Rangers themselves, but against the race from which they come.[20]

Valley residents coined a new word—"rangering"—to describe the summary execution of Mexican Americans suspected of participating in, or even sympathizing with, the rebellion.[21] Long-standing racial antagonism vented in vigilante tactics and arbitrary action on the part of the Rangers in the Brownsville vicinity alone led to the killing of as many as 300 Mexican Americans, "many in 'cold blood.'"[22] Instead of inspiring fear, however, the bloody Texas Ranger terror provoked anger and retaliation on the part of Floresmagonista sympathizers like Tejanos Luis De la Rosa, a former deputy sheriff of Cameron County, and Aniceto Pizaña, a respected rancher from the Brownsville, Texas, vicinity.[23] Over the next year, De la Rosa and Pizaña, subscribers to the anarchist newspaper *Regeneración* and adherents to the Plan of San Diego, attacked the implements of the Anglo Texan modern system of production: their ranches, irrigation pumping stations, railroad trains and depots, and automobiles. Using guerrilla tactics, they burned bridges and railroad trestles, cut telegraph and telephone wires, and ambushed Ranger and U.S. Army patrols, and even struck "the major symbol of Anglo domination, the enormous King Ranch."[24] The seditionists, as they came to be called in a contemporary *corrido* about the rebellion,[25] performed what they conceived as acts of war, intending to reclaim land taken from Mexico by the United States, reject the changes wrought by the Anglo capitalist mode of production in the Rio Grande Valley, and establish a new Border Republic. The upshot of revolutionary action was that "by the fall of 1915, South Texas was on the verge of a race war," as an Anglo "backlash of massive proportions" created a reign of terror aimed at virtually eliminating the Mexican American population in general from South Texas.[26]

The titular story of Paredes's collection, "The Hammon and the Beans," and a number of the following stories involve precisely the Plan of San Diego, its revolutionary creed, and the racial hatred and tension that has persisted to the present in South Texas in the aftermath of the bitter fighting, the "border troubles" of 1915 to 1917. In Paredes we are not immediately concerned with that revolutionary struggle. Instead, the focus is on the effects of struggle and on the end of the heroic past of Mexican American armed resistance to Anglo American hegemony. Paredes's stories look forward to the beginning of a new stage of Mexican American resistance to Anglo American control of the Southwest in the realm of culture and ideology. The stories represent brilliantly the difficult dialogue between a Mexican past and an American future for Texas Mexicans living on the border at the margin of modernity and modernization.

The immediate past is represented by the Plan of San Diego Rebellion of 1915-1917. With its links to the Mexican Revolution, international anarchism, socialism, and the heroic resistance struggle of the Flores Magón brothers, the rebellion represents the phase of "direct action," now part of the legendary past. The future is represented in the stories by the troubled chil-

Introduction

dren who must cross the ever-present border between their parents' Mexican past and an as yet unspecified American future. Squeezed between what has been and what might be, between necessity and freedom, this represented present often seems retrospectively to the narrators of the stories as moments of mere pathos and diminished possibility.

"The Hammon and the Beans" is set in the Lower Rio Grande Valley of South Texas, the region of the most intense border conflict.[27] Paredes's first-person narrator recreates the mood of life on the border in the first two decades of the twentieth century, a historical moment when the heroic resistance of men like the *corrido* hero, Greg⊃rio Cortez, and even of the Plan of San Diego revolutionaries, Luis de la Rosa and Aniceto Pizaña, is already fading into the hazy, and unhistoricized, past. Brownsville, Texas, Paredes's hometown, is depicted in the story as "Jonesville-on-the-Grande," a place of diminished heroic quality and with all the feel of a town suffering under occupation by a victorious foreign army. The narrator reminds us that "It was because of the border troubles, ten years or so before, that the soldiers had come back to Fort Jones".

In the wake of the border troubles, "Fort Jones" serves in the story as a metaphor for the paternal presence of the occupying army, and as a literal reminder of the power behind that presence. With that power comes the prerogative to write history. The "high wire fence that divided the post from the town" is an objective correlative of the political and cultural distance that separates the occupying army from the Mexican American citizens of Jonesville. "[W]e stuck out our tongues and jeered at the soldiers," continues the narrator. "Perhaps the night before we had hung at the edges of a group of old men and listened to tales about Aniceto Pizaña and the 'border troubles'." However, the oral histories told by the old men must compete for the children's allegiance with other official histories of revolutionary resistance that the children are learning from their books in their American schools: stories not about the Plan of San Diego but "about George Washington...and Marion the Fox and the British cavalry that chased him up and down the broad Santee."

In his "Theses on the Philosophy of History," Walter Benjamin argued that "To articulate the past historically does not mean to recognize it 'the way it really was' (Ranke). It means to seize hold of a memory as it flashes up at a moment of danger.... Only that historian will have the gift of fanning the spark of hope in the past who is firmly convinced that even the dead will not be safe from the enemy if he wins."[28] Paredes is here seizing just such a moment of historical memory as it flashes in a moment of danger, the danger of cultural eradication, by concretizing it in the reality of regional local space. Already, even the dead are not safe from this enemy as the social history of the region is obliterated from the narrative of American history. (Indeed, by the time I was growing up in Brownsville in the sixties, all mention of Mexican American resistance had been erased from our Texas history lessons.) In ideological terms, what the scene of everyday life offers is an ongoing dramatization of the conflicts between the residual elements of the child's traditional community and ideals and forces of the newly dominant American culture, a conflict being fought for the hearts and minds of the Mexican American children. That ideological power struggle, as seen through the eyes of the child-narrator and the outcome of which is already painfully obvious, is precisely what the story is about: "And so we lived, we and the post, side by side with the wire fence in between."

The separation between the two is not as inviolable as the initial scenes of the story lead us to believe. While "none of us ever went to Fort Jones," there is one child who does, "a scrawny girl of about nine," named "Chonita." Every evening Chonita would enter the forbidden grounds "to the mess halls and [press] her nose against the screens and [watch] the soldiers eat." The daughter of impoverished working class people who live in a one-room shack provided to them at no cost by the narrator's parents, Chonita is not only more daring than her playmates, she "was a poet too." Every evening she would return from her forays into the fort with the left-overs from the soldiers' meals for her family and with imitations for her friends' amusement of the soldiers "calling to each other through food-stuffed mouths": "'Give me the hammon and the beans!' she yelled. 'Give me the hammon and the beans!'."

Her mimicry and her daring are the instruments of her poetry. The other children, the narrator's friends, to egg her on pretend that Chonita "could talk English better than the teachers at the grammar school." The narrator finds it a very bad joke to tease the poor, ignorant little girl, but loses track of her and her escapades when he is suddenly taken ill.

On the evening of Chonita's death, we learn that her real father had been "shot and hanged from a mesquite limb" for working too close to the tracks the day the "Olmito train was derailed." The reference to Plan of San Diego action identifies Chonita's father as one of the victims of the Texas Ranger terror following the rebellion. In bed, away from adult conversations that he has been overhearing, the boy drowsily muses over what he has heard and only half understood concerning the heroic acts of men who lived and died before he was born. As his mind drifts among contradictory thoughts, all of a sudden he hears "the cold voice of the [post] bugle [that] went gliding in and out of the dark like something that couldn't find its way back to wherever it had been." The stark loneliness of the bugle's homeless notes bring him back to poor Chonita, who according to his mother is now "happy... in Heaven":

> I thought of Chonita in Heaven, and I saw her in her torn and dirty dress, with a pair of bright wings attached, flying round and round like a butterfly shouting, "Give me the hammon and the beans!"

In another age, the fragile, malnourished "butterfly" might have found life not in a deferred vision of a plentiful afterlife, nor by begging scraps from the army kitchens, but in radical politics or collective action, demanding social justice on the picket lines with her oppressed sisters and brothers. "In later years I thought of [Chonita] a lot, especially during the thirties when I was growing up. Those years would have been just made for her. Many's the time I have seen her in my mind's eye, in the picket lines demanding not bread, not cake, but the hammon and the beans," says the narrator. Her poetry might have been real rather than mimicry. "But it didn't work out that way," he admits. The heroic age of direct action "with pistols in hand" seems distant from present reality. Envisioned in the

Introduction

narrator's imagination as a forerunner of Paredes's own childhood heroine, the great Depression Era labor organizer and secretary of the Communist Party of Texas, Emma Tenayuca, Chonita represents the noble possibility of revolutionary social action, deferred. But since it is deferred, there can thus be no falsely victorious ending to the story, as the narrator in later life fully realizes. His night of mourning for Chonita is the source of his memorial to her: the story of her brief life of poverty. That written monument is one that might initiate the conditions for a reawakening of the spirit of direct action and which might eliminate the possibility of other little girls having to suffer Chonita's fate. The text of the story thus becomes, like the *corridos* the narrator overhears, an occasion for the expression of a symbolic solution to the determinate contradictions of history.

The other selection previously published, "Over the Waves is Out," deals with the intersection of generational conflict, the value of the aesthetic, and the formation of the modern American nation in the borderlands after the Plan of San Diego uprising of 1915. A young boy mysteriously hears music in the night and imagines it to be a sign from the muses that he has been elected to be one of the precious few in his rude surroundings on the Texas Mexican border called to their seductive melody. Instead, we learn that the boy has been hearing the noise from one of the newfangled contraptions that have recently begun to invade the borderlands: a radio playing in a nearby bakery. When a disgruntled accordion player willfully destroys the radio by blasting it with his shotgun, destroying it in the spirit of the original *saboteurs*, the young boy is left to reconcile his lost status as one of the aesthetic elect with his pathetic insight that the arts of musical production and reproduction are as liable to the vagaries of mechanical actions as are the relationships between fathers and sons liable to misunderstanding.

As in the first story, the decline of the heroic age of direct action and revolutionary resistance is again the subject here. But while in "The Hammon and the Beans" the narrator's recognition of that decline is linked to the pathos of a child's death, in "Over the Waves is Out" the recognition of the end of the historical moment of direct action with pistols in hand is comic and almost bathetic. As in the first story, the insight to the reduced nature of present reality comes indirectly, from the discrepancies between what the narrator describes, what he hears, and what he later comes to understand. But also as in the first story, the understanding that comes with that view of the past does not preclude the possibility of future victories in the conflict between oppressors and oppressed. It does, however, admit to the necessity of its deferral to other times and other methods.

The degeneration of the heroic revolutionary past is here subtly allayed by Deputy De la Garza's declining age and by his son's intoxication with the sensuality of music. In both cases one senses a certain diminishing of the potential for heroic behavior; and yet, the narrator's gentle irony serves not so much to undercut the protagonists as to express their ambiguous position between two ages and two cultures. Their partial illusions as well as their partial insights about each other serve as critiques of their self-assured visions of themselves and the other. For the father, his rediscovery of his past musical consciousness opens the possibility of a reconciliation with the self that his own father denied

Introduction

him and with the son whom he has perhaps misapprised. For the boy, the seductive power of music survives only while the force of his illusions is strongest, hence his feelings of sadness, age, and solitude at the story's end. But this sense of sadness, age, and solitude might also allow him to participate in his father's history, viewing it now not as the irrelevant songs and tales of nostalgic old men, but as the substance of his own fate.

Significantly absent from this male interchange are all of the women of the family. And yet, in depicting the contradictory truths of patriarchal consciousness, Paredes's story offers unconsciously an image, albeit as a negative truth, of feminist consciousness. The consolidation of male solidarity, with the acceptance of the heterogeneity of male affective response, seems necessarily to entail driving to the margins of narrative any women's presence. Paredes's story shows how oppositional Chicano narrative attains hegemonic patriarchal force by repressing its feminine consciousness.

The next selection, "Macaria's Daughter," composed about 1943 and like the remainder of the stories in the collection published here for the first time, is perhaps the most gripping of these stories, as it attempts to imagine a social revolution tied not to anarchist direct action, nor to cultural or symbolic action, but to the gender and feminine consciousness not represented in the other fictions. The story tells a tale, woefully familiar enough, of the murder of a young Mexican American woman (who "looked like Hedy Lamar") by her singularly unappealing husband. But what separates Paredes's treatment of this plot is the bitter irony that allows readers to view through a dense, multiply-temporal, complex narrative frame, simultaneously the young wife's naively ambiguous desires and her husband's mounting murderous desperation. Marcela, the young wife, has been constructed by her mother's identity (Marcela is known as "Macaria's daughter"), by her mixed Anglo-Mexican blood (her father is an Anglo door to door drummer), by her resemblance to figures of the Hollywood silver screen, and even more powerfully by the limitations enforced upon Mexican and American women by harsh and merciless patriarchal cultures. In the tableau-like ending of the story, a plaster image of the Virgin of Guadalupe with "its brown Indian face" stares down upon the murdered woman from the altar in a corner of their shabby shack. The young wife's mutilated body becomes an extension of the symbology of women's victimization and an abject mark of the terrible power of abstract male ideology. Even though the young husband *would* not, he feels the community's unvoiced ethical imperative that he *must* kill her in order "to keep being a man." Frida Kahlo's approximately contemporaneous painting, "Unos Cuantos Piquetitos!" ["A Few Small Nips"] (1935), depicting not the symbology but the reality of male terror and woman's blood, might well serve as emblem to "Macaria's Daughter". Kahlo's painting was inspired, in part, by Guadalupe Posada's turn of the century illustrations of gruesome murders and ghastly accidents and by a contemporary newspaper account of a brutal murder of a woman by her husband.[29] The poly-temporal vividness of Paredes's narrative similarly echoes Kahlo's indictment of male pornographic fantasies, linking violence and female sexuality in disturbing imagery drawn from the popular imagination. The difference, however, is that in Paredes the callousness of Kahlo's perpetrator is displaced partially from the husband onto the Anglo policemen who see Marcela's exposed, torn body and reflect on its sensual beaty. In both Kahlo and Paredes, to be sure, the issue is the shocking brutality of male power suavely condoned, indeed compelled, by traditional community values.

"A Cold Night," also set in the early 1940's, is one of a group of Paredes's stories entitled *Border Country* that were submitted to and won first prize in a contest sponsored by the *Dallas Times Herald* in 1952. "The judges declared it the best story submitted though the same collection included 'The Hammon and the Beans' and 'Over the Waves Is Out.'"[30] It focuses on a child and another scene of death. Neither his father, a day laborer working to remove stumps from the cleared chaparral to prepare new farmland, nor his mother, whose face "reminded him of the face of the Virgin of Guadalupe," understand why the child is one day suddenly afraid to say the "Avemaría" ("Now and at the hour of our death. Amen"). Having secretly witnessed the brutal beating to death of a man in an alley behind the church, the boy is so disturbed by the merciless violence he has witnessed that he is now also completely repulsed by and can only express his hatred of God, who blithely allows such violence to exist. "Terrified by the thought that at any moment he could become a corpse like the man in the alley," he is not comforted by his mother's advise that he "Just love God." He continues to carry an amulet of the Virgin of Guadalupe, whom he prefers to the white-skinned Virgin Mary because of her "nice familiar Indian face...beautiful... all-embracing, all-forgiving." However, in contrast to the serenity associated with the Indian Virgin, "Christ [who]...writhed bloodily on his cross" with a "bloody head and wounded side," is now too much like

Ramón Saldívar

the man killed in the alley to bolster faith and provide comfort. In a scene reminiscent of Tomás Rivera's short story, "Y no se lo tragó la tierra"[31] but in fact anticipating it by twenty years, the boy systematically curses God and all the saints, and is struck not by divine retribution buy by "the supreme meanness of it all." Left now without transcendental stays to authenticate his being, the child hears only the wind eerily calling his name ("Ramón. Ramón. Ramón.") and imagines it to be "the lonesomest sound" he has ever heard. But as in Rivera, the celestial solitude and universal loss the child feels at story's end is surmounted by a sense of cold determination that might well serve as the ground for a more substantial base for a materially performative authentication of identity.

"The Gringo," written in late 1952 and early 1953, is the most recent of the stories included here. A vignette of historical romance, it takes us back to the opening days of the U.S.- Mexican War. In February 1846, after Texas had sought annexation into the United States, General Zachary Taylor led part of his forces into the disputed trans-Nueces area of South Texas, north of the Rio Grande. Claimed by both the Republic of Texas and Mexico after the Texas War of Independence in 1836, the South Texas region had remained culturally Mexican during that ten-year period, even if geopolitically indeterminate. Taylor's move southward to the Rio Grande was tantamount to an act of war and was matched by the northward movement of a Mexican force led by General Pedro Ampudia to Matamoros, Mexico, across the river from Brownsville.[32]

The titular "Gringo" of the story is a fair-skinned, blue-eyed Texas Mexican boy caught in the midst of these historical events. His story thus partakes in the narrative of nineteenth century American national formation as Paredes situates us within the developing discourses of region, nation, and political community. Having been wounded by real *gringos* in an earlier ambush south of the Nueces, his father and brothers killed while he is spared when mistaken for one of the Americans because of his white skin, "the Gringo" (named Ygnacio) is nursed back to health by the daughter of one of the Americans. When he comes to and attempts to speak to her, she warns him not to as she has already divined the truth of his racial identity and understands that a certain lynching will follow the revelation. The young woman, appropriately named Prudence, tends Ygnacio's wounds, attempts to teach him English, and even tries to convince her father that Ygnacio is "white" and can thus be taught to be "a real Christian." Plainly, his cultural and linguistic contamination as a Spanish-speaking Mexican, not his skin color, are the source of the Americans' hatred. Paredes is here interested in the dynamics of American racism, motivated at times on the basis of racial phenotypes that are never absolutely clear and distinct, while at others on sociocultural factors that try the boundary between what is acquired and what is essential. On the border, racism was but one form of prejudice; religion, class, language and other cultural gestures, were others. The indeterminacy of racist attitudes aside, however, the fact remains that such distinctions are made and acted upon. Thus, at a hint that a romantic attachment between the daughter and Ygnacio might be forming, the Mexican "Gringo" is quickly transformed in the father's eyes into just another "greaser," fair skin or no. With Prudence's help, Ygnacio manages to escape across the Rio Grande.

In Matamoros, wearing identifiably American clothes and boots, and armed with the brace of "horse pistols" given to him by the American woman, "the Gringo" is taken for an American spy, especially when he warns about the might of Taylor's armed force. Intending to recruit irregular (guerrilla) forces to aid Ampudia and his poorly equipped troops in their coming fight with Taylor's invading army of real Gringos, Ygnacio cautions that "Our only hope is if our rancheros fight them the way we know how. In guerrillas." Ygnacio surmises that by maneuvering around the American army deftly, hitting and running to hit again, Indian-style, they just might check the firepower of the Americans' guns. But just as his cultural and linguistic traits set him at odds against the Americans, his fair features mark him for suspicion among the Mexicans. Setting an ambush for a patrolling U.S. Cavalry unit, Ygnacio is finally goaded to prove his Mexican allegiance. When the American patrol stops short of the ambush, Ygnacio impetuously rides toward their position, hailing the Americans, attempting to lure them into the trap, only to be given away again by his own speech: "Thees way, boyss!" It is May 8, 1846, at Palo Alto, Texas, the date and site of the first major encounter between American and Mexican armed forces during the U.S.-Mexican War.[33] When his old-fashioned horse pistols misfire, "the Gringo" unsheathes his machete and charges an American officer who calmly awaits him with drawn pistol. Facing the new American technology of war, a rapid-firing revolver, "the Gringo" rides head-long into history as "the guns of Palo Alto went off inside his head."

Some of the stories, like "A Small Brown Bird," done

in Japan about 1949, turn away from the specificity of South Texas history and return instead to one of the ongoing motifs of the story collection, namely the pathos of enforcing and enacting the macho role of manhood. This motif is especially the subject of the next story of the collection, "Revenge," but on an entirely different register.[34] Here, Anastasio, a country boy affecting the city style, seeks revenge for the killing of his brother. However, word arrives with the figure of his hard-edged country cousin, Apolinar, that Anastasio has already dawdled too long, for the killer has himself been done in by one of the pathetic tragedies of everyday modern life: he has been run over by an automobile! Apolinar subtly goads the increasingly reluctant Anastasio into upholding his suddenly disputable reputation as a *"macho"* with *"huevos,"* as someone "Bigger and stronger and meaner than anybody else," by reminding him that he has sworn to laugh over the dead man's grave.

As in "Macaria's Daughter" where the husband feels compelled to kill in order "to keep being a man," Anastasio's fate too has been plotted for him by the discourses of Mexican masculinity. Norman Mailer claims that there is no injunction more mysterious than "to be a man." With the heightened sensibility of near paralyzing fear, Anastasio feels the indeterminate mystery of that injunction as he walks laggardly through the hot, dusty streets of Jonesville to the dead man's house, as if toward his own funeral. Finally, cowed more by Apolinar's merciless glance and taunting gestures than by the presence of his enemy's family, Anastasio does indeed bring himself to laugh over the coffin. But in a startling development, the dead man's father overhears the laugh, takes it for a heartfelt sob of loving grief, and compels Anastasio to join in the funeral cortege and attend the burial ceremony! All the other toughs in the town, lining the route of the cortege, present to mediate the enactment of revenge and adjudicate the privilege of masculinity, now are treated to the grotesque sight of Anastasio in the ludicrous position of mourning his declared enemy. His laugh taken for a sob, and hence linked to the wailing cries and moans of the women who truly grieve for his enemy, Anastasio is pressed into the feminine social space of grieving. From the perspective of the hierarchized patriarchy, Anastasio is no less than completely undone as a macho. Apolinar, subtle ironist and master of coercion, having surely anticipated the limits of Anastasio's masculinist pose all along, is the interesting figure here, as he witnesses the scene from aside, critically projecting the limits of masculinity and its perversely performative pathos.

Modernity is again the backdrop to the next story, "Brothers."[35] The unlikely "brothers" are a German immigrant boy, Fred, and Arturo, a Mexican American native of Jonesville. According to the boys' teacher, Fred's grandfather left Germany after "the Great War" "to stand up for freedom and justice for all. For the brotherhood of man." At the beach one day, playing cowboys in the "language of the movies," Arturo's Spanish-accented English marks him, but so does Fred's German-accented one. Linguistic quirks aside, the two are consummately linked in child's play as they mimic with refined skill the cowboys-and-robbers romance scenarios provided by Hollywood. The silver-screen medium provides access to a mimetic brotherhood that seems capable of transcending real historical and ethnic differences. However, that illusion is sorely tested by the hypocrisy of Fred's father when "the little white

Introduction

boy and his dark-skinned playmate" ask him whether, since the apparent homonyms, Spanish *ya* and German *ja*, both denote "yes," it is possible in German to say *sí* and mean *ja*. For if such linguistic relations are possible, and since as Fred's father says, "all men are brothers" and "at bottom speak the same language," then as the boys reason, they might turn out "to be related," and brothers in truth. The German father looks at the Mexican American boy and dismisses the preposterous thought, acidly ordering his son to return to his side of the wire fence separating the Mexican and Anglo sections of the beach.

The next selection, "Rebeca," written in Japan between 1948 and 1950, describes two distinct time periods: an early one, depicting an almost idyllic epoch of rural, pre-modern life, on the banks of the Rio Grande, and a later one, representing the rhythms of modern urban space in Jonesville. In the rural scenes, we learn that the eponymous Rebeca, youngest daughter of Don José María Chapa and Doña Cenobia Chapa, is a model daughter and an excellent cook, to boot. Anticipating the sentimental plot of Laura Esquivel's *Like Water for Chocolate* by forty-plus years, Paredes tells us that "the kitchen was her joy, her work of art." As it does for the characters in Esquivel's domestic idyll, Rebeca's serenity comes from a near-total identification with her gendered role of culinary laborer: "Everyone praised her *asado de puerco*. Her *frijoles rancheros* had just the right amount of cilantro. Her *tortillas de harina* were a marvel; her *buñuelos* melted in your mouth. And her way with north Mexican tamales, slender and delicate, was incredible." But her joy as a food producer is blunted by the conditions of her work. While her sisters labor five days a week, from breakfast through before supper doing the general housekeeping, Rebeca works seven days a week, from five in the morning when she makes her father's coffee, until bedtime, after she washes the dishes and prepares for the next day's meals in order to keep everyone happily fed: "she...realized that her beloved kitchen was also her prison." To escape this prison, she dreams of a little house "where she would be the mistress."

That romantic dream of love with a dark, Rudolph Valentino-like countryman named Chano Quintana and the compromised pastoral that it represents ends when Rebeca is pressured by the lure of city life and modern ways into marrying "a pink-faced young man" from the city, Alberto Medrano. Escaping the prison of her country kitchen, Rebeca finds herself in the prison of urban matrimony. In marriage Beto proves cruel, hard to please, and even brutal to their children, so that over the years Rebeca "yearned for the old days at her father's ranch." Now, in the story's present, with her children grown and her gastronomic magic no longer producing the delight it once did, Rebeca has taken up yet another oral means of sublimating her desires and filling her emptiness, by smoking two packs of cigarettes daily. With illusions of romance and serenity completely dispelled, Rebeca is diagnosed to be suffering from terminal lung cancer. But the new serenity she finds in contemplating her own death eludes her when she learns that she is not dying after all. Crushed by the prospect of what others take to be her miraculous good fortune, in the end Rebeca takes up her cigarettes again, to tempt her fate, to provoke an untimely rupture of the imprisoning routine of wife and mother, to fill her emptiness, or perhaps simply to annoy her husband.

Introduction

The remaining seven selections take us from the geographical, if not the social, space of early twentieth-century South Texas and into the World War II Pacific theater of operations and the opening days of the Korean War. In these selections, the issues remain as in the Jonesville South Texas stories, the intersections of race, power and conquest. But now Paredes attempts to account as well for the extraordinarily fierce Manichean nature of the war in Asia by linking domestic American racism with the conduct of its armed forces during the war and the postwar occupation of Japan. What is at issue now is the global nature of the idioms of racism and their role in the construction of an American national subject, suggesting how expressive forms of race hate encountered on the border became imbricated with the effects of colonialism and imperialism in Asia during World War II.

To understand how racism influenced the conduct of the war in the Pacific, Paredes takes us first in the story entitled "Little Joe" to infantry basic training at Camp Robinson, Little Rock, Arkansas.[36] An Anglo narrator named Watson reflects on the curious experiences of a fellow trainee, Little Joe, who hails from the Texas-Mexico border. Watson and the other white recruits cast Little Joe in the role of a knife-wielding killer, like all of his kind, essentially endowed with the bloodthirsty impulses of a savage cut-throat, that is, as a being possessed of special powers of non-human evil. "One must remember," notes Paredes, "that in the 1930s supposedly scholarly studies still were being published in Texas depicting Mexicans as treacherous and cowardly, a degenerate product of miscegenation between Spaniard and Indian."[37] Here, his fellow recruits have created such an exaggerated image and bla-

Ramón Saldívar

tantly racist construction of Little Joe that even the biggest man in the squad, a Minnesotan named Great Big Johnson, is petrified with fear whenever Little Joe cleans his bayonet: "That little guy, he don't look like much, but don't cross him. I'd hate to do that." The reality is that Little Joe is a neat, quiet, polite, South Texas boy, hardly a cold-blooded killer at all. In contrast to the image of the Mexican in American popular culture, notoriously portrayed as a knife-wielding killer during the Zoot Suit Riots of 1942-43, and symbolically presented as a primal brutal force in World War II novels like Norman Mailer's *The Naked and the Dead*, Paredes's Little Joe is not primordially linked to the harsh power of uncivilized savagery but is simply a decent human being attempting to live out from under the constraints of the prevailing Jim Crow, segregationist, white supremacist American ideology that keeps Mexicans and blacks in their subordinate place. C. L. R. James, writing in *The Socialist Appeal*, the Socialist Workers Party newspaper in September 1939, posed the question people of color faced at the onset of the war, implicit in Paredes's "Little Joe":

> Why should I shed my blood for Roosevelt's America, for Cotton Ed Smith and Senator Bilbo, for the whole Jim Crow, Negro-hating South, for the low-paid, dirty jobs for which Negroes have to fight, for the few dollars of relief and the insults, discrimination, police brutality, and perpetual poverty to which Negroes are condemned even in the more liberal North?[38]

Introduction

Denied the core principles of democracy as formulated in the Fourteenth and Fifteenth Amendments which guarantee the political rights of American citizens, or as expressed in Roosevelt's famed "four freedoms,"[39] the experiences of Mexican Americans, African Americans, Native Americans, Asian Americans and other American people of color during World War II exposed the hypocrisy of American critiques of Nazi and Axis racism. Mailer's caricature of a Texas Mexican in *The Naked and the Dead*, Sergeant Julio Martinez, is regularly represented in exaggerated metaphors of animal panic, compared at one point as reacting in conditioned terror to the sounds of combat like Pavlov's dog, or described at another as having the "poise and grace of a deer...nervous and alert as if he were thinking of flight."[40] Called "Mex" and "Japbait" by the other characters, Mailer's Mexican American speaks an infantile English, acts "instinctively," understands "intuitively," and cringes with "inferiority...when he talked to...White Protestant."[41] Like the metaphors linking him to the hunted prey, these qualities reflect the extent to which Mailer's Mexican American is marked by the same category the other Americans usually reserved for the Japanese enemy. Paredes's Mexican American soldiers, by contrast, serve as implied critiques of the Manichean dimension of caricature. They are reflective, doubting, amusing figures, active agents of their own fate, illustrating far more complex versions of the experience of the racialized combat in the Pacific than does Mailer.

This critique is extended in "The Gift," a story set in a Japanese POW camp.[42] Lt. Commander Young, the ranking captured American, is gripped by abject fear of the Japanese. His spirit having been completely broken by the Japanese, the Navy officer shamelessly informs on his fellow GIs nightly to gain himself some small comforts. After several men are brutally beaten and others executed because of Young, his cell mates feel compelled to kill him to save themselves. Identified only as "Mex," a sign of the conflicted racial politics among the American prisoners, the narrator draws the short straw as the executioner. But before he can act, Young, finally pushed too far, breaks through his terror, strikes back at his tormentors, and kills the more sadistic of the Japanese, called "Monkeyface" by the Americans.[43] Facing the executioner's sword, Young accepts his fate nobly. The narrator, spared having to play the fall guy in killing Young and the certainty of execution himself, now finds he must adjust his judgment of Young. Moreover, granted the gift of life both by circumstance and by the good fortune of a young Japanese lieutenant's mercy, he also finds himself in the peculiar position of having been recognized as a Subject by the enemy. Driven by the intensity of racial hatred and fear on both sides, Japanese guards and American prisoners eye each other across an apparently unbridgeable gulf. Paredes here shows, however, that the substantial social space figured as the lived distance between cultures is not an isomorphic one, smooth and continuous in its subject/object dichotomy, but rather is riven by hidden fissures and crossed by uneasy junctures that span cultural borders, making Manichean ethical judgments impossible to justify.

The U.S. occupation force in Japan is the subject of the next story, "When it Snowed in Kitabamba." Captain Meniscus, an unabashed idolizer of Douglas MacArthur, obsessed with neatness and order, sees his duty as Occupation Forces chief of Kitabamba to transform the Japanese into Americans. He keeps the motto of his pragmatic obsessions framed underneath a portrait of MacArthur: "The shortest distance between two points is a straight line." In his zeal to represent the superiority of American ways and to impress the Japanese with the precision of American methods, the captain has turned the delivery of the daily mail from Tokyo into an intricate, arcane, ceremonial ritual, replete with martial music, files of MPs lining his route toward the mail train, and his own march of high solemnity.

From such elevated solemnity only a fall can result. And so indeed, when one day an unexpected snow falls on Kitabamba, the Captain's dogged short march between two points is circumvented when he slips and falls awkwardly in the snow, turning his exalted ritual into a ridiculous farce. His MPs laugh with disdain at the fall of his pretensions. The gathered Japanese are more gentle with their conqueror; at first they too are mildly amused by the man's comic comedown. However, their amusement quickly turns into something else as "with sadness in their eyes" they recognize something much deeper than the suffering pathos of an arrogant, petty tyrant's stumble. In "On the Essence of Laughter," Baudelaire notes that:

> ...the power of laughter resides with the one who laughs, never with the object of laughter. It is not he who falls who laughs at himself, unless he is a philosopher, someone who has acquired, by habit, the ability to reflect upon himself (*se dédoubler*) and attend like a disinterested spectator upon the phenomenon of

his I.[45]

Such a reflective capacity, within consciousness, between two moments of the self, argues Paul de Man, is not an intersubjective relation at all but is in fact essential to the nature of irony itself. However, the laughter of the witness to the fall is to the fallen surely a mark of intersubjective difference, denoting the superiority of one subject over another, "with all the implications of will to power, of violence, and possession which come into play when a person is laughing at someone else—including the will to educate and to improve."[46] In Meniscus's tumble, the superiority implicit in the laughter of his MPs is clear: they disdain his pretensions and mark their distance from him with it. Meniscus himself is hardly philosophical enough to "reflect upon himself (*se dédoubler*) and attend like a disinterested spectator upon the phenomenon of his I." The gentle laughter of the Japanese, however, does tend toward a Baudelarian *dédoublement*, as it designates less hierarchies of superiority and inferiority than an implicit recognition of their own separation from themselves. In laughing at Meniscus, implicitly they lament their own newly fallen state. From this fallenness, they can pity Meniscus's fall, express "fellowship" with his humiliating come down, and force him to contemplate the shallowness of his own understanding of them over whom he has lorded as a stand-in for the haughty Supreme Commander, Douglas MacArthur. Their laughter and their philosophic self-detachment, like the name "Meniscus" itself (denoting a figure of crescent shape formed by the juncture of concave and convex surfaces[47]) ironically subvert MacArthur's truism about "the shortest distance between two points."

"Ichiro Kikuchi," also predicated on a peculiar turn of irony, is based on an actual experience of a young friend of Paredes's wife, Amelia.[48] In the story, Ichiro Kikuchi is the son of a Japanese father and a Mexican mother. Born and raised in Cuernavaca and baptized Juan Guadalupe, he grows to young adulthood on his Japanese father's and Mexican uncle's farm, growing flowers. At his father's insistence that he travel to Japan to maintain his Japanese identity, Ichiro finds himself unable to return to Mexico after Pearl Harbor. The young Japanese Mexican is eventually drafted, sent into action, and immediately captured by Americans in the Philippines. By 1945, the Japanese army is a far cry from the proud, disciplined, able force it once was. Ichiro's unit of old men and schoolboys, ordered to fight to the death, instead surrenders, tragically misjudging the good faith of the American army. But contrary to the notion that it was only the Japanese who wantonly killed their prisoners, the fact was that the war in the Pacific was for both sides "a war without mercy":

> No quarter, no surrender. Take no prisoners.
> Fight to the bitter end. These were everyday
> words in the combat areas, and in the final
> year of the war such attitudes contributed to
> an orgy of bloodletting that neither side could
> conceive of avoiding.[49]

Many Japanese fighting men did die instead of surrendering but they did so in part because of "the disinterest of the Allies in taking prisoners."[50] Ernie Pyle, war correspondent of near folk hero status, having transferred to the Pacific from Europe in February 1945, offered partial explanation for this "disinterest" by noting in one of his first dispatches that "In Europe we felt that our enemies, as horrible and deadly as they were, were still people." He continues, "But out here I soon gathered that the Japanese were looked upon as something subhuman and repulsive; the way some people feel about cockroaches and mice."[51] About to be summarily executed with his entire unit, Ichiro is digging his own grave when a GI assigned to eliminate the prisoners, a Mexican American sergeant, notices the medallion of the Virgin of Guadalupe Ichiro wears. Symbol of a national unity of faith, the Guadalupe icon tears Ichiro from the propaganda narrative of Japanese dehumanization and re-inserts him in the discourse of greater Mexican identity. The medallion identifies the Japanese infantryman not only as a fellow Catholic, but also as a fellow Mexican. When Ichiro responds in Spanish to the shaken Mexican American GI's hailing, he only confirms what the GI has already understood. Later in Tokyo, after the war, the shock of having seen himself partially in the demonized Japanese Other proves too much for the Mexican American GI, as he turns away from Ichiro who is attempting to thank him for the gift of his life. Race hate bred at home, displaced in combat onto a vicious and odious enemy, appears at this moment far too uncomfortably close at hand. By turning away, the Mexican American GI declines to acknowledge the extent to which he too, at home and in Japan, straddles binary oppositions as he stands in the position of the reified and objectified racial Other. Here again, Paredes masterfully represents the situation that C. L. R. James suggested Americans of color would face in World War II and anticipates the contradictions posed for them by other imperial, postcolonial struggles in Korea and Vietnam. In the Manichean struggle between seemingly incompatible antagonists, with merciless extermination the goal of each side's efforts, the defining line between "war crimes" and justifiable action becomes as blurred and ambiguous as the line between fortune and fate.

"Sugamo" takes the issue of "war crimes" one step further, as it examines the fate of a Black American soldier accused of murdering a Japanese civilian during the Korean War. Sugamo is the name of the prison where the Prime Minister of Japan, Hideki Tojo, and other Japanese military leaders were held, tried, and executed for "war crimes" after World War II. The scene is set against the background of American determinations of international justice.[52] As he awaits court martial, Private Jewel C. Jones mulls over what he conceives to be the polite good-natured, childlike qualities of the "gooks" and contrasts their "difference" with the oppressively racist attitudes of the MPs who guard him and of the white supremacist society in which he has been raised. In complex time sequencing, Jones flashes-back first to action in Korea when his unit's frontline troops are overrun, forcing rear area service troopers such as he into combat. After the day's heavy fighting, his commander orders him to escort a prisoner to headquarters, located "far to the south [beyond] the faint rumble of battle" and to "be back in fifteen minutes". Private Jones understands the major's impossible order as it is clearly intended—code words implicitly condemning the prisoner to death. Jones's pride in having been selected as "a man with brains" who "understood" the order is short-lived. The young Korean prisoner also perceives what is about to happen and pleads for his life, uttering the only words he knows in English, "Thank-you-thank-you-thank-you", before Jones blasts him with his automatic weapon.

In a second-level temporal sequence, we learn that after this harrowing moment and back in Tokyo on leave, Jones is refused the services of one of the bar-girls, because he is black. When the bar manager attempts to deflect Jones's anger in his limited English, "Thank you, s'," the distinct temporal realities of then and now merge for Private Jones and he lashes out at the bar manager as he had at the pleading prisoner: this time, instead of blasting the pleading man with an automatic weapon, he beats the man to death. In present time, the black soldier Jones is sentenced to death for the murder of the Japanese bar manager, while being jeered by redneck MPs. But the double-jeopardy of racism, its destructive force whether one expresses it or receives it, remains the unresolved issue of the story.

"The Terribly High Cost," set in post-war Tokyo, continues this exploration of American racism during the occupation of Japan. Really two stories in one, in the frame narrative a particularly vapid university professor, Travis Williamson, and a visiting Indianan friend, Peter Richards, discuss the origin of a rare Hiroshige print that Richards has presented to Williamson. When Williamson misjudges the value of the print because it is not an "original," Richards explains how he received the print (a rare collector's piece from the original nineteenth-century block) in Tokyo after the war as a gift from one Kunio Yoshida, a janitor with the Civilian Property Custodian's office, for which Richards works.

Yoshida's story forms the inner narrative. According to Richards, Yoshida is like all the conquered Japanese:

Introduction

"shabby and sad-looking, always bowing at every American in sight." When Richards gets to know him better, he learns that Yoshida has a degree in American Literature from "an Ivy League school." Labor market conditions in Occupation Tokyo being particularly unfavorable for professors of American literature, Yoshida is obliged to support his war-ravaged family as a janitor. Yoshida's father, an old-style samurai, broken by the war, subsequently commits suicide by jumping from the cliffs at a popular suicide spot, the beautiful nearby town of Otani.[53] The expenses surrounding the death put Yoshida in worse financial straits until Richards gets him a position at Nippon College, a two-year institution for American Occupation personnel, working as a teaching assistant in a course on American Literature offered by an incompetent American professor. The ironic twist of having a Japanese national teaching American literature to Americans is superseded at the ending only when Yoshida's daughter commits suicide after having been jilted by a Hawaiian Nisei corporal. Paredes is here again concerned with the double-crossings of enforced post-war enculturations, defeated Japanese instructing their conquerors and Japanese-Americans victimizing Japanese nationals, anticipating the reversals of fortunes that post-war power realignments would produce.

The final two selections, "Getting an Oboe for Joe" and "The American Dish," are broad farces narrated in a parodically picaresque style by a roguish, salacious character named Johnny Picadero.[54] "Getting an Oboe for Joe" deals with a whimsical attempt to locate an oboe in post-war occupation late-night, party-time Tokyo for a despondent Mexican American baker who refuses to prepare his marvelous breads without his

music. In the midst of a raucous chase involving Key-
stone Kop Army MPs, seedy characters from the Tokyo
underground, and Johnny Picadero's dodging of the
police by donning a kimono and passing as a Japanese,
we are asked to recall South Texas. For the chase
repeats the events narrated in the most famous of
South Texas *corridos*, but as farce, not tragedy: "just
like Gregorio Cortez...So many of them just to catch
one Mexican!"[55] Unlike Gregorio Cortez's, Johnny Picadero's efforts prove fruitless, but all's well that ends
well since it is not high social drama that Paredes is
after in this story but rather low comedic slapstick
intrigue.

"The American Dish," another Johnny Picadero
tale, continues in the picaresque mode as part of what
was intended to be a series of stories featuring our
anti-hero. Back home in "San Cuilmas" (San Antonio,
Texas) after the war and another four years in the occupation army, Johnny Picadero travels to Mexico to visit
his friend Pablo, who like fifteen thousand of his coun-
trymen, saw action in the Pacific serving in American
armed forces.[56]   In this case the satire is aimed at
Americans who think they can pass as Mexicans
because they know how to order "Chile con carne," an
American dish, in Mexican restaurants, and American
venture capitalists looking for sleazy opportunities in
post-war Latin America. The roguish Johnny encoun-
ters "spies," a delectable Miss Ross, another American
dish, and the shady operatives of a fly-by-night American film company attempting to steal Mexican cultural
capital by illegally filming "the tribal dances of the
Culomula Indians." As with the punning names of the
fictional Indian tribe and of the roguish main character,
Paredes's intent in these last two stories is not to

diminish the sting of his earlier satires of American racial mores but to extend the critique into the realms of comedy, burlesque, and caricature.

As in "When it Snowed in Kitabamba," in these last two selections laughter becomes the ironic medium through which the philosophic detachment necessary for the recognition of mistaken, mystified assumptions about superiority and inferiority, and even the acknowledgment of difference, can occur. Related to the comedic spirit that Paredes would in later life celebrate in *Uncle Remus con Chile*, his collection of jests, oral histories, legends, and anecdotes from South Texas, the Johnny Picadero stories explore the vernacular rhetorical modes available to revisionary and contestatory history as it seeks to revise the narrative of American nationhood at the borderlands of culture. In all of the stories collected here, however, whether in the modes of tragedy, comedy, or realistic narrative, the guiding rhetorical force of that narrative is ironic wisdom, the self-knowledge that glimpses the discontinuity and plurality of levels within a subject, caught between two worlds, who comes to know itself by what it is not. Positioned by difference, Paredes' border subjects acknowledge the social dimension of difference. Repeatedly, this acknowledgement occurs aesthetically, in the shapes and nuances of a variety of oral forms, gestures, expressions and styles, that is, in the formulaic patterns, that disguise and sometimes reveal humanity. It is here, surely, that Paredes's virtuosity as a master storyteller and clear-sighted critic of contemporary vernacular eth-

Ramón Saldívar

nic culture and its historiography is most powerfully present. The new, pan-American history that he narrates traverses imaginary border lines and immigration checkpoints to document the imaginative styles concerned with Mexican American struggles for social justice. *The Hammon and the Beans and Other Stories* represents the latest evidence of Américo Paredes's historical centrality as an artist and scholar of that vernacular imagination.

Ramón Saldívar
Stanford University

Introduction

Notes

[1]For further biographical information on Américo Paredes and excellent indications of his preeminent role in the foundation of Chicano Cultural Studies, see José E. Limón, "Américo Paredes: A Man From the Border" *Revista Chicano-Riqueña* Vol. 8, no. 3 (Summer 1980): 1-5, and "Américo Paredes" in *Dancing With the Devil: Society and Cultural Poetics in Mexican American South Texas* (Madison: U of Wisconsin P, 1994); Héctor Calderón, "Reinventing the Border: From the Southwest Genre to Chicano Cultural Studies" (forthcoming); and José David Saldívar, "Chicano Narratives as Cultural Critique," in *Criticism in the Borderlands: Studies in Chicano Literature, Culture, and Ideology,* ed. Héctor Calderón and José David Saldívar (Durham: Duke UP, 1991), pp. 167-180.

[2]José David Saldívar, "Chicano Narratives as Cultural Critique," p. 170.

[3]Bauman, "Introduction," in Américo Paredes, *Folklore and Culture on the Texas-Mexican Border* (Austin: Center for Mexican American Studies and U of Texas P, 1993), pp. 1-2.

[4]Michel Foucault, *The History of Sexuality*, Vol. 1. (New York: Pantheon, 1978), p. 95.

[5]Theodor Adorno, *Minima Moralia: Reflections from Damaged Life* (London: New Left Books, 1974), p. 218.

[6]For a full elaboration of Paredes's participation in the critique of Roosevelt's New Deal liberalism, see R. Saldívar, "Bordering on Modernity: Américo Paredes's *Between Two Worlds* and the Imagining of Utopian Social Space," *Stanford Humanities Review* Vol. 3, no. 1 (Winter 1993), pp. 54-66, and "Modernity, the Nation, and Chicano Subject Formation: Américo Paredes's *Between Two Worlds,*" in Abdul JanMohamed, ed., *Minority Discourse* (forthcoming).

[7]Edward Said, "Reflections on American 'Left' Literary Criticism," *The World, the Text, and the Critic* (Cambridge, MA: Harvard UP, 1983), p. 171.

[8]Homi K. Bhabha, *Nation and Narration* (London and New York: Routledge, 1990), p. 3.

[9]Bhabha, *Nation and Narration*, p. 4.

Ramón Saldívar

[10]David Montejano, "Frustrated Apartheid: Race, Repression, and Capitalist Agriculture in South Texas, 1920-1930," in *The World-System of Capitalism: Past & Present*, ed. Walter L. Goldfrank, Vol. 2, Political Economy of the World-System Annuals (Beverly Hills: Sage Publications, 1979), p. 133.

[11]Montejano, "Frustrated Apartheid," p. 138.

[12]James A. Sandos, *Rebellion in the Borderlands: Anarchism and the Plan of San Diego, 1904-1923* (Norman: U of Oklahoma P, 1992), p. 70.

[13]Sandos, *Rebellion in the Borderlands*, pp. 72-73.

[14]Sandos, *Rebellion in the Borderlands*, p. 74.

[15]Sandos, *Rebellion in the Borderlands*, p. 81.

[16]Sandos, *Rebellion in the Borderlands*, p. 81.

[17]Sandos, *Rebellion in the Borderlands*, p. 83.

[18]Charles H. Harris III and Louis R. Sadler, "The Plan of San Diego and the Mexican-United States War Crisis of 1916: A Reexamination," *Hispanic American Historical Review* 58 (3), 1978, p. 385.

[19]Sandos, *Rebellion in the Borderlands*, p. 91.

[20]Tracy Hammond Lewis, *Along the Rio Grande* (New York: Lewis Publishing Co., 1916), p. 178, cited in Sandos, *Rebellion in the Borderlands*, p. 92.

[21]Sandos, *Rebellion in the Borderlands*, p. 92.

[22]Colin M. MacLachlan, *Anarchism and the Mexican Revolution: The Political Trials of Ricardo Flores Magón in the United States* (Berkeley: U of California P, 1991), p. 57. MacLachlan is citing a contemporary report by U.S. Secret Service agent Edward Tyrell.

[23]Harris and Sadler, "The Plan of San Diego and the Mexican-United States War Crisis of 1916," p. 386.

[24]Harris and Sadler, "The Plan of San Diego and the Mexican-United States War Crisis of 1916," p. 387.

[25]See "Los Sediciosos," in Américo Paredes, *A Texas-Mexican Cancionero: Folksongs of the Lower Border* (Urbana: U of Illinois P, 1976); and my discussion of the ballad in *Chicano Narrative: The Dialectics of Difference* (Madison: U of Wisconsin P, 1990), pp. 30-31.

[26]See Harris and Sandler, "The Plan of San Diego and the

Introduction

Mexican-United States War Crisis of 1916," pp. 390-92; Sandos, *Rebellion in the Borderlands*, pp. 108-110; and Frank C. Pierce, *A Brief History of the Lower Rio Grande Valley* (Menasha, WI: George Banta Publishing Co., 1917), pp. 114-115.

[27]For the publication history and fuller close readings of "The Hammon and the Beans" and "Over the Waves is Out," see *Chicano Narrative*, pp. 48-60.

[28]Walter Benjamin, "Theses on the Philosophy of History," in *Illuminations*, ed. Hannah Arendt, (New York: Schocken Books, 1969), p. 255.

[29]Sarah M. Lowe, *Frida Kahlo* Universe Series on Women Artists (New York: Universe Publishing, 1991), pp. 83-84.

[30]Paredes, personal correspondence, December 13, 1992. The unpublished collection included two episodes drawn from the manuscript of the novel *George Washington Gómez*. Paredes won $500 in books for his efforts.

[31]See Rivera,...*Y no se lo tragó la tierra/And the Earth Did Not Devour Him*. (Houston: Arte Público P, 1987), and the discussion in *Chicano Narrative*, pp. 74-90.

[32]Pierce, *A Brief History of the Lower Rio Grande Valley*, pp. 26-27.

[33]Pierce, *A Brief History of the Lower Rio Grande Valley*, p. 28. Palo Alto, Texas, is located on "an extensive prairie nine miles north of Brownsville, just west of Loma Alta."

[34]"Revenge" was composed in Brownsville, during the period 1940-44, before Paredes left his wartime draft deferred job to allow himself to be drafted. Paredes, personal correspondence December 13, 1992.

[35]The first draft of "Brothers" was completed "in Tokyo on June 25, 1950, the day that North Korea invaded the south." Paredes, personal correspondence, December 13, 1992.

[36]Written in Japan, soon after Paredes landed there in 1945 with the Occupation Army. "Done while my memories of basic training in Arkansas were still fresh on my mind." Paredes, personal correspondence, December 13, 1992.

[37]Paredes, *Uncle Remus con Chile* (Houston: Arte Público P, 1993), p. 11. Paredes adds that J. Frank Dobie in *The Flavor of Texas* "defends the Mexican by switching stereotypes, from treach-

erous knife-stabber to kindly Uncle Remus."

[38]C. L. R. James et al., "Why Negroes Should Oppose the War," in *Fighting Racism in World War II* (New York: Monad P, 1980), p. 28.

[39]See Paredes's scathing poem, of that title, in *Between Two Worlds*; also, my discussion, "Bordering on Modernity: Américo Paredes's *Between Two Worlds* and the Imagining of Utopian Social Space," pp. 54-66.

[40]Norman Mailer, *The Naked and the Dead* (New York: Rinehart & Co., 1948), pp. 18, 63.

[41]*The Naked and the Dead*, pp. 591, 592, and 691.

[42]This story was done between 1946 and 1950 in Japan, with only minor editing for the present collection. Paredes, personal correspondence, December 13, 1992.

[43]John W. Dower, *War Without Mercy: Race & Power in the Pacific War* (New York: Pantheon, 1986) describes how simian imagery was part of the prevalent Allied propaganda effort to dehumanize the Japanese. The epithet "Mex," of course, had already carried a derogatory valence in other American imperial wars.

[44]Done in Japan between 1946 and 1950. Paredes, personal correspondence, December 13, 1992.

[45]Charles Baudelaire, "On the Essence of Laughter," in Paul de Man, *Blindness and Insight: Essays in the Rhetoric of Contemporary Criticism* (Minneapolis: U of Minnesota P, 1983), pp. 211-212. My translation.

[46]De Man, *Blindness and Insight*, p. 212.

[47]*OED, sub verbum* "meniscus."

[48]In personal correspondence, December 13, 1992, Paredes notes that this story, composed between 1948 and 1949, was "Based on an experience to a young friend of [Amelia's] family. He was not half Mexican but had been born in Mexico. Like many Nisei, he was caught in Japan by the war. It was a rosary he was wearing on a chain around his neck when he was digging his own grave along with other members of his platoon. There were plenty of 'war crimes' committed by U.S. forces long before Vietnam and My Lai. Yet we executed the Japanese leaders as war criminals because Japanese soldiers also committed the same kind of atroci-

ties."

⁴⁹Dower, *War Without Mercy*, pp. 10-11.

⁵⁰Dower, *War Without Mercy*, p. 11.

⁵¹Ernie Pyle, *Last Chapter* (New York: Henry Holt & Co., 1945), p.5.

⁵²As political editor for *Stars and Stripes*, Paredes covered the first few months of Far East "war crimes" trials after the war in the Pacific. At one point during the trials, Paredes was granted an exclusive interview with Hideki Tojo at Sugamo Prison. "Sugamo" was completed in Austin, Texas, after his return from Japan in 1950. From personal correspondence, December 13, 1992.

⁵³Paredes had read a newspaper article in the late 1940s about Atami, "Japan's suicide capital...a picturesque little town. The town's authorities were complaining about the extra expense to the town." An early draft done in Japan was completed in Austin between 1952-53. From personal correspondence, December 13, 1992.

⁵⁴"Picadero," derived from *picar* (to prick), suggests various puns in the Spanish, including *pícaro* (traditional knavish adventurer of Spanish fiction), *picador* (horseman who pricks the bull's neck muscles in the bullfight), *picardía* (Mexican oral lore of pungent word-play). Both stories were begun during the first few months that Paredes arrived in Occupation Japan as *Stars and Stripes* correspondent at the 11th Replacement Depot near Okazaki. From personal correspondence, December 13, 1992.

⁵⁵"So many mounted Rangers against one lone Mexican!" from *"El Corrido de Gregorio Cortez."*

⁵⁶See Paredes, *Uncle Remus con Chile*, pp. 146-147 and 175-176.

The Hammon
and the Beans
and
Other Stories

The Hammon and The Beans

Once we lived in one of my grandfather's houses near Fort Jones. It was just a block from the parade grounds, a big frame house painted a dirty yellow. My mother hated it, especially because of the pigeons that cooed all day about the eaves. They had fleas, she said. But it was a quiet neighborhood at least, too far from the center of town for automobiles and too near for musical, night-roaming drunks.

At this time Jonesville-on-the-Grande was not the thriving little city that it is today. We told off our days by the routine on the post. At six sharp the flag was raised on the parade grounds to the cackling of the bugles, and a field piece thundered out a salute. The sound of the shot bounced away through the morning mist until its echoes worked their way into every corner of town. Jonesville-on-the-Grande woke to the cannon's roar, as if to battle, and the day began.

At eight the whistle from the post laundry sent us children off to school. The whole town stopped for lunch with the noon whistle, and after lunch everybody went back to work when the post laundry said that it was one o'clock, except for those who could afford to be old-fashioned and took the siesta. The post

3

was the town's clock, you might have said, or like some insistent elder person who was always there to tell you it was time.

At six the flag came down, and we went to watch through the high wire fence that divided the post from the town. Sometimes we joined in the ceremony, standing at salute until the sound of the cannon made us jump. That must have been when we had just studied about George Washington in school, or recited "The Song of Marion's Men" about Marion the Fox and the British cavalry that chased him up and down the broad Santee. But at other times we stuck out our tongues and jeered at the soldiers. Perhaps the night before we had hung at the edges of a group of old men and listened to tales about Aniceto Pizaña and the "border troubles," as the local paper still called them when it referred to them gingerly in passing.

It was because of the border troubles, ten years or so before, that the soldiers had come back to old Fort Jones. But we did not hate them for that; we admired them even, at least sometimes. But when we were thinking about the border troubles instead of Marion the Fox, we hooted them and the flag they were lowering, which for the moment was theirs alone, just as we would have jeered an opposing ball team, in a friendly sort of way. On these occasions even Chonita would join in the mockery, though she usually ran home at the stroke of six. But whether we taunted or saluted, the distant men in khaki uniforms went about their motions without noticing us at all.

The last word from the post came in the night when a distant bugle blew. At nine it was all right because all the lights were on. But sometimes I heard it at eleven when everything was dark and still, and it made me feel that I was all alone in the world. I would even doubt that I was me, and that put me in such a fright that I felt like yelling out just to make sure I was really there. But next morning the sun shone and life began all over again, with its whistles and cannon shots and bugles blowing. And so we lived, we and the post, side by side with the wire fence in between.

The wandering soldiers whom the bugle called home at night did not wander in our neighborhood, and none of us ever went into Fort Jones. None except Chonita. Every evening when the flag came down she would leave off playing and go down towards what was known as the "lower" gate of the post, the one that opened not on main street but against the poorest part of town. She went into the grounds and to the mess halls and pressed her nose against the screens and watched the soldiers eat. They sat at long tables calling to each other through food-stuffed mouths.

"Hey bud, pass the coffee!"

"Give me the ham!"

"Yeah, give me the beans!"

After the soldiers were through, the cooks came out and scolded Chonita, and then they gave her packages with things to eat.

Chonita's mother did our washing, in gratefulness—as my mother put it—for the use of a vacant lot of my grandfather's which was a couple of blocks down the street. On the lot was an old one-room shack which had been a shed long ago, and this Chonita's father had patched up with flattened-out pieces of tin. He was a laborer. Ever since the end of the border troubles there had been a development boom in the Valley, and Chonita's father was getting his share of the good times. Clearing brush and building irrigation ditches, he sometimes pulled down as much as six dollars a week. He drank a good deal of it up, it was true. But corn was just a few cents a bushel in those days. He was the breadwinner, you might say, while Chonita furnished the luxuries.

Chonita was a poet too. I had just moved into the neighborhood when a boy came up to me and said, "Come on! Let's go hear Chonita make a speech."

She was already on top of the alley fence when we got there, a scrawny little girl of about nine, her bare dirty feet clinging to the fence almost like hands. A dozen other kids were there below her, waiting. Some were boys I knew at school; five or six were her younger brothers and sisters.

"Speech! Speech!" they all cried. "Let Chonita make a speech! Talk in English, Chonita!"

They were grinning and nudging each other except for her brothers and sisters, who looked up at her with proud serious faces. She gazed out beyond us all with a grand, distant air and then she spoke.

"Give me the hammon and the beans!" she yelled. "Give me the hammon and the beans!"

She leaped off the fence and everybody cheered and told her how good it was and how she could talk English better than the teachers at the grammar school.

I thought it was a pretty poor joke. Every evening almost, they would make her get up on the fence and yell, "Give me the hammon and the beans!" And everybody would cheer and make her think she was talking English. As for me, I would wait there until she got it over with so we could play at something else. I wondered how long it would be before they got tired of it all. I never did find out because just about that time I got the chills and fever, and when I got up and around, Chonita wasn't there anymore.

In later years I thought of her a lot, especially during the thirties when I was growing up. Those years would have been just made for her. Many's the time I have seen her in my mind's eye, in the picket lines demanding not bread, not cake, but the hammon and the beans. But it didn't work out that way.

One night Doctor Zapata came into our kitchen through the back door. He set his bag on the table and said to my father, who had opened the door for him, "Well, she is dead."

My father flinched. "What was it?" he asked.

The doctor had gone to the window and he stood with his back to us, looking out toward the lights of Fort Jones. "Pneumonia, flu, malnutrition, worms, the evil eye," he said without turning around. "What the hell difference does it make?"

"I wish I had known how sick she was," my father said in a very mild tone. "Not that it's really my affair, but I wish I had."

The doctor snorted and shook his head.

My mother came in and I asked her who was dead. She told me. It made me feel strange but I did not cry. My mother put her arm around my shoulders. "She is in Heaven now," she said. "She is happy."

I shrugged her arm away and sat down in one of the kitchen chairs.

"They're like animals," the doctor was saying. He turned round suddenly and his eyes glistened in the light. "Do you know what that brute of a father was doing when I left? He was laughing! Drinking and laughing with his friends."

"There's no telling what the poor man feels," my mother said.

My father made a deprecatory gesture. "It wasn't his daughter, anyway."

"No?" the doctor said. He sounded interested.

"This is the woman's second husband," my father explained. "First one died before the girl was born, shot and hanged from a mesquite limb. He was working too close to the tracks the day the Olmito train was derailed."

"You know what?" the doctor said. "In classical times they did things better. Take Troy, for instance. After they stormed the city they grabbed the babies by the heels and dashed them against the wall. That was more humane."

My father smiled. "You sound very radical. You sound just like your relative down there in Morelos."

"No relative of mine," the doctor said. "I'm a conservative, the son of a conservative, and you know that I wouldn't be here except for that little detail."

"Habit," my father said. "Pure habit, pure tradition. You're a radical at heart."

"It depends on how you define radicalism," the doctor answered. "People tend to use words too loosely. A dentist could be called a radical, I suppose. He pulls up things by the roots."

My father chuckled.

"Any bandit in Mexico nowadays can give himself a political label," the doctor went on, "and that makes him respectable. He's a leader of the people."

"Take Villa, now..." my father began.

"Villa was a different type of man," the doctor broke in.

"I don't see any difference."

The Hammon and the Beans

The doctor came over to the table and sat down. "Now look at it this way," he began, his finger in front of my father's face. My father threw back his head and laughed.

"You'd better go to bed and rest," my mother told me. "You're not completely well, you know."

So I went to bed, but I didn't go to sleep, not right away. I lay there for a long time while behind my darkened eyelids Emiliano Zapata's cavalry charged down to the broad Santee, where there were grave men with hoary hairs. I was still awake at eleven when the cold voice of the bugle went gliding in and out of the dark like something that couldn't find its way back to wherever it had been. I thought of Chonita in Heaven, and I saw her in her torn and dirty dress, with a pair of bright wings attached, flying round and round like a butterfly shouting, "Give me the hammon and the beans!"

Then I cried. And whether it was the bugle, or whether it was Chonita or what, to this day I do not know. But cry I did, and I felt much better after that.

Over The Waves
Is Out

He had always wanted to be a musician, but his father would not let him, because his father had once known the man who composed "Over the Waves." They had gone to school together in Monterrey, to a real gentlemen's school. And then the man who composed "Over the Waves" succumbed to drink and women, which led him to a tragic end.

His father knew about the evils of drink and women, having investigated them in his youth. It was dangerous, besides being unnecessary, for the boy to do any exploring of his own. Besides, he was a delicate boy. That girl face of his wouldn't go well in a brothel. And that was the place for musicians, his father said.

But the boy did not want to play in a brothel. He would often lie on the grass of afternoons and dream he was a minstrel in the court of El Cid Campeador. Except that instead of a harp he played a piano, a shiny three-legged piano with a tail. But his father never could understand, because he had once known the man who composed "Over the Waves."

And there was another thing. In his youth, before he lost a finger somewhere, the boy's father had liked the guitar. Once, as he told it himself, he was playing at a funeral. His father, the boy's grandfather, happened by and broke the guitar on his head. The boy's father never played again. He ran away to Tampico, and when he came back he had learned to play cards. It was then that the grandfather stopped speaking to him.

It made it hard on the boy, because he wanted to be a musician. He would sidle up to his father whenever he found him seated close to a window on his days off, reading *The Life and Times of Pancho Villa or God, Grand Architect of the Universe.* His father would sit there reading in his shirt sleeves, the cowboy hat and the heavy pistol in the cartridge belt lying on a table beside him, the linen coat hanging on the back of a chair.

"Papa," the boy would say, "why don't you buy a piano?"

His father would jab a thick, freckled forefinger at the page to mark his last word and look at him over his glasses. "Eh? A piano? You've got a phonograph."

"But I just got to have a piano."

"That again." His father would shake his head. "So many things in the world, and you want to be a musician. Why not a carpenter? Or a mason? Or a merchant? Or a barber even; there's a clean, gentlemanly profession for you."

"No," the boy would say firmly, "I want to be a musician."

"Look," his father would say, "what does a musician make?"

"But I'm going to write music."

"Merciful God! Have you ever heard of the man who composed 'Over the Waves'?"

"Yes," the boy would say. "Many times."

Américo Paredes

So his father would steer the conversation into the technical aspects of music, the different instruments like the clavichord, the clarinet, the drums and the trumpet. Then he would talk about bugle calls and drift into a story of the Revolution. Soon the boy was listening to a colorful account of how his father and Villa took Chihuahua City.

And suddenly his father would say severely, "Now run along and play. I'm busy."

And the boy would go. He was outsmarted every time.

All he could do was dream; so he dreamed of the piano. At night, in his little recess of a room with its one window framing a patch of sky, he would lie awake in the dark, imagining he was a pianist with wild hair and evening clothes, and that he was playing the piano, playing, playing.

And one night it happened. Softly, so softly he could barely hear it, there came a sound of piano music. He sat up in bed. The house and the street were silent, still the piano sounds ran faintly on. The music was coming from inside him! He lay back, breathless, and closed his eyes. His hands ran over an imaginary keyboard. Now he could distinguish the tripping runs, the trills, and the beautiful, anxious chords.

He wanted to shout, to sob; he didn't know which. But he did neither. He just lay quiet, very quiet. Something inside him grew and grew. He was lifted up in a sea of piano music which continued to pour out of him, churning and eddying about him in glowing spirals, slowly burying him in a glittering shower until he fell asleep.

Next morning he awoke with a feeling that the day was a holiday. Then he remembered and he smiled secretly. He tried to put away the memory in a corner of his mind, tuck it away where no one else might get at it. But as he dressed he kept trying to remember the music. It was there, in some cranny of his mind, where he could just barely touch it. It seemed that if he tried hard enough, reached down far enough, he could grasp it, a whole handful of it, and bring it shimmering into the light. But when he tried to do so it would slip away, just out of reach. He went in to breakfast, full of his rich warm secret.

"I'm talking to you," his father said.

"Wha—yessir?" he said.

"No humming at the table."

"Humming, sir?"

"It's bad manners. Eat your breakfast."

He looked down at his plate again and gulped down a few more mouthfuls.

"What if he did hum a little?" his mother said. "You've made him miserable now."

"He will not hum at my table," his father said.

"Your table," his mother said.

"My table," his father said.

"Fine table," his mother said.

"Agh!" his father said.

"I think you like to see him look miserable," his mother said.

"He looks miserable all the time," said his sister.

"You hush," his mother said. "Keep your spoon in your own porridge."

He kept his eyes on his plate. The food he had already eaten lay cold and heavy on his stomach. As soon as he could he excused himself and left the table. He went out, dragging his feet. In the yard he hesitated, looking about him dismally. Then he smiled. He hummed tentatively and smiled again.

Night came at last, and he lay in bed waiting for the house to be dark and still so the music would come again. And finally it came, faintly at first, then more distinctly, though never loud, splashing and whirling about, twisting in intricate eddies of chords and bright waterfalls of melody, or falling in separate notes into the night like drops of quicksilver, rolling, glimmering.

His father left early the next morning, and he, his mother and his sister ate breakfast together. In his father's absence, he could not keep the question to himself any longer.

"Did you hear music last night?" he asked.

"No," his mother said. "Where?"

"A serenade?" his sister asked. "Someone with a serenade?"

He frowned. "Not that kind of music."

"When?" his mother asked.

"Last night."

"I was awake long after you went to bed," his mother said. "There was no music."

He smiled. He looked at his mother and smiled.

"Don't you feel well?" his mother said.

"You didn't hear it at all," he said.

"What was it like?" his mother asked.

He got up from the table, the secret look on his face. "It was heavenly," he said.

"Child!" said his mother.

"He's in love," his sister said.

He included his sister in his rapt smile and walked slowly out.

"Heaven?" his mother said, crossing herself.

His father called him into the living room. The boy

came in and stood before his father. His father closed his book and put it down, took off his spectacles and put them in their case.

Then he said, "Your mother asked me to speak to you."

The boy looked at him.

"You're playing a sort of game with yourself every night, I hear," his father said. "You make believe you hear music."

The boy's face brightened. "I do," he said eagerly. "I do hear it."

His father looked at him sharply. "Don't lie to me now," he said.

The boy looked at his father, sitting in judgment in his soggy shirt and day-old beard, with his memories of Pancho Villa and the man who had composed "Over the Waves." And he knew he could never make him understand about the music, how it came from inside him, how beautiful it was, and how it made everything else beautiful.

"A game is a game," his father said.

The boy looked at the floor.

"Your mother's worried something may happen to you."

"Nothing's going to happen," the boy said.

"Not unless you keep worrying your mother," his father said.

"I won't talk about it anymore," the boy said. "Never."

"You go talk to her. Tell her you really don't hear anything."

"But I do hear!" the boy said.

His father gave him a hostile, suspicious look. "Don't lie!" he said.

"I'm not lying."

"You're lying this very minute!"

The boy directed his angry gaze at his own feet.

"You really don't hear anything," his father said, his voice becoming persuasive. "You just play at hearing it, don't you?"

The boy did not answer.

There was a short silence, and then his father said, "What does it sound like?"

The boy looked up quickly. His father was watching him intently, almost eagerly.

"Oh, I don't know," the boy said. "I couldn't tell just how it sounds."

"I once thought I heard music in my head," his father said. "I was in bed in Monterrey when I heard this piano. But it was only a friend out with music. He had a piano in a cart, so we went out and serenaded the girls. And then the mule bolted and…"

He stopped and looked at the boy.

"I told you I had a musician friend," he added.

"Yes," the boy said.

His father became dignified again.

"You mustn't do things like that," he said. "Think of your mother."

The boy hung his head. His father drummed his fingers on the table beside him.

"I'll talk to her myself," his father said. "I'll tell her the truth, and that you're sorry."

The boy was silent.

"Well, go out and play," his father said.

He was lying in bed, looking out his window at the sky, and listening to the music. He was hovering between sleep and wakefulness, floating about on the beautiful sounds, when all of a sudden he was wide-awake. There had been a dull, thudding noise, as though a distant door had been slammed shut.

He sat up in bed. There was a hubbub of voices in the street. He jumped into his overalls and ran out; people were running towards a light. He ran towards the light too, and caught up with his father, who was hurrying along, buckling on his cartridge belt about his shirtless middle, beneath his flapping coat.

"At the bakery!" his father said to a man leaning out of a window. "Trouble for sure!"

There was anything but trouble in his voice; it was brisk and eager, strangely unlike his father's voice. The boy stayed just behind him, somewhat awed.

It was a bakery where the bakers worked all night making the next day's bread. As his father reached the place, a police car came squealing to a halt in the street.

An excited man in apron and cap shouted above the din, "He ran down the alley there! He's got a shotgun!"

A couple of deputies ran into the dark mouth of the alley, their cowboy boots clomping awkwardly on the pebbles, their pistols drawn. His father started to run after them, but then he saw the sheriff stepping out of the car and he stopped.

The sheriff smiled at his father.

"Stick around, de la Garza," the sheriff said.

The boy's father had his gun in his hand.

"Let me go too, sheriff," he said.

"No, de la Garza," the sheriff said. "I'll need you here."

The boy's father put his gun away very slowly. Then he said to the nearest man in the crowd, "All right, you! Move on!"

He pushed the crowd back.

"Go home to bed!" he said. "Move on! Move on!"

The crowd shifted, parted, and the boy, who had stayed beside his father, almost underfoot, could now look inside into the long shelves of unbaked dough and the glowing ovens. He came closer, trying to see the terrible thing he knew must be inside.

Close to the door he became aware of the piano music. It was bouncing within the bakery's thick walls in a roar of echoes, escaping into the street only as a deep mutter which blended with the mutter of the crowd.

The sheriff walked inside and yelled, "Shut that damned thing off!"

One of the bakers answered in a high, complaining voice.

"We can't," he said. "He shot off the whole face of it."

"Well, pull the string off the wall," the sheriff shouted.

The music was cut off abruptly.

The crowd had now retired a respectful distance, and the boy's father followed the sheriff inside. The boy edged closer to the door. He could see it now, a small brown box. It was pitted and broken by the shotgun blast.

"We was here, minding our own business," a big fat baker was saying, "when he walks in, and bang!"

"Maybe he thought there was a man inside," the sheriff said.

The other two deputies came crunching in as the sheriff spoke.

"Is there?" one of them asked.

"Don't be a cow, Dávila," the sheriff said. "How could he make himself that small?"

"It cost me a lot of money," the fat baker said, "and I want to see him pay for it."

"Where is he?" the sheriff said.

"He got away, sheriff," said Dávila.

The boy's father opened his mouth to say something, then shut it again.

"That's fine," the fat baker said. "That's just fine! A fine bunch of policemen!"

"Let's not get excited," the sheriff said. "You seem to be an excitable man. What were you two fighting about?"

"Fighting?" the baker said.

"Why did he shoot your place up?"

"How would I know?" the baker said. "Ungrateful dog!"

"He used to come here," a younger baker said. "He'd have coffee with us, and we'd always give him bread to take home."

"He'd play his accordion for us and we'd feed him," a third baker said. "And now this."

"So out of a blue sky he shoots your place up," the sheriff said. "I ought to take all of you in for questioning."

The fat baker pursed his lips angrily, but he did not say anything.

The sheriff yawned. "But I think I'll forget it this time," he said. He yawned again. "Let's go," he said. He smiled. "He's across the river by now."

At the door the sheriff stopped and looked at the boy.

"Yours, de la Garza?" he asked.

The boy's father nodded.

"Fine young man," the sheriff said, and yawned.

"I guess so," his father answered, "except for him thinking he's got a piano inside his head."

"A what?" the sheriff said, almost waking up completely.

"A piano," the father said. His face glowed with revelation, and he turned to his son. "The music!" he said. "That radio thing. That's your music!"

"It isn't!" the boy said. "My music never came out of a box!"

"Now, now," his father said. "You know it did."

"Stop saying that!" the boy cried. "I'll...I'll run away if you don't stop!"

His father took his arm and shook it playfully.

"Temper," his father said, in high spirits. "Temper."

"It's all your fault," the boy said, shaking loose. "It's all your fault if I never hear it again."

"Best thing that could happen to you," his father said.

"But I don't want to stop hearing it," the boy said. "And now you've made it happen. It won't come back again, I know."

"Let's go home," his father said. "Your mother will be worried."

"Wait a while," said the sheriff. He looked thoughtful. "I see," he said, with the air of one who discovers a vital clue. "He thinks he hears music, is that it?"

"That's about it, sheriff," his father said.

"Why don't you get him a piano?"

"Well, I don't see how I...ha-ha, you're joking, sheriff," his father said.

"Tell you what," the sheriff said. "I'll see he gets a piano. We've got one at home, and the kids just play the damn...well, I think I should get them something different. One of them radios, for instance."

His father looked as if he had suddenly swallowed something unpleasant.

"Sheriff," he said, "we just couldn't impose on you

like that."

"No trouble at all," the sheriff said. "Fact is…Well, I think I should get the kids something else. It's one of them player pianos, you know. You pump it with your feet and the music comes out."

When the sheriff said it was a player piano, the boy's father lost some of his sickish look. But he said nevertheless, "I just couldn't allow it, sheriff. It's just a silly idea of his."

"Stop being polite with me, de la Garza," the sheriff said. "I'll have that piano at your house tomorrow, and you'd better not refuse it."

"But sheriff," his father said.

"Let's ask the boy," the sheriff said. "Do you want the piano, sonny?"

"Does it play 'Over the Waves'?" the boy asked.

"No," the sheriff said.

"I'll take it," the boy said.

His father pursed his lips and sighed.

"Where's your breeding?" he said. "Say thank you, at least."

After the sheriff left, they went down the dark street, leaving the lights behind them. His father took out his gun as he walked, cocked it and uncocked it, sighted along the barrel, twirled it around and put it back in its holster.

"That Dávila," he said. "He couldn't catch the scabies." He laughed. "If the sheriff had let me go, I would have caught the man. I remember once when I was young, I ran down a Carrancista officer. We both lost our horses…"

"It was a Federalist officer," the boy said.

"Was it?" his father said.

"It was the last time," the boy said.

"Ah well," his father said. "Maybe it was, at that. It's hard to remember at times, it's been so long ago. So long, long ago."

He sighed, and for a few moments they walked together in silence.

After a while the boy said, "Papá, will you give me a dollar?"

"A dollar?" his father said. "What for?"

"To buy a book."

"A book? A whole dollar for a book?"

"A piano book. Now that we'll have a piano I think I should practice."

His father made a strange noise in the dark.

They walked a few paces in silence.

Then his father said, "You don't have to practice with that kind of piano. You just pump the pedals. Fact is..." His voice brightened. "Fact is, I think I'll try it myself."

The boy jerked his head toward him.

His father smote one hand against the other. "By God!" he said. "You know what?"

"What," the boy said.

"I'll get 'Over the Waves' in one of those rolls!"

The boy stopped in his tracks.

His father did not notice. He kept right on walking, saying, "I'll get it tomorrow. By God, I will!"

The boy watched his father disappear into the night. He felt very sad and very old and very much alone. Somewhere in the dark, ahead of him, his father was whistling in a very ornate tremolo.

*"In the
Immensity
Of the waves, of the waves of the sea ..."*

Macaria's Daughter

The two police cars came screaming down the street and skidded to a stop at 18th and Miraflores. Four men in suntans and stetson hats stepped out into the midmorning sun. The sirens died out, the dust settled, and the street was quiet again. The shacks lining the hard-dirt sidewalk leaned crazily toward each other on their slender stilts. They seemed to be deserted.

"Which one is it, Mac?" asked one of the policemen.

"This one here," Mac said, pointing to a weather-blackened box. He walked in past the fallen gate, and the rest followed. The door was open. Standing on the grapefruit crate that was the doorstep, Mac looked inside. The woman was lying on the floor between the head of the bed and the altar. The altar was a high shelf nailed into the corner and decorated with varicolored tissue paper, spangles, little mirrors and ornate white candles misshapen by the heat. In the center was a plaster image of the Virgin of Guadalupe, quarter-life size, its brown Indian face staring down on the woman. A second policeman climbed on the step and peered over Mac's shoulder.

"God, she's a mess," he said.

The man was in the far corner of the room. He was sitting on a kitchen chair, his elbows on his knees and his head in his hands so that only his long tangled hair was visible. He looked up at the second policeman's voice and, seeing Mac's bulk in the doorway, he rose. He was short and squat with long powerful arms and a very dark, pushed-in face that was almost noble in its ugliness. The sweat trickled down his pock-marked features in tiny rivulets.

"Hello, Tony," said Mac.

"Hello," the man said.

Mac walked into the room. "Where's the knife?"

"There." Tony pointed toward the bed. Another policeman came in and looked at the woman. A car drove up outside, and the driver yelled to the patrolman standing in the doorway, "What is it, Pete?"

"Mexican killed his wife," shouted Pete.

"Oh," said the man in the car. He drove away.

The others were looking at the woman. "He tried to cut her head off," one of them said.

"Naw," said the other, "look at them breasts. He worked on them more."

"Geeze! There's more'n thirty, forty cuts on that body."

Mac went over to Tony and patted his shoulder. "Too bad, Tony," he said. "Was she in love with another guy?"

Tony's ugly face came alive. "No!" he said savagely. "No!"

"Now, now," Mac said, "we all know why a man kills his wife."

The youngest of the policemen was looking at the woman's thighs, which her tattered skirt did not wholly cover. They were white and incongruously whole. "Gosh," he said, "she must have been pretty."

She was too pretty. Tony had thought of that when he sat in the kitchen chair looking at her, his right hand pressed against his side. She was lying on the bed reading a comic book. Now she took the book away from her face and looked at him. "Are you sick?" she asked.

He stared at the length of her, from her shapely little feet to the white face with the big eyes and the childish mouth. She was as pretty as the movie stars whose pictures she clipped from magazines and pasted on tinseled cardboard for the shelf opposite the altar. She looked like Hedy Lamar. Did Hedy die in any of her pictures? He couldn't remember.

"Why don't you answer?" she complained.

"I'm sick," he said.

"Oh." Her mouth was a red circle of concern. "Do you want me to fix you something?" she asked without stirring. "Maybe a cup of coffee will make you feel better. Ever since you came in this morning you've been sitting there." She sat up suddenly. "Are you mad at me?"

"No," he said.

She flopped back on the bed. "Well, I am mad," she pouted. "Every morning you come in and kiss me and pet me, and this morning not even a smile."

The hollow of her throat was soft and smooth. He wondered why it was necessary for him to do it. To keep on being a man, they said. The withered old men would sit around in the shade, smoking their cigarettes and talking about him. But it wasn't her fault; she was Macaria's daughter. A great surge of pity choked him. Life had given her such a bad deal, and now he had to kill her. It was too awful to think about, and he wanted to kneel at the edge of the bed and put his head in her lap and sob. He clamped his teeth over his trembling lips.

But they were waiting out there, especially the women. When he came home that morning there was nobody out on the street, nobody in the yards. He knew they were all inside, waiting for him to do it. Nobody wanted to be hauled into court as a witness, so they were hiding and watching. The women especially. Until they heard her screams, telling them that justice had been served, that their own virtue had been affirmed.

The first time he saw her he was a boy of eleven and already looked more like a monkey than a boy. She was on the front steps of the house at the alley corner, a small house built at the sidewalk's edge with no fence at all, Macaria's house. She sat chin in hand looking up the street toward the pavement several blocks away. Next evening she was there again with her baby brother, a pale little skeleton of a child with a belly bigger than his head.

Tony's mother had told him to stay away from Macaria's house, but the lonely little girl with the frightened eyes attracted him. He soon made it a habit to sit with her and her little brother as soon as it was dark. They sat and looked up the street, and she would ask him what his mother was like and what he had for supper. He never asked questions, just answered and looked at her in the dim light.

Her little brother whimpered occasionally, but he

never cried. When a pair of headlights swung off the pavement, the girl would say, "There they come now, there they come." The little boy would repeat, "They come now." But the automobile would rock past them on the bumpy street, and the little girl and her brother would peer after it in the gloom. After that they would be silent for a long while. The bugle in Fort Jones would blow for nine o'clock, and Tony had to go home. Half a block away he always turned and looked back. The lights in the houses around them were going out one by one. But the little girl and her brother still sat on the steps, pressing their bodies against each other. Tony would run home because his mother was waiting.

One Sunday there was an especially good show at the movies, and he saw it over and over till he was sleepy. He hurried home, fearful because the Western Union clock said eleven. Inside the barrio he was stopped by two men in sweaty work clothes.

"Say, kid," one of them said, "do you know a woman by the name of Macaria that lives on this street?"

"She's in the push-and-pull industry," said the other one.

"In the alley," Tony said and showed them the house. There was a light inside and the door was open. Macaria was standing in front of a mirror putting on an earring and talking to a third man. She was as pretty as a china doll. The man with Macaria was laughing, and he slapped her playfully on the rump. Fascinated, Tony followed the other two men and stuck his head inside the door, looking for Macaria's daughter.

"Say," the third man said, "aren't you Antonio's little boy?"

Tony said he was.

"You'd better go home," the man said. "You've got no business in a place like this."

It was about this time that Macaria's little boy died. Not long afterwards, she married a middle-aged American drummer named Sam Polk, who sold clothing and household goods from door to door. In a couple of years she and Sam Polk were well-to-do. She had the little house painted a bright yellow and put red shingles on the roof, making it one of the best-looking houses in the neighborhood. She dressed her daughter in bright organdie and sent her to school. The neighbors were scandalized. Macaria was still Macaria, and she had no right to live so well on the wages of sin. And though her daughter now called herself Marcela Polk, she was still Macaria's daughter. Too pretty for her own good, with her big dark eyes, her white skin and her pouting red mouth. The housewives looked at her when she passed by, and they shook their heads. It was written plainly on her face, and it showed in the way she walked, they said. She was her mother's daughter and she was fifteen now.

Macaria knew what the neighbors said, and she defended her daughter with misdirected zeal. She beat Marcela often, to keep her from making friends with the boys. The boys did follow her home from school, making obscene jokes and pushing one another against her from behind. Older men whistled at her, and if she turned up her nose, they would say, "How does she get that way? For all she knows I'm her father." The girls hated her because she was pretty, because she wore brightly colored dresses, and because she was Macaria's daughter.

Tony had quit school at thirteen. At sixteen he was almost full grown and had a job nights at the ice plant. One evening when he was going by the yellow-painted house on his way to work, Macaria beckoned to him from the door. "Come in," she said, and he went because there was nothing else he could do. Sam Polk was sitting in an easy chair looking at the ceiling, and Marcela was on the sofa looking at the floor. Macaria waved Tony into a chair.

"You're Tony," she said.

"Macaria," Sam Polk said.

"Shut up," Macaria said. Sam Polk sighed and looked at the ceiling. "You've been walking my daughter home lately," continued Macaria. "Two, three times a week now, and I'm getting tired of beating her." She glared at him. "You love her?"

Tony was too embarrassed to answer.

"Want to marry her?"

He managed a half nod.

"All right," said Macaria, "she's yours."

Tony stared incredulously.

"What's the matter, damn you?" Macaria said. Then with drunken satisfaction, "She's a virgin. She better be."

"Macaria, for God's sake," said Sam Polk.

"Shut up," said Macaria and Sam Polk shut up. She put up a fat thigh on the arm of Tony's chair. "You're ugly, see? That's why I like you, because you're so goddam ugly and hardworking and strong."

"Macaria," pleaded Sam Polk.

"Damn you, I said shut up! You see," she confided to Tony, "Sam can't beat me and make me be good. But you can beat her. You can make her be good all the time. It's wearing me down. If I keep her another year, some goddam pachuco will take her out into the bushes and I'll kill her, by God, I'll kill her."

Tony felt the outlines of the clasp knife beneath his shirt. He looked at his wife, lying on the bed reading her comic book like a child, and his eyes watered. They had got married at the courthouse, with Macaria and a couple of hangers-on as witnesses. His parents had refused to come, and they did not visit them in the one-room shack Tony had rented in the poorest part of the barrio.

He had never beaten her, never shouted at her even. He gave her the finest things ten dollars a week could buy. Candy, second-hand magazines and comic books, and little presents from the five-and-ten. But except for him, she was alone. The neighbors would not speak to her, although they talked about her in loud voices whenever she ventured outside. They knew who she was, Macaria's daughter. Still, she had been a good wife. Until now.

He took his hand away from his belt, rose and went toward her. She looked up at him expectantly. At the edge of the bed he dropped on his knees and caressed her hair. She dropped the comic book and put her hands on his shoulders.

"I love you," he said.

She smiled indulgently.

"I'd give anything to make you happy," he continued. "That sounds like the movies, don't it? But maybe the way they do things in the movies is the right way, after all. What's the difference between you and Hedy Lamar, anyway?"

"Aw, now, Tony," she said.

"Do you suppose I don't think sometimes?" he said. "You're so pretty. You should have pretty things, and what have you got?"

"I have you," she said.

His flat, ugly face twisted comically. "Don't do that," he said. "Don't do it, please!" Then more calmly, "Tomorrow we'll get us a divorce."

Marcela raised herself on one elbow. "What are you talking about?"

"I know all about it," he said.

She stared. "All about... All about what?"

"The plant broke down last night. We passed by the Black Cat, and you and him were in the car."

Marcela tried to say something.

"You were drinking and laughing. And then you drove away." He choked and closed his eyes momentarily. When he opened them again, he saw she was trying to crawl away from him. "Don't be frightened," he said. Then, awed by the thought, "I might have killed you. I almost did. That's what everybody expects me to do, you know."

She made a squeaking sound.

"But I can't do it. I can't get mad at you, not killing mad." He breathed deeply. "When me and the boys saw you the first thing I thought was 'Well, I've got to kill her now. When a man's wife falls for someone else, it's got to be done.' One of the boys said, 'Got a knife?' I said, 'No.' And he said, 'Here's mine.' I took it and they went away and left me alone. But all along I knew I couldn't do it. I've thought it all out and falling in love is no sin."

"Don't, don't." The words were finally dislodged from Marcela's throat. She sat up and began to cry.

"I knew you weren't in love with me, as ugly as I am. Only I wish you had told me from the start. We would have got us a divorce, and then it wouldn't be so bad. As it is, after tonight, they'll say I'm a born cuckold. They'll say... I don't care. It's time the breaks came your way." He put his hand under his shirt to close the clasp knife. "Tomorrow we'll fix it so you can marry him."

"But I can't," wailed Marcela.

"Why?" He stopped with his hand half inside his shirt.

"I don't love him. I never saw him before. I went because I wanted to get out! To get out!"

He moved back, away from her.

"I was sorry afterwards! I swear!"

The coroner came in, and Mac pointed toward the altar. "Over there," he said.

"Nice piece of work," the coroner said. He knelt before the body and asked without turning, "What was it? Same old story?"

"Yep," said Mac. "Wasn't it, Tony?"

Tony did not reply.

"All right," Mac said. "Come along now." He took Tony's arm and led him toward the door.

The youngest policeman was standing behind the coroner. "Pretty little wench she must have been," he observed.

"You should have seen her mother when she was young," the coroner said.

A Cold Night

The boy was playing on the floor, close to the tub full of glowing charcoal. Because the lip of the tub was hot, he sat tilted sideways, a buttock against the lower part, the rest of him leaning away, propped on one hand. With his other hand he played. He was a quiet, skinny little boy; his arms and legs looked like the limbs of those mechanical Mickey Mouses sold in the ten-cent stores: black, straight and very thin.

On the other side of the tub his father sat in a backless kitchen chair, hunched elbows-on-knees over the coals, smoking a cornhusk cigarette. Occassionally he spat into the tub. The coals sizzled and steamed for a moment and then glowed red again. The room would be quiet after that, except for the subdued noise of dishes, which the boy's mother was putting away. And now and then her hollow cough.

The boy was playing with an oblong piece of wood, whittled roughly at both ends to make it taper. The tapering made it look like a short, fat cigar. Or a boat, or a racing car or an airplane. That was the beauty of this piece of wood, it could be so many things. It was the boy's favorite toy and his only one, and because of that it was dirty and discolored from long handling.

Its rough edges, where the boy had worked it clumsily, were beginning to smooth away.

Outside it was cold, one of the coldest nights of the year. The wind shook the little two-room house. There was a broken windowpane, into which an old pillow had been stuffed. Sometimes the wind would force its way inside. When it did, it caused a chill eddy in the room, especially along the floor, where the boy played, his sharp little nose close to the piece of wood, his big eyes soft with dreams.

Three days before the weather had been mild, and the boy had been playing outdoors. That was a long time ago. He had been squatting in the alley behind the church then, teasing a big red ant that was in a hurry to get home. He had been waiting for the church bells to talk to one another in the soft, warm twilight. That was when he saw death. But that was long ago. He tried not to think about it, not to let the thought interfere with his dreams about the oblong piece of wood.

Now the wind blew against the house in a mighty gust, and the pillow in the windowpane could not withstand it. The pillow pulled away slowly from the broken glass and slid to the floor. The boy shivered and looked at his father. His father did not move. He sat on the backless chair, his half-burned cigarette in one hand, his other hand stroking his swallow-wing mustache, his shoulders hunched. His matted hair was pressed down along his forehead where his hat had been. The boy looked at him, a half-smile on his thin, pointed face. Some day, he thought, some day I will have a beautiful mustache like that. His father did not notice him. He was dreaming too.

His mother left the dishes and crossed the room in

A Cold Night

heavy, clumping steps. She picked up the pillow and jammed it back in place in the windowpane, pushing so hard that the broken glass cracked a little more. His father looked up and met her eyes.

"I was getting up," he said. "I was going to do it."

"Tomorrow," she said. "Tomorrow you were going to do it."

"I'm tired too," he said. "And my back hurts pretty bad. You don't know what it's like, pulling stumps out of the ground from dawn to dusk."

"I guess I don't," she said.

The man turned back to the fire, his feelings hurt. He dragged on his cigarette and slowly let the smoke out through his nostrils. The boy stared at the smoke, fascinated.

His father said, "Why don't you go to bed? Or play with something else. All you do is slide that piece of wood back and forth."

"He doesn't have anything else to play with," his mother said. "He could have, if you had let him go downtown last week to see Santa Claus."

"Come along," she told the boy. "It is time for you to go to bed."

"It's cold in bed," the boy said.

His mother smiled thinly. "It will be warmer in bed. After a while."

The boy knew it would be warmer in bed. But the bed was in the other room, and it was dark. He was afraid of the dark, but he was even more afraid to say so. Perhaps if he did not mention it at all, she would not make him say the prayer this time. So he left his toy and went with her, and after he had creaked into bed, he burrowed about in the cold bedclothes to warm them as quickly as possible.

His mother said, "Haven't you forgotten something?"

He stopped burrowing, and pushing away the covers he knelt on the bed. "Not the one about the Virgin Mary!" he said. "Please!"

His mother smiled her thin, distant smile. Her brown face seemed to float above the flame of the candle she was holding. It reminded him of the face of the Virgin of Guadalupe in the church. Except that his mother's smile frightened him. "It's a very important prayer. The Virgin Mary will look after you all your life."

"I don't want *her* to look after me!"

"Say the words with me." His mother's voice was firm. He straightened his back, shifted his knees and repeated the words after her. The Padrenuestro first and then the Avemaría, down to the last terrible words. "Now and at the hour of our death. Amen."

His mother blessed him, kissed him and said, "Now go to sleep." And she went back into the other room, taking the stump of a candle with her.

But he couldn't sleep. He was thinking about God. Through the chinks in the wall he could see the light in the other room, and he wished he were there, watching his father smoke and playing on the floor with his piece of wood. He did not like it at all, lying in the dark with nobody but God. It made him think of things he didn't want to think about. But he couldn't stop thinking them, because they were God's business. That's what his mother had called it, God's business. "One must leave God's business to God," she had said when he told her that evening three days ago. But now he was alone with God, and he had to think of all those things.

He had seen death, that was why. He had come

home, still shaking, and he had told his father, "I just saw death."

His father was sitting on the doorstep, smoking. He had been surprised into a quick upward glance. After that one glance his father had settled back to his smoking. "Hush," he said. "Don't talk wild talk."

His father was a dreamer, he did not believe in death. But his mother, who spit blood into a dirty rag, was not a dreamer. When she heard what the boy had said, her eyes glittered with a feverish interest, a hint of recognition. She called him inside, questioned him.

He had been in the alley, squatting, his back against the brick wall at the rear of the church. Just beside him was a door, and in front of him were two garbage cans belonging to the church. He was squatting there, teasing the red ant and waiting for the bells to ring before he went on home through the alley.

A man had come down the alley, hatless, the end of his tie over his shoulder as he hurried along. He stopped to light a cigarette and looked about but did not see the boy. After puffing on his cigarette, he started off, then stopped. There was another man standing at the mouth of the alley. The man with the cigarette swung about and started walking back the way he had come. Then he stopped. Still another man was at the other end of the alley.

The man with the cigarette just stood there. The other two men quietly came up to him. No one said a word. The two men took something out of their back pockets and beat the other man over the head. There was no sound except for the whack-whack of the blows and the men's heavy breathing. The beaten man put his hands on top of his head. The others tore the hands away, and the whack-whacking sound went on.

Again the man put his hands on his head, again they pulled his hands away. Then they began to push at him after each blow. The man staggered this way and that but he didn't fall. Finally one of the two men took out a knife and stabbed him in the side. Now the man fell.

The other one kept looking at the fallen man until the one with the knife said, "Come on, let's go. He's dead."

The one who was looking muttered something. The other one said, "God damn! Haven't you ever seen death before?" Then they went away.

The boy came out from behind the garbage cans. He had never seen death before, so he went and looked at the man on the ground. Lying in his bed in the dark, alone with God, the boy wished he had not looked. But he had looked, a long, long look, and then he had run home and told his mother. She had listened eagerly. When he finished he exclaimed, "Why did they do it, Mama?"

"God knows," his mother said. "It's God's business."

"It was awful!" he said. "I wish I hadn't seen it."

His mother had looked at him calmly. "Awful?" she said. "There's nothing awful about death. All of us have to die sometime. Some day you'll be like that man in the alley."

"Oh no!" he cried, "I don't want to die! I'm not going to be like that!"

His mother gave him a hungry smile. "Of course you'll die. When God wishes, not one moment later or sooner. You don't know how or where or when." She paused to cough. "It's time you learned how to pray, no matter what your father says."

That night he had prayed with her, terrified by the thought that at any moment he could become a corpse

like the man in the alley. She had taken a grim satisfaction in his terror. "There's nothing to be afraid of,"
she had said. "Just love God."

But lying there in the dark that cold night, he
could not love God no matter how much he tried. Fear
choked him, he wanted to get up and scream. But he
remained quite still. He wondered how God could be
so cruel to be like He was, and he said to himself, "Oh,
I hate Him! I hate Him!"

It came out before he could stop himself. He felt he
was sinking, and he started to pray, fervently and
with trembling lips. Cupping his amulet of the Virgin
of Guadalupe in his hand, he kissed it over and over.
It was a tin likeness of La Guadalupana, which hung
around his neck on a string. This image of her, though
just a lump of tin, was a constant reminder of the Virgin that stood in church to the left of the altar. He
liked her much more than he did the Virgin Mary. She
was the most beautiful thing in the church, she and
the bells.

It would have been very dull in church, except for
La Guadalupana. She was dressed in red and green
robes. The moon and the stars were at her feet, and
there was a blue canopy above her, decorated with
glass pendants shaped like huge drops. The inside of
her robe was painted gold, and there was a frame of
gold all around her. Below her there was a table with
a white lace cloth, and on it there were little glass
cups filled with short, fat candles in many colors,
flickering and throwing all sorts of shadows on the
wall, making the colors of the Virgin's robe sparkle,
and the glass drops on the canopy too. It was a beautiful sight.

But best of all was her face. It was a nice, familiar

Indian face, brown and smiling. It was beautiful, that smile, all-embracing, all-forgiving. When he was in church, the boy always fixed his eyes on the Virgin's smile, and he prayed to her instead of to the Christ that writhed bloodily on his cross at the right side of the altar. This was before he had seen the men in the alley. Since then his mother had sent him to church once, and he had not been able to look toward the right of the altar without shuddering.

So now, lying in the dark, in the cold of the night, while the wind pried at the window and at the cracks in the wall, he stroked his image of La Guadalupana and tried to see her not as she was in his tiny medallion but as she was in church, brilliant and colorful, smiling down on him. He had done this before, on other nights when he lay alone in the dark, and it helped him go to sleep. He tried to do it now, but tonight he could not see her. Instead, the writhing figure on the cross kept swimming into his vision, with its bloody head and wounded side. Except that the face was like that of the man in the alley.

He was alone with God and God's business. And it made him very much afraid. He began to weep, silently, and with the tears there came rebellion, exasperation with himself and everything else, and he said to himself over and over, "Goddam! Goddam!"

The words became monotonous, meaningless, and he tried to give them new force. "Goddam everything!" he said. "Goddam everything! Goddam God!"

His mouth twitched violently. He put up his hands as if to avert a blow. But nothing happened.

He waited. He did not even think of praying, he knew he was beyond any such help.

Above the foot of the bed, close to the roof, there

was a little window not much larger than a picture
frame, and beyond it was a square of sky. It was a
clear, bright piece of sky, and in it were several stars.
The stars were white and shiny, and they seemed to
wink at him. There was no sound outside except for
the swirling wind. It seemed to be calling his name.
"Ramón. Ramón. Ramón."

In the other room his father hacked and spit into
the coals, and after the coals had hissed, there was no
sound except the wind calling his name, "Ramón.
Ramón. Ramón." It didn't sound angry, it didn't seem
to care at all.

Whatever there was inside of him that had
crouched and shivered suddenly stood up, courageous
and erect. He took a deep breath and said deliberate-
ly, "God damn God!"

A wild spasm seized him, shook him violently,
then passed away, leaving him weak but victorious.
No thunderbolt. In the sky the stars still shone. He
tried again, adding the names of Christ, of Saint Peter
and Saint Paul. After that he added the Holy Ghost.
He was delighted with the supreme meanness of it all.
He lay there, saying the words over and over to himself until he got tired. He closed his eyes, for he was
very sleepy, and soon he was floating about on the
edge of sleep, thinking. His father had been right, after all.

His head was dipping and rising in airy blackness.
What was he...trying.... He blinked into half-wakeful-
ness again. What was he trying to... oh, yes. He was
trying to call the Virgin of Guadal... But no! He sat up
in bed. That wasn't it! That wasn't...

He sat there with his mouth open, catching his
breath. Cupping the image of La Guadalupana in his

hand, he raised it to his lips. But before his lips touched the piece of tin, he closed his fist about it in a quick, almost violent movement. He pressed his clenched fist against his chest and sank down on the pillow, staring at the dark. The wind sighed and swirled about the house. "Ramón. Ramón. Ramón," it said.

It was a lonesome sound, the lonesomest sound he had ever heard.

The Gringo

He was standing on the brick sidewalk along a street close to the plaza. Looking. Thinking. Down the walk came a group of girls dressed in the *china* style worn by working-class women of the cities. Low-cut blouses, flared skirts. Not much underneath. They came chattering toward him, and he stepped into the dust of the street to give them room. They stopped talking as they came near him and looked him over. No shy, downcast glances with these city girls. They took in his face, his clothes. Especially his clothes, as so many other people had done that day.

As they went by, one of them said in an affected lilt, "¡Ay, qué chulo!"

"Pretty boy, yes," said another, "for a Gringo."

A third looked back at him. "What's a *gademe* doing here? Now?"

"Go ask him," the first one said. They all giggled.

He felt like going after them and telling them, "I am not a Gringo! I am not a Gringo!"

If he could only find some place in town where he could get some decent clothes. He couldn't change his skin, or the color of his eyes. But if he could only get rid of the floppy black hat, the Gringo farmer's boots with their round toes and stove-pipe tops. But he knew no one here. Only his cousin Eutimio, and he was waiting in the chaparral close to the river.

Once the girls were gone, a group of ragged urchins moved closer to him, their eyes bright in their dirty faces. "Are you a Gringo?" they asked him. "Are you a Gringo?"

He stepped back onto the sidewalk. "No!" he shouted. "No!" They scattered, laughing, and once they were a safe distance away, they threw clods at him. His brother Leandro must be about the age of the biggest of the boys. If he was alive. From Eutimio he knew that his father and older brothers were dead, and that his mother and the younger ones had gone to Padilla, many leagues to the south. Eutimio had tried to convince him that he too should go south and look for them.

"This is no business of yours, Ygnacio," he had said. "The army will do the job." But he knew the army by itself would not be able to do the job.

A crowd was gathering around him. They were not staring at him, though; they were looking down the street. Then he heard the drums. Up the street came a body of infantry. People were shouting, "¡Viva el coronel Ampudia! ¡Viva el coronel Ampudia!"

So this was Ampudia's brigade, or part of it. The crowd yelled even louder as they went marching by. Only the officers were wearing boots. The soldiers were in huaraches, but there were smart little shakos on their heads. He wondered how many of them had ever fired the muskets they carried. And how many would be dead tomorrow or the next day, cut down by the Gringo cannon. But it was evident that to the crowd they looked invincible. A middle-aged man was standing next to Ygnacio, his blanket folded over his shoulder. He had a patch over one eye and a loud, hoarse voice. "Kill the *coyones!*" he yelled. "Don't let me one of them alive!" He turned and looked at Ygnacio with his bleary eye. "Ampudia will cut them to pieces! He'll sweep them away! Isn't that so, *joven?*"

"I... don't know. The Gringos have so many guns!"

The one-eyed man peered up at him. "Who are you, anyway?" Then he noticed the brace of pistols in Ygnacio's belt, and he moved back a little. Ygnacio edged into the crowd, and the one-eyed man started cheering again. It was no use talking to people like these. There were no recruits here. And an army of irregulars was the only hope.

He had ridden south, staying at some distance from Taylor's army, until he ran into a detachment of their cavalry. They took him for a Gringo living thereabouts, so he risked coming closer. It was a powerful army, fearsome yet beautiful to watch. He didn't stay long because he knew he would give himself away if he spoke more than a few words in English. So he rode until he got to the great river, hoping to bring some useful information. But nobody would listen to him.

He threaded his way through the crowd to a side street that led to the edge of town. There was a cantina at the end of the street, a mud and thatch *jacal* beside a clearing. A couple of empty oxcarts rested in the clearing, and there were a dozen skinny horses tied to the mesquite branch that served as a hitching post. Perhaps he might find some recruits there. He would drink with them, buy them drinks perhaps. He felt the money pouch in his pocket. He had the coins Prudence had given him before they parted.

There was loud talking in the cantina. About the Gringo army north of the river, about Gringo spies supposed to be in town. All the foreign merchants were spies, someone said. They saw him then, standing at the door, and the talking stopped. He went to the near end of the bar. The bartender was a tall, wiry man. His sallow skin was stretched out over a bony face that looked like death's head. He was looking at Ygnacio's belt and the two horse pistols stuck into it as Ygnacio came up to the bar.

"Un mezcal, por favor."

The bartender poured the drink into a clay cup, and Ygnacio laid a coin on the counter. The bartender rang the coin against the wood, then held it up for everyone to see. "Good silver," he said. "A whole silver *real*." He put a little pile of copper coins on the counter. "Your change," he said.

The men began to talk loudly again. "There are a lot of Gringos in town these days," said the man standing closest to Ygnacio. He was a long-faced man, dark but with white spots all over his face and hands.

"That's right, Pinto," said a man farther down the bar. "They're all spies. Gringos *gademes*! We ought to turn them over to the army!"

El Pinto belched noisily. He was somewhat unsteady on his feet. "We ought to round them all up," he said. "Round them up and hang them. That's what we're going to do." He focused his eyes on Ygnacio. "You speak very good Spanish, *joven*."

"Why not?" Ygnacio said.

El Pinto smiled a humorless smile. "You speak English?"

"I'm a Mexican, just like you!"

"No need to get sulfurous, *joven*," El Pinto said,

still smiling. "You can't blame me for making a mistake, you being a stranger here. Where you from?"

"From up north, close to the Nueces."

"Gringo country. You a friend of theirs?"

"No, I am not their friend, though I have come to know them well."

"So it appears, *joven*, from the looks of you. Did you run away from them?" The others grinned.

"Yes, I did. I ran away from them. Perhaps you and your friends will go the other way with me and run into them." There was a moment's silence, and Ygnacio added, "I slipped away from them. I was a prisoner. On the way down here I camped close to their army a couple of times. They didn't bother me because of the way I'm dressed. And..."

"And because you are one of them," said a short man with a beard.

Ygnacio ignored him. "And I have come all the way down here to join Antonio Canales and his guerrillas. How many of you are ready to go with me?"

"To fight the Gringo army?" El Pinto said. "Why? That's what our soldiers are for."

"Without some help from us, our soldiers are going to lose."

The short man with the beard said, "What did I tell you? He's a traitor!"

"Listen to me! You haven't seen the Gringo army! Our only hope is if our rancheros fight them the way we know how. In guerrillas."

"I'm not a ranchero," El Pinto said.

"No! You are a coward!"

El Pinto looked around and then sidled closer to Ygnacio. "You know?" he said softly, almost gently. "You are just a boy, you lack experience. If you were full grown, I would show you that you are mistaken."

"About what?"

"About many things. Like going around acting like a *caudillo*. Being a warrior chieftain is not for boys like you. And if you were a grown man, I would show you I'm not a coward."

"I'm old enough. Show me."

"Will you go outside with me?"

"With you and all your friends?"

"Without my friends. And without your pistols. Just you and me and our knives."

"Very well. I'll put my pistols aside once we get where we're going."

El Pinto turned toward the others. "My friend and I have some business to settle. All of you stay here till I come back." He tossed off the rest of his drink and led the way out of the cantina. At the door he stumbled and almost fell.

The sun was setting as they came out of the cantina. El Pinto was mumbling something about boys who needed to be taught a lesson. His speech was getting slurred. They went down a trail in the brush until they came to a large clearing.

" 'Sgood place here," El Pinto said indistinctly. He threw aside his blanket. He was staggering so much that it looked as if he would fall down at any moment.

"You're too drunk to fight," Ygnacio said. "I don't want to kill a drunken man."

" 'M all right," El Pinto mumbled "No pistols. No pistols."

Ygnacio put his hat on the ground behind him and placed the pistols on top of it. El Pinto yelled, "Now, boys!" and he rushed at Ygnacio, knife in hand. Ygnacio turned, his pistols still in his hands, and kicked out at El Pinto, knocking him on his back. "I know you're there!" he shouted. "And I know exactly where you are! You make more noise than a bunch of cows."

El Pinto got up and ran into the chaparral at the far side of the clearing. He and his friends retreated noisily through the underbrush. Ygnacio put one of the pistols in his belt and picked up his hat. He took a quick look at his right leg. El Pinto's knife had scored the boot but had not cut through the leather. There was something to be said about farmer boots.

It was dark by the time he came to the spot where his cousin Eutimio was waiting. Eutimio had found a sheltered place by the trunk of a fallen tree. He had a small fire going, and a coffee pot was on the fire. Their horses were tethered nearby—Eutimio's roan and Ygnacio's buckskin that had carried him all the way from the other side of the Nueces.

Eutimio and Ygnacio leaned toward each other across the fire so they could talk in low voices. Eutimio's round, usually cheerful face was somber. Every once in a while he would pass his hand through his stiff Indian hair and push it back, but immediately his hair would stand up straight again.

When Ygnacio told him about his encounter with El Pinto, Eutimio exclaimed, "You did a very foolish thing! Those people at La Calavera's cantina are the lowest scum in town. I told you going into the city was a hare-brained idea."

"I just wasn't lucky," Ygnacio muttered.

"You were luckier than you think. After showing them a bag full of silver *reales*, it's a wonder you still are alive."

Ygnacio was annoyed by Eutimio's scolding, but he held his tongue. Eutimio was only his cousin, but he was a good thirty years older. Eutimio filled an old tin cup with coffee and handed it to him. "Where did you get all that money?" he asked.

"Prudencia gave it to me when we said goodbye."

"A horse and saddle, a pair of pistols, and money as well? She must have been very much in love with you. Was she pretty?"

"Yes."

"No wonder you decided to stay with the Gringos so long." Eutimio was again his cheerful, playful self.

"I told you I had no choice but staying," Ygnacio replied testily. "The bullet that killed my horse went through my thigh first. It was a very bad wound and took a long time to heal."

"There must have been many of them."

"We thought they were just five, and we were a dozen. So we went after them with our machetes, except for my father and Don Mariano Hernández, who had blunderbusses. All we wanted to do was run them off. We didn't know there were more of them hiding in the brush, so we were ambushed like stupid greenhorns. Besides, they had those new revolving pistols."

"I've heard of them. I've never seen them, though."

"I saw them, all right."

"Why was Don Mariano with you? Were you expecting trouble?"

"Oh, no. We were home, sitting at the table, celebrating my birthday," Ygnacio said bitterly. "The older men were joking that now that I was sixteen I should get married. Then Manuel Vázquez, the sheepherder, came running in and told us the Gringos were rounding up our cattle. We thought we would just chase them off, since it was the first time they had bothered us. But they hadn't come just to steal a few head of cattle. I don't remember too much, except the surprise and the rapid firing. Then my horse was falling, and the next thing I knew I was coming to in the preacher's house."

"With your head in Prudencia's lap? Looking up into her pretty face?"

"Let's not joke about it. Let's not talk about it anymore."

That was the first thing he had seen. Her face as she looked down at him, pink cheeks and blue eyes. For a moment he thought he was in Heaven and that she was an angel. Then he was fully awake and saw he was in a strange house. People were talking, but not in Spanish. He was on a cot, his head bandaged and his left leg in a splint. He tried to say something, but she put her finger on his lips. Later he would know she had been tending him for the better part of two days and a night.

"The men you tried to recruit in La Calavera's cantina..." Eutimio was saying "...they're brave enough to rob a drunk, but they can't fight. They can't even ride. And that's all you'll find in the city now, as I tried to tell you. Those men of fighting age who didn't join Canales have been rounded up by Arista's officers."

After the fight, the Gringos had taken home their wounded, and they took him along, thinking he was one of theirs. When no one knew who he was, they took him to the preacher's house.

"I don't know what to make of you," Eutimio said. "You may be right. Arista will get whipped and it will be up to Antonio Canales to destroy the Gringos bit by bit. But why do you have to raise your own band of guerrillas?"

"I hate the sons-of-bitches. They killed my father and my brothers. Isn't that enough?"

She had known from the very first that he was not one of her people. And she kept it secret as long as she could. Meanwhile, she tried to teach him English. But it wasn't long before her father knew. There was a meeting, and most of them wanted to hang him, but her preacher father would not have it. So it was agreed he would be spared, but the preacher would be responsible for him. He was moved out of the house to quarters with their Mexican workers.

"I've got you some men who can ride and fight," Eutimio said.

"Good! Where did you find them?"

"On the other side of the river. They are highwaymen who operate on the road between here and the river mouth."

"Robbers."

"What else can you get around here?"

"The men with Canales are not outlaws."

"True, but El Gato Negro and his men feel patriotic enough to fight as guerrillas. What they want is booty, but as long as they fight the Gringos, Canales will not care."

"When do they join us?"

"Tomorrow morning, on the other side of the river. They have their own horses and weapons, of course."

"Why do they call him the Black Cat?"

"Because he looks like one. His name is Tomás Villegas. Very dark, but he has these yellow eyes that make him look like a cat peering at you from behind a bush."

"He's white, Papa," Prudence told her father. "He's

learning English, and when he knows enough, you can make a real Christian out of him." And she kept on nursing him. When he began hobbling about, he started doing chores around the house.

"All right," Ygnacio told Eutimio. "We'll take them with us. How many are there?"

"Eight. No more. El Gato Negro picks his men very carefully. But for now, drink your coffee and let's get some rest. We'll go across before dawn."

"Drink your milk," she said. "You need to build up your strength, now that your leg is healing."

"All right now," he said. "Healed long ago."

"Shush! Don't say that!"

They were standing by the gate leading to the barn, very close to each other. In plain view. If they had intended to do something bad, they would have hidden somewhere. It was completely innocent. He took the wooden bowl from her hands, drained it, and gave it back to her. As she reached out, their fingers touched and intertwined. The bowl fell to the ground, and they came closer together.

"After we cross tomorrow," Eutimio was saying, "don't forget to check the powder in those two cannons of yours. Make sure it didn't get wet."

"I know, I know," he said. He lay down on the sacahuiste grass, using his saddle for a pillow.

They jumped apart at the sound of her father's voice. "You goddam Greaser!" he roared. He picked up a piece of firewood and beat at Ygnacio's head. Ygnacio fended off the blows, and this enraged her father even more. He dropped the stick and stomped toward the side of the house, where he had left his buggy, and he drove away.

"I'll take the first watch," Eutimio said. "I fed your

horse, by the way. He's had more rest than you have."

It was a buckskin with a black stripe across his shoulders, the best horse the preacher had. As soon as her father was gone, Prudence led the horse out of the barn and started to saddle it herself. He took the saddle from her and was going to put it away, but she said, "Saddle up! Hurry!"

While he saddled the buckskin she ran into the house and came back carrying a water bottle, a bag of hardtack, and some weapons. Two old horse pistols with powder and shot, a knife, and a machete. "Hurry!" she repeated. "He went to get help. They'll kill you."

He rode away, without even kissing her goodbye. Not even that. Once across the Nueces he felt safe. He was in familiar country, where he had learned to hide from raiding Indians ever since he was a little boy. He knew they would look for him at his father's ranch, but he went there anyway. The houses were burned, the rails of the corrals down.

Eutimio was shaking his shoulder. "It's almost light," Eutimio said. "We must cross now."

"You didn't wake me at all."

"You needed the rest. Come on, we must hurry."

They swam their horses across and waited in the brush. The sun was already high when Villegas and his men showed up. They came quietly enough through the chaparral, as guerrillas and highwaymen should.

Villegas looked at Ygnacio suspiciously, his yellow eyes half-closed. After Eutimio introduced them, Villegas said, "There will be ten of us. Good. But I am not going with you, *joven*. You and your cousin are coming with me."

Ygnacio swallowed his pride. "As long as we are seeking the same ends, and that we agree on the means, it is all right with me."

"Good," said Villegas. It was hard to tell whether he was pleased or amused. He added, "We have information that a Gringo patrol will be coming this way, going upriver. If they follow the river, as we expect them to, they will leave the open road and enter the chaparral at this point."

"Things are going well," Eutimio said.

Villegas said, "As soon as they are well into the brush, we'll hit them."

"This morning?" Ygnacio exclaimed.

"Of course. When do you think. Tonight?"

"Yes! We let them bed down, and then at dawn we hit them. That is the best way."

"It is the best way, Villegas," Eutimio said. "They'll be so sleepy they won't put up much of a fight."

"You and your cousin may be afraid of a fight," Villegas said. "We aren't. And anyway, we don't want to hit them too far upriver. We want to get hold of the horses and saddles close to the city."

"Close to the city?"

"We already have a buyer for whatever we can take from the Gringos."

"I told you, Eutimio!" Ygnacio cried. "Thieves! That's all they are!"

Villegas looked thoughtfully at Ygnacio's pistols. He was about to say something when a mourning dove cooed down the road. One of Villegas' men rode up. "They're coming now," he said.

They moved into the brush, all of them, not far from where the road opened out into the flat country. They waited. Nothing happened. Villegas sent one of his men on foot to see what the soldiers were doing.

"They are stopped about fifty paces from the entrance into this road," the man reported.

"Perhaps our patriotic friend here has let them know we are waiting for them," said Villegas. "Perhaps he's one of them."

"I am not one of them," Ygnacio said wearily.

"But you look like them," another man said. "Why don't you ride out there and tell them the road is safe?"

"I will do it," Ygnacio said, spurring his horse into the open road. "Ho, there!" he shouted as he approached the soldiers, trying to say the words as he had heard them not too long ago.

The soldiers moved forward at a slow walk, their point man trotting ahead of them. The point came up to Ygnacio. He was very young and looked more like a girl than a man. Ygnacio swallowed and then shouted, "Thees way, boyss!"

An officer coming up behind the point urged his horse into a canter. "Hold!" he shouted. "That's not a white man!"

Ygnacio drew one of his pistols and shot the boy in the face. He aimed the other one at the officer, but it misfired. At the same time the officer shot at him but missed.

"¡Arma blanca!" he cried, sliding his machete from its sheath. But the officer galloped forward without drawing his saber. Then he saw the revolving pistol, and the guns of Palo Alto went off inside his head.

A Small Brown Bird

"You there! Boy!"

His mother's voice brought him to a sitting position.

"Yes ma'am."

"Go out and play!"

"Yes ma'am."

Her spare form moved away from the door, and he leaned back on his cot again, grimacing. For a while he lay there in hot-throated resentment, thinking nothing at all, just staring out the window. A sound of subdued voices came from the front part of the house, and he hardened into attention, straining. Perhaps they had a present hidden in the house somewhere. Perhaps... His mother's voice rose, sharp and tinny.

"It isn't enough, I tell you! For the whole week it isn't enough!"

His father's voice answered, conciliatory, and the boy turned to the window again. It was sunny outside; the guayaba bush was green and cool against the window. What a lousy day, he thought.

He heard his mother's footsteps, and he began tying his shoe laces.

"Didn't I tell you to go out and play?" she said.

"Yes ma'am."

"Well, why don't you?"

He bent over his shoe laces.

"And don't scuff those shoes." The shoes were scuffed already, but it was the only pair he had.

She went into the kitchen, and he sat on the edge of his cot again. If only it wasn't vacation time, he thought. Then he remembered the comic book he had hidden under the cot. He reached down for it and leafed through it, but his mind would not stay on the pictures. His thoughts wandered, and the little girl who lived next door crept into them. At first she watched while he went through heroic acts. Then she was in peril herself, and he rescued her, while her small brother watched. Now she was beside a mountain stream; the whole class at school was there too. Suddenly five bears came tearing out of a thicket.

A bird sang.

The boy looked out, annoyed. It was a small brown bird, a little ball of feathers chirping and hopping about on the bush outside the window. He put an arrow to his bow. Zing. The bird fluttered to the ground. The wall dissolved, and the boy leaped forward onto the jungle floor. There lay the bird, transformed into a tropical thing of rare and brilliant plumage. The boy picked it up and took it to the little girl next door. She clapped her hands with delight.

He did not hear a knock. The first thing he knew there were voices in the parlor, and his father was shouting to his mother that her brother was here. He sprang from the cot and made a dash for the parlor, galloping blindly through the door before he realized his mistake. Then he stopped, confused, a few steps inside the room.

"Oho!" his uncle shouted. "Give him the spurs! Pull his head back!"

The boy opened his mouth in a smile, but he glanced at his father at the same time, and the smile froze on his face, leaving his mouth foolishly open.

"Close your mouth," his father said wearily. "Close your mouth... how many times... Oh, God!" He passed his hand over his scanty hair.

The boy clicked his mouth shut.

"You know better than that," his father continued, still in the same tired voice. "Rushing in like that when there's company."

"Hah!" his uncle said. "I'm not company."

"You hush," his mother's voice came from behind the boy. "You spoil him."

"Hah!" his uncle said.

"It's your fault, too," she told his father.

"The boy's sick," his father said.

"He looks pale, all right," said his uncle.

"His mouth open all the time," his father said.

"You should have his tonsils taken out," said his uncle.

"Yes," his father said with a kind of diluted bitterness. "Have them taken out. Just like that."

"He won't go out and play," said his mother. "All he does is sit and sit."

"There isn't much yard to play in," said his uncle.

"He could play if he wanted to," his mother said.

"Where?" his uncle asked. "Out in the middle of the street?"

"Oh, quit taking his side," his mother said.

The boy still stood where he had stopped on entering, his mouth rigidly shut, his forehead wrinkling and unwrinkling as he followed the talking. His mother looked down at him.

"March right back and come in as you should," she said.

The boy shuffled out and came in again, very slowly and quietly.

"What do you say?" his father said.

"Good afternoon, Uncle. I hope you are well."

"Louder," said his mother.

He repeated the greeting and was allowed to sit on the edge of a chair.

"Well, well," his uncle said. "You look pretty healthy, now that I look at you close. And big too. How old are you getting to be now?"

"Ten," the boy said, his voice very low.

"Speak louder," his mother said. "Sit up straight."

"When were you ten?" his uncle asked.

The boy looked at him. "Today," he said, his voice lower still.

His uncle rubbed his shiny bald head. "Today? Did you get any presents?"

"No," said the boy, his voice scarcely audible.

"Well," his uncle said. "That's too bad."

"He was expecting a party," his mother said. "Just imagine. A birthday party."

The boy hung his head.

"Maybe it isn't as bad as that," his uncle said. He reached behind his chair and produced a long cardboard box taped at the ends with glued paper. "Here," he said.

"You shouldn't waste your money," the boy's mother said.

"This isn't wasting money."

The boy looked hungrily at the cardboard box. "Go ahead and open it," his uncle said.

The boy looked at his mother. "Go ahead," she said.

A Small Brown Bird

He fumbled and tore at the glued paper until the rifle came out of the box. It was a shiny new Daisy. The boy held it in his arms and stared at his uncle, the wrinkles on his forehead working up and down.

"What do you say?" his father said.

"Thank you. Thank you, Uncle."

"Like it?" said his uncle.

The boy swallowed and nodded.

"Well, go out and play with it," said his father.

"Go on out," his mother said.

The boy hurried out of the parlor, the rifle in his arms. As he reached the door of his room, his uncle was saying, "There are only two kinds of wars..."

His room came alive in a swirl of uniforms. Rifles glittered blackly. Then they were upon him, with cold steel. He attacked. Parry! Thrust! Hopskip, parry, thrust. They had him down on one knee, but he was up again.

The bird sang.

There it was again, the same little brown bird, perched on the guayaba bush. The boy loaded his rifle, mumbling under his breath because the lever worked hard. While he loaded he kept one eye on the bird. It perched on a slender branch, its shiny-eyed little head turning this way and that. The boy raised the rifle and took aim, slowly and carefully. The bird flew away.

"Damn!" he said to himself.

He was going to sit down on his cot but changed his mind. Instead he went out, and he saw the bird sitting on the red picket fence between his house and that of the girl next door. But before he could get within range it flew off the fence and into a large tree growing in the front. He inched his way up the narrow lane between his house and the red picket fence. The bird hopped from branch to branch in the tree, mingling its chirruping with the whiz of tires in the street beyond. Now he was under the tree, pointing his rifle up at the bird. The bird stopped hopping and looked down at the boy. He took careful aim. His mother leaned out of the window and yelled, "What are you doing there!"

He lowered the rifle. "If you don't behave, I'll take that thing away from you!" she shouted. She disappeared inside, and the boy looked from the window to the bird, which was singing happily in the tree.

"You! You!" he said.

The little girl who lived next door and her little brother came up to the tree on their side of the fence. The brother had a metal thing around one of his legs and he limped.

"What's the matter?" the girl asked.

"Look," said her brother. "He's got a gun."

The boy stared contemptuously. "Bird," he said gruffly, pointing upwards.

"Oh," said the girl. "I bet you can't hit it."

"I can too," he said.

The bird flew out of the tree, skimming low over the ground until it reached another tree in the back of the yard. The boy moved along the fence after it with exaggerated care, while the girl and her brother kept pace with him on their side.

"He's got a gun," her brother said.

"Shhh!" said the boy.

"Shh," the girl said.

Her brother shushed, and the three drew close to the bird. Again the boy drew a bead on his target, and again the bird flew away. The boy cursed under his

A Small Brown Bird

breath.

"What did you say?" the girl asked.

"Blasted bird," he said.

"That isn't what you said."

He turned his back on her. The bird was on the topmost twig of a large mulberry tree that grew where the alley fence made a corner. The twig could scarcely bear its weight, and the bird swung to and fro on the slight afternoon breeze as if it were on a swing. The boy advanced, his eyes on the swinging, bobbing form, and he stumbled on a coil of wire and fell noisily to the ground. The rifle went off close to his ear. For a moment he lay face down, paralyzed with fear, not knowing where he hurt. When he rose, he was pale and shaken. He had bruised his leg.

Behind him the girl's brother was chanting, "He fell down, he fell down." He bit his lip angrily. On top of the mulberry tree, the bird sang and swung back and forth. The boy looked up at it and shook his fist. "I'll get you!" he said. "I'll get you if it takes a hundred years!"

While he reloaded, the bird flew out of the mulberry and disappeared among the trees in a neighbor's backyard. "To the ends of the earth," the boy said.

He opened the gate separating the two houses and stole into the neighbor's yard. The bird was sitting on the branch of an elm, chirping. "I'm coming to get you," the boy whispered fiercely. "I'm coming."

There was a pattering rush of feet, a click of nails on the hard ground. He had forgotten the dog, the bird had made him forget the dog. Terror-stricken he stuck the rifle before him and waved it. The dog growled and snapped at the rifle muzzle. He fell back toward the fence, weak-kneed. The dog followed him, venturing under the rifle to snap at his ankles. In the boy's throat a scream began to form. Then his hand found the open gate behind him. He backed through the gate and slammed it shut against the dog's snout. The dog tried to bite his hands through the screen mesh of the gate. Weakly the boy fumbled with the latch and fastened the gate securely. Then, in fury, he picked up a clod and threw it through the fence. Bits of dirt showered on the dog, and it retreated deep into its own yard, barking loudly.

The boy walked away on trembling legs, trailing the rifle on the ground behind him. He stopped and looked at his dusty shoes. He inspected a small tear in his knickers. Nothing to do but go inside.

"Psst," said the little girl. He looked up and saw her beckoning. "Are you hurt?"

He started to nod, then shook his head.

"I saw you fight the dog," she said. "You are very brave."

He looked as grim as possible.

She pointed to the gate that led from her yard into the alley. "Come over and play," she said.

He had often imagined himself playing in her yard. Now he went out of his backyard, along the alley and into her yard, expecting something terrible to happen. It was a large yard with many plants and flowers and fruit trees all around. Where there were no plants or trees, there was grass, evenly cut and lying like a rug along the ground. It was like a picture in a magazine. The girl looked even prettier up close and without the fence between them.

"Let's sit under that tree," she said. "It's nice there."

"Are your parents home?"

A Small Brown Bird

"They aren't home," she said. "But they won't mind." She smiled a dimpled smile and his heart pounded.

"Father will come," her brother said. "He'll make you go away."

He followed her to the tree, a great hackberry that covered the ground like an umbrella, and sat down with his back against the trunk, his rifle between his knees.

"The dog bit him," her brother said.

"It didn't either," the boy said.

"Will your mother punish you?" the girl asked.

"Will she! Just look at my shoes. She'll whale the daylights out of me. She'll…" He saw the look on her face and stopped. "Aw," he added, "it won't be that bad."

"I'll bring you a rag," the girl said. She ran to the house, her yellow skirt bobbing up and down over her fat legs. He leaned back against the tree trunk and looked about him. It was beautiful in there. He turned his head and looked at his own house across the fence. The sight gave him an unpleasant feeling, so he looked away.

"Father spanked me," the girl's brother said.

"I bet you had it coming."

"I don't like him," the small one said.

The girl came back with a rag. While he dusted his shoes she went back into the house and returned with a tall glass. "Do you like grape juice?" she asked.

He hesitated, not wanting to admit he had never tasted grape juice.

"Go on," she said. "It's good. I put ice in it."

He took the glass and drank. "It's good," he said. "It's very good." He smiled at her.

"He's got a gun," her brother said, reaching for the rifle.

"Don't," the girl said.

The boy moved the rifle out of the small one's reach. "Children shouldn't play with guns," he said.

Her brother scowled. "The dog scared you," he said.

The boy laughed. The girl laughed too, and he felt warm inside. "Listen to that," he said. "Why, that poor dog never had a chance."

"You were scared, too," her brother said.

"You should have seen that dog," the boy said. "He came at me, and I went at him like this! Then he came at me again and tried to grab my foot, so I kicked him right in the teeth. You should have seen that dog!"

The bird sang. It was in the tree, directly overhead.

"Quick, quick!" the girl said. "Shoot!"

He raised the rifle and fired. Splat! went the rifle. The pellet caught the bird as it hopped from one branch to another. For an instant it was stopped in midair.

"Got him!" shouted the boy. "Got him!"

The bird fell with a plop. And there it lay, almost at their feet, a mess of feathers and blood. The boy stared. He had never thought there would be blood. He shut his eyes and opened them again. The bird was still there, on the ground. The girl began to cry. She knelt on the grass and placed the dead bird on her handkerchief.

"I'm glad I did it," the boy said. "I'm glad. I'm gonna kill every bird on the block."

"Oh, you cruel thing!" the girl said. "You cruel, cruel thing!"

"Well, it's just a bird," he said. "Just a bird."

A Small Brown Bird

He turned to her brother, who was staring at him. "Come close and look at it," the boy said. "It won't bite you."

The small one limped over and looked. The girl stopped crying and said, "You leave my brother alone!"

Her brother found his voice. "The cat will eat it," he said.

The girl said, "No, he won't. We'll bury it."

"I'll dig a hole," the boy said.

The girl ran to the house, and the boy began to dig under the tree, using a piece of broken glass. As he dug he looked up at the girl's brother. "Such a fuss," the boy said. "After all, it's only a bird."

"The cat will eat it," her brother said.

"Ah, shut up!" said the boy, and he resumed his digging.

The girl came back with a cardboard box and some green paper. She made a coffin with these things, working quickly and competently, her eyes intent on her task. She placed the bird inside the box and put the box in the hole.

"Don't cover it yet," she said. "We have to pray first."

"That's a silly thing," the boy said, "praying over a bird."

She stood over the bird and prayed. The boy closed his eyes and prayed too, under his breath. It gave him a pleasant feeling, saying the words at the same time she did.

Then the girl stopped. "Look!" she cried. "Look!"

The bird was moving. It stretched one uplifted leg in a spasm, and its beak moved soundlessly. The boy snatched his rifle and, struggling with the lever, loaded and fired, loaded and fired, loaded and fired into the creature in the hole.

The girl began to cry again. "Oh, you're horrible!"

she said. "You're horrible!"

The boy dropped his rifle. "It was you!" he said. "You made me do it! 'Shoot! Shoot!' you said. It was you!"

"Go away!" she cried. "Get out of my yard! Go away!"

He picked up his rifle and walked out of her yard. He felt such a great sense of loss that it was all he could do to keep himself from crying.

Revenge

Anastacio was lying in the red half-dark of his rented room. The board window and the doors were closed, and it was very hot inside. In spite of the glossy pamphlets put out by the Jonesville chamber of commerce, it gets very hot during the summer in the Golden Delta of the Rio Grande.

Anastacio sought relief from the heat by moving as little as possible. He was in his twenties, long and flat-chested, with a sad face that showed pale beneath his dark skin. He was in his undershirt, his legs spread wide to keep his shoes off the quilt which served as a mattress on his canvas cot. His trousers were of the "city" type, narrow at the hips, belled at the bottom, and held to his waist by a wide belt with a large gilded buckle like those used for saddle cinches.

He was engaged in studying a small hole in the shingled roof, which showed between two bare rafters. The intensely brilliant sun struck at this hole with concentrated force and exploded inside in a diffused gush of golden rays. Around the golden halo the shingles were pink, made semitransparent by the force of the sun. He watched this phenomenon with a complete absorption, though he had seen it many times before.

As the time slipped away, the fiery hole in the roof lost its brilliance. Anastacio sat up and rubbed his eyes. Then he went to the other side of the room, poured some water from an old white pitcher into a wash pan, and washed his face. That close to the wall he could hear the woman who lived in the room next door, and from the muffled sounds guessed she had a visitor. She was still young, pretty in a slack sort of way, pretty enough to have men visit her in the heat of the day. He heard the sounds, the stifled laughter. Listened mechanically, without interest, as he dried his face.

After he had washed, he put on a starched white shirt with built-up shoulders and wide cuffs. He touched up his hair at the mirror hanging from a nail on the wall, paying special attention to his sideburns. The mirror reflected a long, delicate face ending in a dimpled chin, a narrow nose under which pouted a small red mouth that looked more like a woman's than a man's. I don't look so well today, he thought.

He went to an old bureau leaning against the rear wall and took out a deck of cards. As he did so, he happened to glance at the corner where, over the head of his cot, his mother had made him place an altar during her last visit from the country. It was just a shelf nailed to the angle made by the walls. On it was a picture of the Virgin of Guadalupe in a gilded frame. He frowned at the altar and returned to his cot. As he sat on the cot, he riffled the cards through his hands, staring at the closed window. Now and then his stomach rumbled.

A fly circled lazily about his head, mingling its dull buzzing with the deadened, heat-drowned sounds of the afternoon. Next door the man left, and after a while the woman opened her back door and threw out a pail of water. The water made a bright, splashing sound, like a dash of color spilled on gray. After that the heat and the dullness returned. Finally a breeze sprang up. It came in through the cracks in the wall and blew fitfully across his face. He breathed deeply, with a catch at the end, as if he had sighed.

There was a knock on the door. Anastacio reached under his cot for a machete and cautiously opened the door. It was his cousin Apolinar. Apolinar was a tiny young man. He wore tiny blue trousers, wide at the hips, narrow at the cuffs in the country style, and short enough to show his socks, which peeped from the tops of his high shoes. Beneath an old linen coat that had survived many washings and pressings, he wore a blue work shirt, without a tie but carefully buttoned at the neck. His features were large and rugged, his nose knobby. Only his mouth was in keeping with his size. It was a red, feminine mouth, very much like Anastacio's.

Anastacio opened the door a little wider so Apolinar could slip through. He quickly shut and fastened the door, while Apolinar put a paper bag on the cot, took off his stetson and wiped his red face with a red bandanna.

"What heat, cousin," Apolinar said.

"Truly," Anastacio said.

"Worse than year before last. The holes are drying up, and those that are left are turning brackish. If it doesn't rain soon, the stock will die."

"Yes," Anastacio said.

"It's fine for the cotton farmers. The bolls burst open and the leaves are burned away by the sun."

"True," said Anastacio.

"I got your message," Apolinar said. "That's why I came."

"I'm indebted to you, cousin. What's in the bag? Something to eat?"

Apolinar shook his head.

"You didn't bring me anything?" Anastacio exclaimed. "I haven't eaten all day!"

"I brought you what you wanted most," Apolinar said. He reached into the paper bag and took out two snub-nosed revolvers. Anastacio swallowed nervously. Apolinar stared at his cousin for a moment, then turned his protruding, copper-colored eyes back to the revolvers. He checked the loaded chambers and laid the guns side by side on the cot.

Anastacio found his voice. "Why two of them?" he asked.

"The other one is for me, so I can back you up. I'll be right behind you, as I always have been."

"I am grateful. But I wish you had brought something to eat."

"How long have you been holed up in here?" Apolinar asked.

Anastacio shot his cousin an angry look. "Two days. Ever since he came back. But listen, I've got to eat something!"

"We could go out and have some *menudo*."

"Are you crazy?"

Apolinar began to roll a cigarette. "Why not?" he said. "We both got guns now." He bent over the cigarette. "Unless you'd rather not."

"I'm not afraid of him! I'm a man with balls! He killed my brother and he's got to die! But I'll kill him at a time and place of my own choosing."

Revenge

"You're a *macho* and you've got *huevos*," Apolinar said quietly. "Who's denying that?" He lighted his cigarette.

"He's dead," he added.

"What?"

"Dead."

"I don't believe it."

"It's true. I saw the body."

"You did? Who killed him?"

"You'd never guess. He was hit by an automobile. Two of them really. One knocked him down and the other ran over him."

"You're sure he's dead?"

"The second car ran over his head. Mashed it flat like a tortilla."

Anastacio sat down on the cot.

"I thought I'd come anyway," Apolinar said. "And bring the guns. So we could go to his funeral and laugh over his body."

"I don't know. I don't know about that."

"What's wrong with you today?" Apolinar said mildly. "You've always been the brave one. Bigger and stronger and meaner than anybody else."

"But at the funeral?"

"That's what you've said you wanted to do these past two years, when he was in the pen. Kill him and laugh over his body. You didn't get a chance to kill him, but you can still laugh over his body. If you really want to, that is."

"What about his kin?"

"They don't know us. We can go in, laugh, and get out before they know what's happening. And if there's trouble, we got these little firecrackers with us."

"I don't know," Anastacio said.

"Are you afraid of the dead?" Apolinar said.

Anastacio turned on him. "I'm not afraid of anything!" he shouted, his face twisted with rage. Apolinar took a couple of steps backward. Anastacio turned his back on him and stared at the wall, his mouth still contorted, his big eyes moist.

Apolinar touched him lightly on the arm. "Get your hat and coat," he said, "and let's go."

Once, when he was much younger, Anastacio had gone to Morelos by himself and drunk beer for the first time. As he was riding the bus back to Jonesville, a strange thing happened. His face felt numb, but his senses were sharper than they had ever been. He noticed everything about the other passengers. Their clothes, their mannerisms, the color of their hair, the shape of their noses. The way they smelled, the individual sound of each of their voices. It had never happened again to him until now, when he and Apolinar left his room, their revolvers struck into their belts under their coats.

He breathed deeply as they stepped outside. The day was bright as it moved toward evening. The dusty streets had begun to cool, and the grass of the sidewalks was reviving. Children came out and played as the two men walked slowly along the street. In the distance a dog barked, belligerently, insistently, but the sound came soft and peaceful to them.

A girl caught up with them and marched past. A girl of about fifteen, wearing an old pink slip that must have belonged to her mother. She was on her way home from one of the grocery stalls in the neighborhood, and she carried a paper bag in her arms, pressed against her plump breasts. She walked ahead of them, barefoot, grace in her bare brown legs, her haunches rippling under their thin covering as she walked.

"Nice little piece," Apolinar said.

"Yes," said Anastacio, without much enthusiasm.

"I bet he was dreaming of something like that all those months he was locked up," Apolinar said. "Can you imagine what it must be like? Two whole years without a woman. A Casanova like you, now. You'd go crazy."

Anastacio grunted.

"I hear that's what happened to him," Apolinar said. "He was half-drunk and on his way to Lupita's place, like a stud in heat. Didn't even see the cars."

Anastacio did not answer. He was looking at the girl as one looks at a picture, or at something very far away.

"That's life for you," Apolinar said. "You never know when your number will be called. You never know."

The girl turned a corner away from them, and they walked in silence after that. The breeze brought a faint suggestion of flowers blooming in someone's yard. Somewhere a woman was calling her child. Her call began low, lost in the bottom of the distance. Then it rose to a high bellow that became a scream.

They entered a wide, graveled street with sidewalks made of wooden blocks and came to a white house with green shutters and a red shingle roof. There were many automobiles parked in front of it. It was shaped like an L. The inside of the L faced the street and enclosed a small, carefully clipped lawn, on which a number of metal chairs had been set up. In the long shadow cast by the house sat sweaty men in tight suits. There were other chairs on the porch, where sat women in black. The men on the lawn occasionally passed small flat bottles back and forth, and chuckled now and then over a joke or a double-meaning. The women on the porch talked in whispers.

People were continually rising and going inside to see the body. Then they came out again and sat down, the men to drink and crack jokes, the women to gossip, as was the custom. Only three old women sat inside with the body at all times, the professional weepers. They could be seen from the lawn through the open door, dressed in black and with shawls over their heads, sighing and saying prayers.

Anastacio and Apolinar hesitated for a moment, then turned into the cement walk leading up to the porch. Anastacio's face was stiff. He cast glances at everyone out of the corners of his eyes. He and Apolinar reached the porch, and an old man in a black suit and white, stiff-collared shirt came out to meet them.

"Good afternoon, *señores*," the old man said. "We thank you for your presence in this house."

Apolinar stepped back, and Anastacio answered the greeting. The old man's watery eyes peered at Anastacio.

"Are you my cousin Pablo's boy?" he asked.

"No," Anastacio said.

"Ah, yes," the old man said. "I don't think he's as tall as you are." He pulled at the smoke-yellowed mustaches hanging limply on the sides of his mouth. "Will you take a seat?"

"I think not," Anastacio said. "We would rather see him."

"Come in then," the old man said. "A few minutes more and you would have been too late."

He entered the room where the dead man lay, and Anastacio followed him, smoothing his coat to disguise the bulge of his revolver. Apolinar followed them to the door.

Revenge

The old women in black sat with their rosaries at one end of the room. At the other end, close to the windows, was the coffin, almost hidden behind a profusion of jasmine, tuberoses, and white lilies. The sun, coming in through the glass of the closed windows, threw a red glow over the flowers. It had been shining on them all afternoon, and their smell was very strong. The odor of the body rose thin and penetrating through the cloying smell.

Anastacio stood before the coffin, looking sideways at the door where Apolinar stood.

"Come up closer," the old man said, "if you want to look at him."

Anastacio stepped up to the coffin and looked down on the dead man's face. It did not look at all terrible. The embalmers had made it handsome. They had covered the bruises, disguised the crushed skull, penciled clearly the little black mustache. They had even shaped the dead lips into a smile.

"So many flowers," the old man said. "He had many friends."

Anastacio nodded. Apolinar was motioning to him from the door.

"All white flowers, too," the old man said. "That's the kind that smell the sweetest."

Anastacio did not reply. He was looking down at the dead man, his chin against his chest. The old man must have thought he was praying, for he bowed his head in prayer too. He was a man already on the road to death. Once he had been fleshy, but age had taken the flesh away, leaving the skin hanging in folds on his face and body. So now he stood beside Anastacio, old and sagging, his head bowed in prayer, while Apolinar beckoned from the door.

They stood there so long that the old man finally said, "You must have been one of his closest friends. He had all kinds of friends, you know, and they all loved him."

Apolinar was gesturing from the door. He had put his fingers in the corners of his mouth and was stretching his lips into a grotesque smile. Anastacio turned toward the coffin and laughed.

The old man looked up quickly. "You sobbed," he said.

Anastacio smiled a twisted, bitter smile.

"You sobbed," the old man repeated. "Not even my sons, his brothers, have done that."

Anastacio lowered his head. When he raised it again, Apolinar was gone from the door. "I think I'll go outside," he said.

"Oh, no," the old man said, taking hold of his arm. "You must not go at the end of the procession. You were too good a friend of his."

Two bright, bustling young men came in. They brought the rubber-tired vehicle on which the coffin would be wheeled to the hearse.

"But I... " Anastacio began

"You will walk beside me, right behind the hearse. My sons and their cousins can walk behind us."

"But I shouldn't!"

"You are too modest," the old man said, still clinging to Anastacio's arm. "You deserve that humble courtesy from us."

The undertakers' assistants screwed the lid of the coffin shut. This was proclaimed to the people outside by the sudden wail of the three black-clad women, a wail which broke abrupt and fierce through the quiet murmur of the funeral. Other women joined them.

Revenge

When it seemed that the air could no longer bear its shrillness, the wail crumbled into a series of explosive screams of unbridled desperation. The screams softened, then became a hoarse clamor of moans.

The wailing rose again, and Anastacio would have bolted out the door, but the coffin barred his way. It was slowly moved out to the waiting hearse, and he followed close behind it down to the cement walk, waiting for a chance to move ahead and disappear into the crowd. But the old man's hand fell upon his arm again. "Come," the old man said.

Anastacio sighed and followed him. The funeral cortege formed out on the street to begin its long, slow march to the cemetery. The people attending formed a long line of twos and threes, first the young girls, then the boys, then the women, and finally the men. Behind them stretched a line of automobiles, loaded with flowers, their engines straining under the slow pace. At the head was the black hearse. A priest and two acolytes walked before it. The pallbearers walked on each side, and behind the hearse, close to the door through which the coffin had entered, walked the old man and Anastacio, with bowed heads. After them came the dead man's brothers and cousins. The cortege moved in silence except for the shuffling of feet and the labored puttering of motors.

After they had walked some distance the old man said, "I'm so glad you came. He had many friends, but none loved him like you did."

Anastacio did not answer. He was extremely conscious of the weight of the pistol concealed under his coat. He hoped none of his friends would see him walking behind the hearse, that no one would see the bulge of the pistol. He wondered where Apolinar was, but he was afraid to raise his head and look at the crowd lining the sidewalk for fear of looking into a familiar face.

Finally the streets ended, and they entered the iron gates of the cemetery, down through the maze of graves to the spot where two sweaty men waited for them, leaning on their spades beside an open hole. The coffin was placed on some planks over the hole, and the priest began his ceremony. They all bowed their heads, and Anastacio thought his chance had come. He would slip away very quietly while everyone prayed. But as he started to edge away his stomach rumbled loudly. The old man looked up.

"You are hungry," the old man whispered.

Anastacio shook his head. "I have stomach trouble," he replied, also in a whisper.

The old man looked at him narrowly in the fading light. "I hadn't noticed before how thin you are," he whispered. "You must come to our house and have something to eat."

"I'm not hungry, I tell you," Anastacio hissed.

"It won't be anything fancy," the old man said.

"I tell you I'm all right," Anastacio said out loud.

The people about him raised their heads and looked sternly at him. He lowered his head and waited, weak and angry. The priest had finished, but still they did not lower the coffin. The lawyer had yet to make his speech.

The lawyer was the most prominent man in the neighborhood. People considered him a great orator, and he was much in demand for funeral speeches. The lawyer was particular about his timing, because his funeral orations had a special high point which people expected with a thrill that never grew old. He liked to reach his climax as the first stars twinkled in the heavens over the grave. Then he would point to the brightest star and say, "I see you now, my brother! You are not down here! You are up there, shining over us!"

But it was not yet dark enough for stars, so they all waited around the grave, their heads bowed, everyone except the priest and his helpers, who silently went away. After a while the dusk deepened, and the first stars shone palely in the blue-gray sky. The lawyer began, with a flourish as was his wont. The people raised their heads and watched him, drinking in his every word, though they had heard all of it before. Even the old man became absorbed in the lawyer's words, and Anastacio was able to slip away.

He was hurrying toward the gate when Apolinar stepped out from behind a gravestone, as suddenly as if he had risen from the ground.

"Ugh!" Anastacio said, stopping with a jerk. "You startled me!"

Apolinar chuckled.

"Where have you been?" Anastacio demanded. "Where were you when I needed you most?"

"There was nothing I could do," Apolinar said, "except stay close by in case you really needed me. But you did pretty well without me."

"You really think so?" Anastacio sounded half-convinced.

"You kept your promise. You laughed over his dead body."

"That's true. But that old man!"

"Why didn't you drop out once the procession started moving?"

"With his brothers right behind me?" Anastacio shivered and gave his head a shake. "I hope nobody who knows me was watching."

"Oh…. I don't think so. At least not many."

"Who?"

"Well…the Mercado brothers were on the sidewalk in front of the house. Also the Arellanos and the Vázquezes."

"Damn!"

"And the Villegas, close to the cemetery gates. And a few others."

"Oh, my God!"

"Perhaps they didn't recognize you," Apolinar said without conviction.

"What am I going to do? The whole *barrio* is laughing at me by now!"

"You could go back home to the country."

"Back home? It would be worse there!"

"How about moving to San Pedrito? Almost nobody knows you there."

Anastacio stopped in front of a *barrio* grocery store. His legs were shaking. In the light shining out of the store, he could see Apolinar's face looking up at him in a curious sort of way.

"Let me take back these two little popguns," Apolinar said, "to the people who lent them to me. And then we'll go have some *menudo*."

"I don't think I want any *menudo*," Anastacio said. "I'll just go in here and get some bread and a few other things and eat supper in my room."

Apolinar grinned. "As you wish, cousin," he said.

Anastacio turned away and entered the store. Behind him Apolinar was laughing softly.

Brothers

Fred and Arturo had known that their families were coming to the beach that Sunday afternoon. They had talked about it on the school playground the Friday before. Fred liked to play with Arturo because Arturo spoke Spanish. Fred was new in Jonesville-on-the-Grande and was in Arturo's class only until he got used to school in the United States. Then he would go to a much higher grade, because German schools were different. Not that Fred had to learn English. He spoke English, French, and Spanish, besides German.

"In Germany," Fred had told Arturo, "I started learning English, French and Spanish from kindergarten on. But that was only for three years. We speak German and French at home, and I get much practice in English here at school. But I don't want to forget Spanish, that's why I like to play with you. And because I like you, of course."

Arturo's parents spoke only Spanish. He wondered what it would be like to live in a family where everyone spoke three or four languages. He had never visited Fred's house or seen his parents. He and Fred lived in opposite sides of town and saw each other only in class and on the school playground. So he looked forward to playing with Fred away from school.

It was nice to have Fred for a friend in school because everybody in class thought Fred was something special. Even the teacher. Sometimes the teacher would talk about what was going on in Germany, and she would mention Fred's father. Fred's grandfather had been a German officer in the Great War, but Fred's father did not believe in war, so he had left Germany and come to the United States.

"It took a lot of courage," the teacher would say, "for Fred's father to stand up for freedom and justice for all. For the brotherhood of man, even if he had to leave his home and bring his family to live in our little town."

Everybody would look at Fred, and Fred would look uncomfortable. His red face would turn even redder, and the teacher would change the subject.

So it would be even better than school to play together on the beach. They sought each other out as soon as they had eaten lunch. They played in the water, going up and down parallel to the beach, now swimming, now wading in the surf. From Washington Beach, with its old tents and dilapidated trucks, they went past the wire fence stretched from the water's edge into the sand dunes. All the way to Miraflores Beach, where there were shiny automobiles and beach umbrellas. At Miraflores Beach, they came out of the water and raced each other.

Men shiny red from the sun and women with long white legs looked idly at the little white boy and his dark-brown playmate as they ran back and forth among the cars. Every once in a while Arturo would stare at a girl's legs, and he would feel funny inside, though he didn't know exactly why. Then he would run more slowly and Fred would catch up with him. Otherwise Arturo was always ahead. Fred was not much taller than Arturo, but he had very short legs, short legs and big feet. He looked funny when he ran. He was tanned a yellowish brown, and his hair was almost white. From the sun, Fred said. He loved the sun. He didn't seem to mind the girls with the long white legs, and though they were good friends Arturo had never asked him about his feelings when he looked at girls.

Soon Fred got tired of chasing Arturo and never catching him, so he said, "Let's go back into the water." He could beat Arturo easily at swimming. Arturo liked playing on Miraflores Beach and didn't want to leave, but he was afraid that Fred would think he didn't like to be beaten at swimming. So they went into the water. They swam back to Wahington Beach, Fred far in the lead, and when they came out Fred said, "That was a good swim! How about playing something else?"

"Let's play at the movies," Arturo said.

"Very good," said Fred, "but what will we use for guns?"

"I got a couple of them in the truck," Arturo said. He led the way to the truck in which Arturo's family had come to the beach with several other families. The truck was deserted, since all the older people were in the water. In one corner of the flat bed was a brightly painted straw bag which belonged to Arturo's mother. Arturo took a couple of sticks out of the bag. They were pieces of knotty pine whittled roughly to look like pistols. Once armed, they moved away from the beach and into the sand dunes, which offered a setting that, with a little imagination, could look much like the scenery in cowboy movies.

"Don't go that way," Arturo said, as Fred veered off into the dunes toward the left.

"Why not?"

"Down between those two dunes, that's where people go to the toilet."

"I don't see any rest rooms."

"Of course not. We just make a hole in the sand."

"And what if you step into it?"

"You don't. Not if you're careful."

"Anyway, that's not a place to play in."

"That's right. Some kids who didn't know went sliding down those dunes." Arturo laughed.

"Ugh!" said Fred.

"They spent the rest of the day in the water, washing themselves off."

They both laughed and moved away, toward some high dunes to the right. They climbed up to the ridge of the largest dune. From there they could look down to the bottom of a little valley a few yards below.

"The rustlers will be coming down there," Fred said. "As soon as they are below us, we open up on them."

"Sure thing, pardner!" Arturo said. They lay on their stomachs at the brow of their imaginary hill, not particularly conscious of the fact that they had slipped from Spanish to English, the language of the movies. For a few moments they lay there, scarcely breathing, until Fred called out, "Here they come!"

"Pow! Pow!" Arturo shouted. "I got one!"

"I got another one!" Fred answered. "Pow! Pow!"

They mowed down dozens of rustlers, springing up now and then and taking cover at another spot on the ridge. Finally they ran out of breath. Arturo stood up and looked around. "I think we got all of them."

"No! Look out!" Fred shouted. "There's one behind you."

Brothers

Arturo whirled to his right and fanned his revolver. "Pow! Pow! Pow! I got him! Thees is a very dead rustler."

Fred laughed. *"Thees, thees,"* he mocked good-naturedly. "You don't say *thees*. You say *this*."

Arturo grinned. "What about you? *Vee* did this and *vee* did that."

"I never say vee. Not anymore."

"¡Ya, ya! ¡Que lo dices!" Arturo said.

"What did you say just now?" asked Fred, also switching back into Spanish. "You said *ya*. What do you mean by *ya*?"

Arturo thought for a moment. "I think it's the same as saying *sí*," he said. "Yes, that's it. Sometimes you say *ya* when you mean *sí*."

Fred was delighted. "That's the way we say it in German!" he exclaimed. *"Ja* means *sí*!"

"Do they ever say *sí* in German?"

"I never thought of that, but I bet you they do!"

"Maybe German and Spanish are the same after all."

"That's what my father means!"

"What?"

"He always says that all men are brothers. He says that at bottom we all speak the same language."

"Then there must be times when you say *sí* in German."

"Say! Wouldn't it be fun if we turn out to be related?"

"Why don't you ask your father?"

"Let's go right now and ask him," Fred said.

They started toward the wire fence at a trot. Before they reached the fence, Fred cried, "There's my father! He's coming this way!"

Fred's father was on the Washington Beach side of the fence and was walking toward them. Arturo stared. He had heard so much about Fred's father from their teacher that he expected somebody different. Somebody tall and strong and good-looking. Like Superman, perhaps. Fred's father was a paunchy, not-so-tall man with a pair of hairy legs beneath his shorts. Bulgy blue eyes looked down at Fred through horn-rimmed glasses.

"Where have you been?" Fred's father said peevishly. "I have been looking everywhere for you."

"I was playing, Father," Fred said. "This is my friend Arturo."

Fred's father seemed to notice Arturo for the first time. He glanced at him and looked away, saying something that Arturo did not understand. "Well, come along!" he said. "Why can't you stay on your side of the fence where you belong? Why do you have to..." He looked at Arturo and stopped. "Come along," he repeated in a softer tone. "Your mother has been asking about you."

"Father," Fred said, "there's something we wanted to ask you."

"Yes?"

"Do they ever say *sí* in German when they mean *ja*?"

Fred's father looked startled. Then he snorted. "Of course not!" he said. "Certainly not! How could you think of such a thing?" He laughed shortly. "Go get whatever you brought with you and come along." He turned around and went back to Miraflores Beach.

Fred stared after his father, who had waded into the surf and come out on the other side of the wire fence. Then he sat down and began to knead a lump of wet sand. Arturo sat down beside him.

"There's thousands of words in German," Fred said, "thousands and thousands. He was angry and he didn't listen. He didn't stop to think. I'm sure there are times when you say *sí* in German."

"It's all right, Fred," Arturo said gently. "It's all right."

"Well, I have to go," Fred said. "Here's your gun."

"It's yours," Arturo said. "I want you to keep it."

Rebeca

As Beto eased the car into the driveway, Rebeca looked with satisfaction at the low, neatly trimmed hedges on each side of the drive. She liked the way their front yard looked. It was like a picture in a magazine. For almost a year now, they had been paying some men to take care of the yard. Beto had decided the boys should not be doing manual labor. They should spend their time studying so they could go to college. Not just any college, either, but really good schools.

They had enough money to pay for yard work, he had said firmly, overriding her objections that it would cost too much. It was true. They had enough money. And a comfortable house, full of things she had never heard about when she was a girl on her father's ranch. Good furniture, machines for washing dishes and drying clothes, a vacuum cleaner. The only heavy work she had to do around the house was ironing and cooking. Especially cooking.

All her children were there in the living room when she came into the house. Beto must have called home when he left the prescription at the drugstore. Elisa led her to the easy chair in front of the TV, and

Rebeca

Cenobia brought her a stool so she could prop up her feet. They all gathered about her and kept looking at her as if she were some rare bird they had never seen before. Panchita, the eldest, named after Rebeca's grandmother Francisca, was chewing gum as usual, her dead-white face expressionless. She will get fat soon, Rebeca thought. Perhaps she will never have the energy to raise a family. Elisa, named after Beto's mother, was taller than Panchita, and darker. Tense, silent Elisa. She was the efficient one, the one who would always work the hardest and get the least out of life. Cenobia, named after Rebeca's mother, was trying hard to put a somber expression on her cheerful, freckled face. She would always be happy, whatever she did.

Of the boys, Alberto Jr. did not cause Rebeca much unease. He was taller and heavier than his father, but he had Beto's blue eyes and fair skin. Unlike his father, he was self-assured and easygoing. His life should be prosperous and happy. José, named after Rebeca's father, was dark and good-looking but extremely shy. He looked up to Beto Jr., and that was a comfort to Rebeca. Young Beto would be a good influence on him.

Only Rofito was missing. He had been christened Rodolfo, not a name in either of the families. But Rebeca had insisted on the name, though she did not tell anyone why. She had named him after Rodolfo Valentino. Frail, sensitive, the youngest of her children, he was not living at home. Where Rofito was she did not know. Nobody was allowed to talk about him at home. But she would see about it now.

Beto bent over her. "Are you comfortable?" he asked. "You just sit there and rest," he continued, not waiting for her to answer. "The girls will take care of everything." He kissed her on the cheek and went into the front bathroom, where he stayed for a long time.

He had kissed her. Right in front of everybody. It was the first time he had ever kissed her when anyone else was around.

"But who will do the cooking?" she said to no one in particular. "My daughters?" The idea amused her.

"Of course we will, Mama," Elisa said briskly. "We'll share the work. You just tell us what we have to do."

Rebeca smiled and said, "We'll see." She leaned back in the easy chair. It was good to be doing nothing at all.

"We'll share the work," Elisa had said. "Just tell us what to do." That's the way it had been on the ranch before she married Beto. She and her sisters shared the housework under their mother's supervision. Before that, there had been early girlhood, when life had been pleasant and lazy. She tried to summon up the fragrance of the huisache, the retama and the honeysuckle on those summer evenings, the smell of the willows along the riverbank at nightfall, when she and her sisters went to watch Chano Quintana row people across from the Mexican side. A cool breeze would be blowing in from the coast, as people came up the steep bank by the dim light of a hooded lantern.

Her father's house was like one long party to her in those days, with people always coming and going across the river. At times girls her age would come across and spend the night, cousins who slept on the floor with her and her sisters. They didn't do much sleeping, though, spending the night in whispers and suppressed giggles.

There had been three of them, three sisters, and

Rebeca

Rebeca was the eldest. There were also five brothers. She remembered them now as five places at the table, five sets of heavy work clothes to be washed, mended, and ironed. Her mother, Doña Cenobia, was a broad, husky woman. She had spent her younger years raising them all, and cooking not only for her family of ten but for the three or four vaqueros her husband, Don José María Chapa, usually hired to help him and his sons on the ranch. Then there were the friends and relatives from the Mexican side of the river, who used the Chapa ranch as a stopping place on their trips to and from Jonesville.

The ranch not only was by the river but near a spot that was easy to cross, except during flood time. People from the other side came over after dark. They had supper and breakfast as guests of her father, a jolly man who loved company. Early the following morning, they would go into Jonesville, which was a few miles up the road that went down to the beach. On their way home the travelers arrived at the Chapa ranch in time for supper. They visited until well after dark before crossing to the other side. And if river guards were spotted in the vicinity, the guests might spend the night there and all of next day, crossing the following night.

Scarcely a week went by that the house was not full of visitors an evening or two. A couple of the Chapa boys played the guitar, and so did some of their cousins from the other side. The young men played and sang; the old men smoked and talked, and the girls gossiped among themselves. It was a happy life, except perhaps for Rebeca's mother. With the years, she grew old and tired. But by then her three daughters were big enough to help her.

Sara and Raquel were broad and strong like their mother. Rebeca, on the other hand, was slender. Delicate, her mother thought, though country life had made her tough enough. But for Doña Cenobia, for whom strength meant bulk, Rebeca was too weak for hard house work. Sara and Raquel were made responsible for washing, ironing, and cleaning house, while Rebeca became her mother's helper in the kitchen.

Rebeca discovered she had a special gift for cooking and baking. Her mother was known as a good cook, but the daughter soon outshone her. Everyone praised her *asado de puerco*. Her *frijoles rancheros* had just the right amount of cilantro. Her *tortillas de harina* were a marvel; her *buñuelos* melted in your mouth. And her way with north Mexican tamales, slender and delicate, was incredible.

Rebeca's kitchen skills became known throughout the countryside. People began to say she would make a wonderful wife for some lucky man. How proud had she been when her mother gave her the run of the kitchen and assumed for herself a secondary role. But she quickly realized that her beloved kitchen was also her prison. Sara and Raquel worked hard, but their tasks occupied only part of their week. Five weekdays was more than enough for the two of them to do the washing and ironing and to keep the house clean. And their workdays were short. They started their chores after breakfast and were through before supper.

For Rebeca every day was a workday. Her days began at five in the morning, when she got the coffee ready for her father. They ended at night, close to bedtime, after she had washed the supper dishes and prepared for the next day's meals. She was a worrier by nature. The more her cooking was praised, the more she fretted over the next meal. She was not systematic about anything. No written-down recipes, no hard and fast rules about quantities of ingredients and cooking times. She did everything by feel and was always relieved when each meal was a success.

Yet, the kitchen was her joy, her work of art. If only there weren't so many people to cook for all the time. When people praised her cooking, she could not help dreaming of a life away from the bustle and noise of her father's house. How beautiful would it be to live in a little house far from her father's ranch. A little house where she would be the mistress, and there would be only one other person, the man she would marry. The house would be on the Mexican side of the river, not too far from its banks but far enough so you could not see it from the other side. It would be set in the middle of the fields belonging to Donaciano Quintana.

Chano Quintana was a frequent visitor at her father's house. Brown and muscular from swimming in the river and rowing people across, he was a friend of her older brothers. He played the guitar and sang very well. When he played at her house, she always came from the kitchen and stood listening by the door. He was very handsome, and he was in love with her. She knew it, although he had not yet spoken for her nor given any direct sign of his intentions. But when he sang love songs, he was doing it for her, even though he never looked directly at her, closing his eyes and turning his face away, as his respect for her and her family required. From the side he looked just like Rodolfo Valentino, the movie star, as the lamplight shone on his beautiful Indian face.

They would make a good pair. She was not Indian,

but she was the darkest of her family; her father called her his little Aztec princess. She thought of Chano at night before she went to sleep. Soon he would give some sign, she was sure. But the sign was long in coming. He was too shy, perhaps. So she waited and worked in the kitchen.

Late one Saturday afternoon, a Ford touring car from Jonesville drove up to their house. A pink-faced young man in a suit and tie got out of the car. He was not very tall but he stood very straight, as if to look taller than he really was. Rebeca and her sisters watched from behind the curtains. He looked at the house, his lips pressed tightly together as if he disapproved of something. Then he straightened his shoulders even more and walked up to the porch. Don José María came out.

"*Buenas tardes*," the visitor said. "You are Don José María Chapa."

"*Servidor*," Don José María replied.

"I'm Alberto Medrano."

"Ah, yes," Don José María said. "Now I recognize you. I haven't seen you since you were a boy. Come inside; this is your house."

Alberto Medrano took off his short-brimmed hat, came into the living room and sat down somewhat stiffly. "I'm here to pick up my Uncle Eligio," he said.

"Yes," Don José María said. "What kind of work do you do, Alberto?"

"I work in a lawyer's office. Will Uncle Eligio be here soon?"

"Oh, no. Not until well after dark. Then we'll all have supper before you go."

"We'll be giving you a lot of trouble."

"Trouble? Of course not."

Rebeca

Alberto Medrano did not answer, and after a while Don José María said, "Of course, we old men like to talk about old things. But my boys will be coming in soon, and they will be pleased to meet you. You can talk young men's talk with them."

After a pause, Alberto said, "It has been hot today. Very soon we'll be in the dog days."

"It's true," said Don José María. "And the sun hits this side of the house in the afternoon. Do you want to take your coat off?"

"No, thank you. But I would like to have a glass of water."

Don José María raised his voice, "Rebeca! Rebeca! Bring our visitor a glass of water." No need for him to shout. Rebeca, her sisters and their mother were within whispering distance.

Rebeca came in promptly with water in one of their best glasses. He did not rise, just looked up at her. Pale-blue eyes in a sober, almost severe face looked steadily at her. "Thank you," he said gravely, still looking at her. She was pretty then, dark and slender. His staring embarrassed her, and she didn't like him very much because of that.

Her brothers came home, and after they had washed they came to the living room. While the men talked, Rebeca and her mother were busy making supper. Sara and Raquel were in their bedroom combing their hair and talking in whispers. Rebeca knew what they were talking about, whether they could get away with putting on a little rouge once it got dark.

Silly, she thought, making so much fuss over this unpleasant man. But she took special pains with her cooking that afternoon. After dark, Don Eligio Medrano and his wife were rowed over by Chano Quintana.

Chano was introduced to Alberto, and they shook hands. Chano was invited to stay for supper, as he usually was when he brought people over, but he said he couldn't stay this time.

As the daughters of the house served supper, Alberto Medrano sat silently at the table, stealing glances at Rebeca. But once he tasted the food, he became talkative. "This is delicious," he said. "I have never eaten such good food."

"It's Rebeca's doing," Don José María told him. "My daughter's a very good cook, just as good as her mother."

Alberto looked at her steadily. "It's true. You are a very good cook." Rebeca managed to say, "Thank you." Throughout the rest of the evening, he stared at her every time she came out of the kitchen.

On Sunday evening he returned, bringing back his uncle and aunt and some other people who wanted to go across. Again he looked and looked at her. During the next three weeks, he came back several times to pick people up or to take them back. "That's odd," Rebeca's mother said. "That young man had never come before, and now he's here so often."

Then came that Sunday, less than a month since Alberto's first visit. It was early in the afternoon, and the house was quiet except for the cackle of the chickens seeking comfortable spots in the dust of the backyard. The boys were visiting friends down river. It was Raquel who first saw the car, coming along the dirt road that led from the highway. Her mother woke Don José María from his nap. He put on a shirt and was ready to receive the three men in suits and ties once they got out of the car.

They talked in low voices in the living room until

Rebeca

her father called Rebeca to bring the visitors some coffee. She served them without looking up at their faces. After they left, her father called them into the living room—her mother, her sisters and herself. He told them what they already had guessed. The men were a *comisión*. They had come to ask Rebeca's hand in marriage for young Alberto Medrano.

"Ah, the quiet one!" Sara said. "How did you manage it without us knowing anything?"

"Not a thing!" Raquel chimed in. "How sly she is!"

"Hush!" their father said. "Well, young lady, what do you have to say for yourself?"

She did not know what to say; she had not expected this. She was not doing anything behind their backs.

"Has he talked to you about this?" her mother asked.

"When? How?" she replied.

"Has he sent you messages with someone?" her father said, looking at her sisters.

"No," she said.

"Well," her father said. "Do you want to marry him?"

"I'm not sure," she said. "Can't I have some time to think about it?"

"You have until the end of the week," her father told her. "The *comisión* will be back for an answer next Sunday."

As soon as they were alone in the kitchen, her sisters started working on her. "Say yes! Say yes!" said Raquel, the youngest. "Think of the dance we can have! There will be hundreds of people in the house!"

"You must get married sooner or later," Sara said. "How can I until you do? It wouldn't look right."

"He looks very nice in those suits he wears," Raquel said.

"He may not be the handsomest man in the world,"

Sara said, "but you won't have to get up at five in the morning to make breakfast and feed the pigs." Chano had some hogs he was fattening.

"I bet he doesn't get up before seven or eight in the morning. People who work in offices start at nine."

"Living in the city. What more do you want?"

"You can go to the movies anytime you want to."

"And you won't be washing any heavy work clothes. Those suits he wears go to the tailor shop to be cleaned."

"You could have one of those machines that wash clothes."

"And electric lights."

"Stop! Stop!" she said. "I need time to think."

"About what?" Sara said. "That other one will never speak up. You say no to this one, and you may end up an old maid. That's what will happen to you."

Rebeca started getting ready for supper, banging pots and pans around until her sisters left the kitchen.

Her sisters did not badger her anymore, but during the rest of the week they talked to each other in Rebeca's hearing about the beauties of city life. The following Saturday her father took her aside. *"Mi hijita,"* he said, "have you made up your mind?"

"I am not sure, Papá," she said. "I just do not know."

"Tomorrow is Sunday," he said gently, "and the *comisión* will be back for an answer." She looked at the floor. "I know this is difficult for you, but you must make up your mind by tomorrow."

"Why tomorrow?"

"Because that is the custom. If I send them away without an answer tomorrow, they will understand that you are willing to marry the boy. They will come back a week from tomorrow for the formal answer. If you refuse the offer then, it will be an insult not only to the boy and his family but to the members of the *comisión.*"

"I didn't know that," she said.

"That is the custom," her father said. "If you have any doubts, *hijita*, it is best that you say no tomorrow."

She took a deep breath. "A week from tomorrow I will say yes."

So they were married, and although there were not hundreds of people at the wedding, as Raquel had hoped, there were enough. Her father slaughtered two fat steers and half a dozen *cabritos.* There was dancing, and there was singing. Chano came over with his guitar and sang. He also accompanied Chicho, the accordion player, in an afternoon of polkas, redowas, waltzes and schottisches. Alberto did not dance to that kind of music, so she didn't dance either. All the guests enjoyed themselves, including Chano Quintana, who—she later learned—drank more than he usually did. The fiesta was still going strong when she and Beto Medrano put their suitcases in the back of his Ford and drove away to San Antonio.

She no longer had to get up at five to make coffee for her father. She got up at six to make breakfast for Beto, who left at seven-thirty for his job downtown. There was a bakery nearby, but he insisted on having her *tortillas de harina* every morning with his eggs and Mexican sausage. She spent most of her time in the kitchen, despite there being fewer people to cook for. There were his relatives, however, who would drop by at supper time, eat and then leave. Her own people rarely came to see her, since Beto was not very friendly when they did come. He became hard to please; everything had to be just so. And he was jealous of every male who visited the house, although few ever did. She felt so lonely that she yearned for the old days at her father's ranch, when she had no time at all to herself.

She welcomed the birth of her children, but that brought about other problems. Beto was a strict, often brutal father. He was not a wife beater, as some other husbands were, but he could be very cruel with words. After all, she was just a country girl with only four years of grammar school. Her children got slapped around, even the girls. But he was especially hard on little Rodolfo, her youngest—Rofito, as she called him. Because he stayed out late. Because Beto didn't like his friends, who were from the poorer barrios. Later, because he wore his hair too long. Until the time the boy came home after midnight, smelling of alcohol. Beto beat him with a piece of broomstick, relentlessly, while she stood dumbly by and watched, until the boy snatched the stick from his father, pushed him aside and ran out of the house. When he came back at supper time two days later, his father opened the door and told him, "You no longer live in this house. Go away or I'll kill you."

That had been five years ago, or was it six? She did not dare even to ask about him. It was then that she started smoking. At first, one or two cigarettes a day. But in a month she was up to two packs daily. Beto, who did not smoke, ordered her to stop, but she just ignored him. When they went to the supermarket, she would gather several cartons of cigarettes in her arms, take them to the check-out counter and have them bagged separately from the rest of their purchases. Soon Beto was begging her to quit, but she just smiled and kept on smoking. Finally he gave up, and life went on as before, except for the smell of tobacco smoke in the house.

If he was hard on his family, Beto was even harder on himself. Work was his only vice. He had risen from typist to legal clerk at the law firm where he worked, having done so by reading every law book he could get his hands on, every document he was allowed to see concerning criminal trials and lawsuits handled by the firm. This she knew because he had told her about it in detail. Many times. That was all he talked about, himself and his work. He was always at home when he was not at the office or away some evenings and weekends seeing to repairs on houses he bought and sold in the barrios. But he had little to do with the running of the house. That had become her job.

The kitchen still was her favorite room in the house, but cooking no longer gave her much pleasure. There were too many other problems that went with keeping the family going. They kept her awake at night and occupied her thoughts during the day, so that she felt she was always skimming over the surface of life. At times, she felt it was more than she could bear, but one day followed the next, and she always found the strength to meet each morning with the same silent patience. Smoking helped. It became for her a restful niche in her daily living. Until that visit to the doctor.

She had not been feeling well for some time, short of breath and dizzy at times. Nobody noticed it and she did not complain. But she did not get any better, so she thought that perhaps she should see the doctor. Finally, she mentioned it to Beto one morning just before he left for work. He looked closely at her. "You look old and tired," he said.

"I *am* old," she told him. "Hadn't you noticed?"

"I'll call Pepe Freyre as soon as I get to the office," he said. "I'm sure we can see him early this afternoon."

Beto and Dr. José Jaime Freyre had been in high school together, and they had been good friends ever since. Pepe Freyre had been seeing their children since old Dr. Zapata died, but Beto and Rebeca seldom saw him as patients, because Beto did not believe in going to doctors unnecessarily.

Pepe was a pleasant little man, with a smile always on his ruddy face. "Come in! Come in!" he said, looking at them over his gold-rimmed glasses as the nurse led them into his office. For a moment Rebeca expected him to say, "You are in your house." After shaking hands, he sat back in his chair and brought his fingertips together. He listened while Rebeca described her symptoms.

"Now, let's see what we can do about that," he said after she had finished. He examined her very carefully under Beto's wary eye. He whistled softly when he looked at her fingers, stained a deep tobacco-yellow. "We must take some X-rays," he said. "We certainly must."

The nurse took her to another room and did the X-rays. When she came back into the doctor's office, Beto and Dr. Freyre were talking quietly, but they stopped as soon as she came in the door. "Come back tomorrow afternoon," the doctor said.

They went back the following afternoon, and this time Pepe Freyre was not smiling. "Beto," he said, "she has cancer. Cancer of the lungs." She felt as if her chair had moved suddenly, and she grasped the arms to steady herself. After that she was all right.

For what seemed like a long time, nobody said anything. Then Beto asked, "How bad is it?"

"Well," Pepe Freyre said, "one cannot really tell, Beto. One can always hope. I mean, there is always a chance."

"Tell us the truth!" Beto said harshly. "How bad is it?"

"Very bad," Dr. Freyre replied. "The cancer has affected more than half of her lungs, as you can see from these plates."

Beto waved them aside. "Is there nothing you can do for her?"

Dr. Freyre looked at the wall beyond them. "We could try radiation. Or chemicals. But the cancer is too far gone for that. The truth is that I don't know how she has managed this long. She doesn't have much time."

There was another silence, and then Freyre said, "I'm going to prescribe some capsules for the pain. Let her take them only when she absolutely has to. Otherwise she will get used to them. Let her rest as much as possible." The doctor looked directly at her for the first time and said, "It was the cigarettes." He shook his head. "The cigarettes." Then turning again to her husband, "There is nothing more I can do, Beto. I'm sorry."

They left. Beto was white and trembling. She felt calm. The world outside looked somewhat unreal, it was true. Everything was more clearly defined, sharper. The colors were brighter. But she felt at peace with herself as they walked to the car.

At home all her children had been waiting for her, all except for Rofito. She would talk to her husband about that. Now that she was dying, he could not deny her. Meanwhile, she began to enjoy life. The house was quieter than it had been since the children were born. It was nice to sleep late and to have things done for her. Elisa surprised her by turning out to be a pretty good cook. After a couple of days in bed, she spent most of her time watching TV and walking around the house, supervising the things her daughters did.

Since she was not in pain, she did not take the pills Pepe had prescribed. She felt sorry for Beto, who looked pale and worried and walked around acting like an old man. To please him she stopped smoking, though it should have made no difference at this point. Dying was not so bad, really. Thinking about it did not frighten her. Instead she felt a wonderful sense of release. She was living in a special world. Everyone was kind and considerate. The nagging little cares that had meant so much to her were unimportant now.

It was more than a week after their last visit to the doctor, when she was sitting in the living room watching TV, that the doorbell rang. She opened the door, and there was Dr. Freyre, looking redder than usual.

"May I come in?" he said.

"Certainly." She opened the door wider. "Please do."

Dr. Freyre stepped just inside the door, looked around and took a deep breath. "I am terribly ashamed about what has happened," he said. "I don't know what to say, how to atone for the anguish we have caused you. But at least I bring you good news. That is why I hurried over to tell you the moment we were sure."

"News?"

"Things like this should never happen, but you

don't know how hard it is to find decent help these days. I fired the laboratory assistant before I came over here."

"What is the trouble, doctor?"

"Trouble? Trouble? The fool, the negatives, the plate...Your X-rays, Rebeca. The fool got them mixed up with those of another patient of mine who just died, of lung cancer. I happened to look at those that were supposed to be hers, and I knew a terrible mistake had been made. They show a perfectly sound pair of lungs, Rebeca. Yours!"

"I don't understand."

"You are perfectly healthy. You do not have cancer."

"Thank you, doctor," she said dully.

"There is nothing seriously wrong with you. You are tired, that is all. Take things easy, and in a few weeks you should be as good as ever."

"Thank you, doctor," she said.

"I must hurry off, but I wanted to let you know as soon as I could."

"Thank you, doctor," she said and closed the door after him.

Panchita and Elisa came in from the backyard with a bowl full of ripe tomatoes. "We heard voices," Elisa said.

"Visitors?" Panchita said. "Do we have visitors, Mamá?"

"Obviously not," Elisa said. "There's no one here, can't you see?"

"Oh, it must have been the set. Is that right, Mamá?"

"Yes," she said. Her daughters went back into the kitchen, talking softly. She turned off the TV and sat for a while looking at the empty screen.

It could not be, it could not be. That big lump of ice in her stomach, which she had accepted unflinchingly, almost eagerly. It was breaking up into sharp little pieces inside her, jagged fragments that would bite and tear at her as before. Then a thought came to her. Beto! It was all Beto's idea! He was so sensitive behind that grim face he showed the world. He had got together with Pepe Freyre about this. They wanted to make her last days happier by telling her there was really nothing wrong with her. That was it! She was certain.

But there was the lack of pain. From all she had heard, people who died of cancer suffered terribly. And she had felt no pain at all. Perhaps later? But if her lungs were so badly damaged, why no pain yet? Then she remembered her cousin Florentino. He had died of cancer and had suffered no pain until the very last. There might be something about it in the medical book Beto kept on the shelf.

She was looking for the book when Beto came into the driveway, honking and honking. He burst into the living room and hugged her.

"Rebeca! Beca! I just heard! I just heard!" There were tears in his eyes. "Pepe called me and told me about it." He turned toward the girls, his arm still around her waist. "There's nothing wrong with your mother! It was a mistake! All a mistake!"

She knew he was not pretending.

"What a wonderful day!" he shouted. "Let's have a big dinner to celebrate!"

She went to the bookcase and found a pack of cigarettes behind the encyclopedia. Her hands trembled just slightly as she opened the pack. After she had inhaled, she smiled and said, "Yes, let's celebrate. What do you want to eat tonight?"

Little Joe

That night all six of us were in the hut, getting ready along with everybody else to say goodbye to good old Camp Robinson. We had one last twenty-mile hike the following morning, a kind of going-away present from the cadre. After that, two days to have a final dip into the fleshpots of Little Rock, Arkansas. And then we were shipping out. Little Joe was sitting on his bunk, working saddle soap into his combat boots, trying to make them soft. You tried to be as kind to your feet as you could when you had a twenty-mile hike ahead of you, especially if you would be carrying a full field pack. And a full field pack weighed almost half as much as Little Joe did.

Great Big Johnson was stretched out on his bunk, looking up at the roof with those vacant blue eyes of his. His legs were sticking out of his bunk into the doorway. He was probably thinking of his milk cows back on the farm in Minnesota. We liked it when Great Big Johnson just lay on his bunk. Whenever he sat up and stretched his legs, there wasn't very much room for the rest of us. There were three Johnsons in our company—Little Johnson, Big Johnson and Great Big Johnson. Little Johnson was six feet tall. Why

Great Big Johnson was assigned to our squad I don't know. But he was an obliging sort of guy and tried to keep his feet out of the way. Little Joe was his number one buddy.

Luke had a wooden box in front of him. He was writing a letter. Luke wrote a lot of letters, but he would never tell us who they were for. He was from Oklahoma, and he thought Arkansas was a backward state. Roth was reading a book. He read lots of books. When he wasn't reading, Roth would tell us about his wife's bare ass. You look at her from behind, he would say, and she looks like she's sixteen. They had two children already. Roth was a good bit older than the rest of us. The Army was really scraping the bottom of the barrel.

Kantner was kneeling on the floor rolling his field pack and singing the Notre Dame fight song, as usual. He was a gangly, freckle-faced kid from Gary. I was sitting on my bunk, opening a package of cookies my mother had sent me.

"While her loyal sons are marching...Onward! To victory!"

"Shut up, Kantner!" Roth said. "Stop singing that silly song!"

"Hey! It ain't silly!" Kantner said. "'Tis the song of the Fighting Irish. My favorite football team and my favorite school."

"You don't look Irish to me," Roth said. "And you're not going to that school, for sure."

"I'm not Irish but I'm Catholic. One of my cousins went to Notre Dame."

"He went there on a sightseeing bus," I said.

"Come on!" Kantner said.

"Hey, Watson!" Roth said. "Toss me a couple of

those cookies. Don't you know how to share?"

"I'll toss you half a dozen," I answered, "if you'll let me meet your wife come Saturday."

"He means meet as in M E A T," Luke said.

"Screw you, Luke," Roth said. "Screw both of you."

I got up and passed the cookies around. I knew Little Joe wouldn't touch them while his hands were full of saddle soap, so I laid a couple of Oreos on his bunk. He looked up at me with his sleepy-looking eyes and said softly, "Thank you. Thank you very much." When I got to Great Big Johnson, he sat up, and the hut became smaller than it was before. I wished Little Joe would take out his bayonet and clean it, as he was always doing, because then Great Big Johnson would get up and leave the hut as fast as he could, and there would be lots of room.

Not that there was anything between Great Big Johnson and Little Joe but friendship. They were always together when we were off duty, and their bunks were next to each other. It was just that Great Big Johnson couldn't bear to see Little Joe with his bayonet in his hand. At least, not in the close quarters of the hut. So when Little Joe took out his bayonet to clean it, Great Big Johnson would walk out of the hut, where he didn't have to see Little Joe handling the damn thing. Little Joe cleaned and polished his bayonet every day, and then he shined his dress shoes. He took his M1 apart and oiled it every evening, and not just on the days we were having inspection. He washed his hands every chance he had. All of us shaved every day; we would catch hell if we didn't. But we skipped showers pretty often. The platoon sergeant didn't much care how we smelled as long as we looked sharp. Little Joe showered every single day, whether he needed it or not. He had this thing about staying clean all the time.

Little Joe came from down on the Texas border with Mexico. None of us could pronounce his name, so we just called him Joe. Little Joe, because he was little, no two ways about it. At first the platoon sergeant wondered whether he could finish a march carrying a field pack. But he did it every time. A couple of times Great Big Johnson offered to carry his rifle for him, and his entrenching tools. The second time Little Joe told him to mind his own business. It was the first time we had heard him lose his temper. We were surprised, even though the day was hot enough. In the platoon ahead of us a soldier had just hit his buddy over the head with his canteen.

Great Big Johnson gave us all the details that night while we were having a beer at the post canteen. All of us except Little Joe, who was back in the hut putting liniment on his ankles. "It was his eyes," Great Big Johnson said. "They shot sparks."

"What the hell!" Roth said. "Nobody's eyes shoot fire."

Great Big Johnson looked at Roth, his face very serious. "You mean I tell a lie?"

"Oh, no," Roth said, "of course not. They shot sparks."

"Sparks they shot," Great Big Johnson said. "That little guy, he don't look like much, but don't cross him. I'd hate to do that."

"I didn't think he'd get mad at anybody," Luke said. "He's always so polite."

"That's the way those people are," Kantner said. "I know. My uncle was down in their country most of his life. It's not like us, always horsing around and making a lot of noise. They're quiet all the time. Then, when they blow their stack—oh, brother! Isn't that right, Watson?"

"I'm from Dallas," I told them. "That's a long way from the Mexican border. But from what I hear, that's the way they are."

Great Big Johnson kept nodding his head. "Yah," he said, "yah." He smiled like a father who hears somebody talking nice about his kid.

"It's no good to cross a guy like that," Kantner said, looking at Great Big Johnson.

"No good." Great Big Johnson kept nodding his head. "No good."

We all were nice to Little Joe. He was a likeable sort of guy. And we didn't short-sheet him, either, or play any other tricks like that on him. Perhaps it was because we liked him. Or because we thought that Great Big Johnson just might be right. No sense picking on somebody who might stick a knife in your belly if you make him mad. As Great Big Johnson said, it was no good crossing a guy like that. It was no good crossing a guy like Great Big Johnson either.

Behind Great Big Johnson's back we laughed. And we kidded him along. "Look how Little Joe throws a grenade," we would tell him. "Just like he's throwing a knife."

"Yah," Great Big Johnson would say. "I know. I know."

Little Joe made like he didn't hear.

Another time, during bayonet drill, Great Big Johnson said, "Look. See how Little Joe comes in from under? Sticks the dummy right in the belly, way down." He shuddered. "I couldn't do that."

"Of course you can't," Roth told him. "You're built too far off the ground." He always was a spoilsport.

"You couldn't do it yourself, I betcha," Great Big Johnson said.

Little Joe didn't say anything. He just looked the other way.

Word got around that Great Big Johnson was afraid of Little Joe, and the whole platoon thought that was about the funniest thing outside the movies. But Great Big Johnson didn't pay no mind. He kept on trying to do things for Little Joe, and Little Joe kept saying, "No, thank you," and Great Big Johnson kept walking out of the hut every time Little Joe cleaned and polished his bayonet.

It was about this time that Little Joe started looking sort of grim, as if he had something on his mind. You would ask him something, and he didn't answer right away, as if he didn't hear you or he was thinking of something else.

"He must have got a letter from home with bad news," Luke told me and Kantner once when we were on KP. "That's what it is."

"I don't know," I said. "It's hard to figure it out. He never says much."

"Maybe somebody from another platoon called him names," Kantner said.

"Names? What kind of names?"

"You know how dark he is. Suppose somebody called him a colored man."

"Colored man?" said Luke. "You mean a nigger?"

"Could be," I said. Little Joe was so dark you had to be pretty close to him to know he sported a tiny black mustache. "If that's so, we'd better get ready for a real free-for-all one of these days. It will be their platoon against ours."

"Not if Little Joe starts cutting some of them up," Luke said. "That's not the kind of fight I want to get into."

"Me neither," Kantner said. "So what are we going to do?"

"We'll have to watch him all the time," I told them. "Keep him from getting into a fight with this guy in the first place. Let's get Roth into this, and two of us will try to stick close to him all the time."

"Nah," said Roth when we told him. "Little Joe isn't mad at anybody in or out of our platoon."

"Could be," Kantner said. "How do you know he isn't?"

"Ever see him with anybody outside our platoon? Or outside our squad, for that matter. He and Great Big Johnson are always together."

"You never know," Kantner insisted.

"Okay, okay," Roth said. "I'll help you."

"What about Great Big Johnson?"

"Let's keep him out. He'll just make things worse."

So we kept a close watch on Little Joe, but nothing happened. And now, at last, our sixteen weeks were just about over. Three more days and we'd be ready to ship out. Out of basic and into the meat grinder.

"Where do you guys want to go?" Luke said, his mouth full of my cookies. "Europe or the Pacific?"

"What difference does it make where we want to go?" I said. "We'll go where they send us."

"Me, I don't want to fight the Japs," Great Big Johnson said. "I just think about them little guys and I feel creepy all over."

Little Joe put away his combat boots and went out the door. "He's gone to wash his hands again," Kantner said.

"You ought to wash yours once in a while," Roth told him.

Kantner paid him no mind. "I'd like to go to Europe," he said. "They got some nice-looking babes over there."

"As good as Roth's wife?" Luke wanted to know.

"You guys are just envious. Come Saturday you'll be chasing all over town trying to pick up a case of the clap, while I'm shacking up with my sweet one-and-only."

Little Joe came right back in. He went over and picked up his bayonet. Great Big Johnson got to his feet, but before he could move Little Joe had jumped around him and blocked his way out of the hut. Little Joe was smiling. "I'm going to cut you open," he told Great Big Johnson.

Great Big Johnson put out a hand in front of him. "No!" he said. "No!" His big jaw was working up and down. "Please, Little Joe!" He tried to back away, but there was no place to back into. Little Joe came closer to him, showing his teeth. Great Big Johnson gave a kind of squeal, hit at the bayonet with the back of his hand and ran outside. Little Joe picked himself off the floor. He was still smiling, and it was not until then that we noticed. There was no blood anywhere, because the bayonet was still inside the sheath.

It took us some time before we could talk Great Big Johnson into coming back inside the hut. "Little Joe won't hurt you," we told him. "It was all a joke. He wants you to come in with us so you two can be buddies like always."

He said, okay, he would if we went in ahead of him. Little Joe was standing in the middle of the floor. "Look," he told Great Big Johnson, "I did all that just to show you. I had the bayonet in my hand, didn't I? Like this, no? Did I cut you? Of course I didn't. You hit me and knocked me down, and I didn't cut you. I never could do a thing like that, do you understand? Never."

Understanding lit up Great Big Johnson's face. "To show me? You just did it to show me?"

"Yes. To show you, to show you..."

"Another guy you would have cut to ribbons," said Great Big Johnson breathlessly. "But your buddy, no. That's why you did it, little buddy. Just to show me. Somebody else, watch out! But your buddy, no."

Little Joe pulled the bayonet out of the sheath. "Ah, you animal!" he shouted, his face twisted with rage. "You stupid cow! Get out of my sight before I throw this knife straight into your belly!"

Great Big Johnson left again. He almost took the door frame with him on his way out. Little Joe sat down on the floor and stuck the bayonet into the wood between his legs.

"I couldn't even hit him with the handle," he said, "no matter how hard I tried. I never threw a knife at anybody or anything in my whole life. I don't like knives! I don't like knives!"

"Why don't you eat your cookies?" Roth said.

"Ah, that bastard!" Little Joe jabbed viciously into the wood with the point of his bayonet. "I hate him! I hate him! I hate him!"

The Gift

When the guard came and kicked me out of the latrine, I knew Lt. Commander Young had something to do with it. But I sure was surprised when I found out what it was. You may wonder what a GI like me was doing in the same POW camp with a hoity-toity officer of the United States Navy. Well, this was no Geneva convention camp, if there ever was one like that. We were out in the jungle, in the middle of nowhere, living in a bunch of huts inside a stockade. Ten men to a hut—soldiers, sailors and civilians. Lt. Commander Young was the only officer. How he happened to end up with us I don't know, but since he was the only officer in camp he was supposed to be responsible for us. And it was my bad luck to be in the same hut with him.

Even though the Japs didn't give him separate quarters or nothing, Young wouldn't let us forget he was an officer and in charge of things. He never joked with us or joined in the griping when the guards weren't around. But he didn't give us no trouble, and so we let him be. There was no harm if he wanted to act like he was walking the bridge of a battleship. He must have been smart and handsome once, like so

118

The Gift

many of these Navy guys, but that was before the Japs got hold of him. His toes were showing out of his shoes, and the seat of his pants was torn. But that was his business, like his case of dysentery.

Then one day Lt. Commander Young had to go and steal a peach that was sitting on the military commander's window sill. A big juicy peach from China. The guards came that evening and took Young away. We heard him screaming for a while; then he stopped and we guessed he was dead. But some time later he showed up. They had roughed him up, that was all. He had a puffed eye and a fat lip, and he limped a little, but he wasn't hurt bad. Except that all the starch was gone out of him.

It didn't surprise me at all. I had always thought that in spite of his superior ways, Lt. Commander Young was a very scared man. We were all afraid—of being beaten or killed some day. But he was afraid in a different way, I thought. Of having to be dirty forever, of losing what remained of his dignity, of having dysentery for still another week. When he was at his starchiest, there had always been a rabbity look in his eye. It was like a crack in a thick wall through which you could see the scared soul of Lt. Commander Young. Now the Japs had broken the wall, and fear poured out of him, drenching him from head to foot. We could see it as we watched him wobble to his bunk and lay down. We let him be.

Then Monkeyface and four of his guards came in. Monkeyface was the sergeant of the guard. We called him Monkeyface because he had a monkey face. He carried a little sword, like an officer, and he used the flat of it on us whenever he felt like it. Monkeyface came in and Lt. Commander Young jumped from his bunk like he was getting ready to run. Monkeyface grinned a 14-karat grin.

"All right! Take it easy," he said, proud as hell of his English. "Latham and Bullard!"

There was so much silence you could have heard the temperature drop. Latham and Bullard stepped forward and the guards took them away. They didn't say a word. All they did was look at Young. Young looked at the floor between his feet.

Next morning before breakfast, we were treated to a show, all of us in the stockade. We were lined up in front of a new-dug trench to watch Latham and Bullard get executed for trying to escape. Latham was a GI, a green kid from Detroit with buck teeth and freckles. He cried the whole time until the sword came down. Bullard was a crusty old Australian with false teeth. His upper plate jarred loose when the blade hit his neck. Breakfast tasted worse than usual that morning.

It didn't make sense, chopping off their heads for trying to escape. There was no place to run to, in the middle of the jungle. It was true, both of them often talked about it when we were in our bunks after lights out. But that was part of a sort of dreaming out-loud we all played at, except for Lt. Commander Young. We would lie there in the dark and tell each other the things we would do when we got out of that camp, and the rest would laugh and joke about the things we said. Some would talk about women, others about food or about going to places and seeing things. Latham and Bullard would team up and tell us about the funny plans they had for all of us to escape. They would take turns in giving us all kinds of details, each one trying to come up with a sillier plan than the oth-

The Gift

er. It was just a way of keeping us from going crazy. Lt. Commander Young never joined in the fun. He just listened.

So it was not hard to guess who had told the Japs about Latham and Bullard. And you can guess how we felt about Young after that. But he didn't seem to care what we thought or what we called him once we were by ourselves in our hut. He was too scared of Monkeyface to care.

Soon he was telling the Japs everything we said and did. We knew because Monkeyface would call him over every evening after supper. Young would come back shaking, and next morning we would catch hell for whatever Young told him we had said the night before. We decided to keep our mouths shut after lights out, but then Young started making up things to tell Monkeyface. And we would catch hell anyway. I'm sure Monkeyface knew they were lies, but he must have thought of the whole business as a big joke.

It was only guys from our hut that got punished. Mostly we got extra details or a few hours in the bamboo cage that was in front of the camp commander's office. But then we started getting knocked around a bit by the guards, one of us at a time just before breakfast. Finally a boy was beaten so bad he had to be taken away because he was too hurt to work. It was after that boy that big Pat Malloy went after Lt. Commander Young. Pat was a sailor, and he had always called Young sir. That was before what happened to Latham and Bullard. After the boy was taken away we had lined up for chow, when Malloy went for Young without saying a word. Young didn't even put his hands up. But two guards came running and stuck their bayonets into Malloy so many times he looked like a bundle of bloody rags when they were through with him.

We stayed in line and watched. There was nothing else we could do. Monkeyface came out and made it plain that nobody was to lay hands on Lt. Commander Young. Then he kicked Young and told him to get up and quit making trouble.

So we started making plans to kill Young. His dysentery made him go to the latrine several times after supper, and during the times he was out we talked the whole thing over. Our idea man was Mort Stickle, who had been a T/5 in the medics. Stickle was a boy with a good head on his shoulders. He said that one of us must sacrifice himself to save the rest. If we let things go on as they were, everybody in the hut but Young would be dead before the war was over. One guy must kill Young, Stickle said, but he must do it in the latrine when the rest of us weren't around, so the Japs wouldn't know all of us had been in on it. Of course the guy who did it would have his head chopped off, like Latham and Bullard, but he would save the rest of us.

What if one of the boys from the other huts was around, somebody said. He'd be sure to lose his head too.

Tough luck, Stickle said, but the odds were nobody else would be in the latrine late at night.

I didn't especially like the idea, but I had to go along with the rest. So we drew straws, and of course I got the short one. I knew it would happen; all my life I've got the short end of the stick. "Bingo!" Stickle said. "You're it, Mex." And he gave me the knife he had stolen from the kitchen.

For a minute I thought of backing out of the deal. How did I know the whole business hadn't been rigged?

The Gift

A kind of odd-man-out sort of thing. Then the guy close to the door signaled that Young was coming back, so I put the knife under my shirt. Young came in and lay down for a while. I waited. Finally he sat up, and I went to the latrine.

Nobody else was there. I waited there in the stink, wishing I was somewhere else. I thought about how the edge of the sword would feel when it hit the back of my neck, and I wondered if I'd feel giddy staring down into the trench where they would bury me. Then I really was afraid, and I knew how Young felt and why he ratted on us all the time. I felt sorry for him, too. I also thought how it would feel when I stabbed him. I wondered if he would yell and put out his hands in front of him after I cut him the first time.

I waited for a long time. Then I heard shouting and somebody running toward the latrine. I barely had time to drop the knife down the hole when a guard came and drove me out. I ended up with Stickle and the other three in a little cell behind camp headquarters. Young wasn't with us. This time he rated separate quarters. We spent the night in that cell, and they told me what had happened.

Just after I left for the latrine, Monkeyface paid a visit to our hut. He was in a joking mood, and he went and sat down beside Young. When he did so, he noticed a dirty little bag Young had in his hand, a little thing with a drawstring around the mouth. Monkeyface made a grab for it and Young pushed him away. Monkeyface hit Young in the mouth, and Young took Monkeyface's little sword away from him and killed him with it. Right in front of everybody in the hut. That is, everybody but me. I was in the latrine. I couldn't have stopped Young from killing Monkeyface, even if I had wanted to.

That's why I lived through it all, until you guys came. But I had to go watch, even though I could hardly stand after the going-over the guards had given me. The men from the other huts were there too, and they were cursing me under their breath. The Japs took care of Stickle and the other three first. By the time Young's turn came, I was sick of watching heads half-chopped off. I'm sure the Jap lieutenant in charge of the execution felt the same way I did. He was a very young man with big glasses that made him look more like a student than a soldier. And he was very pale by then. The calmest man there, I think, was Lt. Commander Young. All his starch had come back.

When the sword fell on his neck, his fist opened and the little bag with the drawstring around its mouth fell from his hand. One of the guards picked it up and gave it to the young lieutenant. He opened the bag and looked inside. Then he smiled a melancholy smile and came up to me where I was standing with the other POWs. "Here," he said. "Gift. I give you."

I took the bag and squeezed it. It felt like a diamond was inside. Or a gold nugget. But I didn't open it until I was alone. You'd never guess what was in it. A kid's tooth, the kind you lose when you grow up. I kept it as a good-luck charm. After all, I felt lucky. I should have, shouldn't I? All the others in my hut were killed, but I was in the latrine so they just beat me and made me watch. I couldn't have done anything else, could I?

But those guys from the other huts think it was all my fault. That I ratted on the others, that's why they all were killed and I wasn't. And that the Jap officer made me a gift of a diamond or a ruby after the executions to pay me for the job I had done. It was the other way around. But when I think of it, those guys never cared much for me. Here. You can have the damn thing. A fine good-luck charm it was. See? Inside the little bag it feels like a diamond. Or a gold nugget, at least. It would fool anybody.

When It Snowed In Kitabamba

Captain Meniscus was a man who dearly loved order. One had to see him at his desk, his neat little profile bent over his tidily stacked papers, his rimless glasses shining in the light that came in through the spotless windows. He kept the town of Kitabamba as neat as a brand-new pin.

The captain loved to issue his little orders. The town, from such and such a street to street such and such, was hereby declared Area Number That. The inhabitants of Area Number That would comport themselves in this and this manner from hours A to B. Occupation personnel would comport themselves in the following manner in relation to indigenous personnel. This man could go so far down this street and no more. This one must not enter this building, but that one might. After a certain hour, certain people might not do certain things.

It would have pleased the captain if he could have believed that the world stopped in its tracks when he was not looking. But he was a practical man; he knew that these creatures he moved hither and yon, put in this square and that, had the annoying habit of creeping and crawling out of place the moment his attention was engaged elsewhere. But he did his best. No one could say that Captain Meniscus did not always do his best. And he worked hard.

Such was the case one cold day shortly before noon, the last day of the year to be exact, of a year that would live in history forever. Much had been accomplished, much had been done toward the making of a better world. Captain Meniscus had begun the year fighting the people he now governed. He was ending it in his office, working hard for them, for their reform. He had decided that he and all his staff would work late that New Year's Eve. It would set a good example, it would show the natives what was being done for them. His light would shine brightly until after midnight, while they played at their New Year's festivities.

And in working late on important days, Captain Meniscus was but following in the footsteps of the Old Man. The Old Man. Reverently he raised his eyes toward him, when Corporal Hogg interrupted by coming in. The captain, who never smoked, was conscious of Corporal Hogg's presence before he saw the man, just by the stale pipe odor.

Corporal Hogg was the company clerk, or sergeant major as the captain preferred to call him. He typed outgoing reports, filed incoming ones, and managed relations with interpreters and the other native help that was necessary for the captain to govern Kitabamba. Hogg spoke with a Texas drawl, a lazy way of speech in the captain's opinion. His uniform was buttoned and clean, yet it was not sharp as a soldier's should be. He was sloppy, Meniscus thought as Hogg's long bony figure approached his desk. But sloppy in a subtle sort of way that Meniscus found hard to reprimand because he could not quite define it.

The corporal came up, drawled a good morning and laid some papers on Meniscus' desk. He stood waiting, not quite lounging and not quite at attention, but somewhere in between. It irritated Meniscus, so that he looked out the window to control himself. He knew that he could easily come to hate Corporal Hogg. But Captain Meniscus had long ago decided he must never allow himself such a disorderly emotion as hate. It was not for an officer. Hate was out of place in an ordered mind which knew where it was going. So he gazed out the window until he was sure he could look at Hogg without a feeling of irritation.

He turned from the window to meet Hogg's lively, jeering eyes. Meniscus looked away again.

"You have the draft of the proclamation," Meniscus said. He preferred to make his questions sound like statements.

"Yes sir," Hogg answered. He spoke in a very respectful tone, but he pushed the paper rudely at the captain. It was Meniscus' New Year's proclamation to the citizens of Kitabamba, to be published the next day. Tame enough in style, dignified but tame, the captain thought. He would have liked it in a more lofty tone, something on the order of Themistocles to the Athenians, "To you then, o citizens, I wish to advise what it is best to do." But the thought that Corporal Hogg must type the draft had stopped him. It would be just like Hogg to remind him, rather innocently, that Themistocles had been a Navy man. So he had begun it in a more routine fashion, "In the name of the Supreme Commander, I wish to extend, to the people of Kitabamba..." He read the draft carefully, making a few penciled corrections in a neat, almost feminine hand. Then he looked up at Hogg.

"You have the report from the village association."

"No sir," Hogg replied. "It hasn't come in yet."

"It has not come in," the captain said sharply, annoyed now at something with a definite cause. "There is no excuse for that."

"It got held up along the way...sir. One must realize that it takes time, that it has to go round to many people...sir."

Meniscus carefully noted Hogg's delayed "sirs," and the part they played in keeping Hogg from definite disrespect.

"Hogg," he said. "I hate this circumlocution, this circumnavigation of things." He pointed, looking Hogg straight in the face. Hogg turned to the wall with what was almost but not quite a faint smile. Hanging before the captain's desk was a large picture of the Old Man in a massive, hand-carved frame. It was a popular picture of him, one he liked himself, in which he was shown looking far into the distance, his chiseled profile raised as though he were sniffing the wind, a white silk scarf around his throat to hide the wrinkles on his aged neck. No one knew how old the Old Man was, and since it was rumored that he dyed his hair, it was hard to guess. But he looked very impressive, with his handsome, dignified face and his haughty expression, the cluster of stars on his shoulder and the shining, gold-braided cap hanging like an aureole over his high olympian forehead. Or like bay leaves. Captain Meniscus always thought of bay leaves when he looked at the braid on the Old Man's cap.

Under the Old Man's portrait was a long bamboo frame which contained a single sentence in large gothic print. The Old Man had once said those words in

Captain Meniscus' presence, not to him but in his presence. Very close to him too.

Corporal Hogg kept his eyes dutifully fixed on the space between portrait and inscription while Meniscus said in his precise tones, "Look at those words, corporal; the words of him we all serve. Look at them, never forget them."

The inscription read, "The shortest distance between two points is a straight line." Hogg stared at the wall with a very sober face.

"Doing things after his manner is not at all impossible, corporal, if we keep those words in mind," Meniscus continued. "The *shortest* distance between *two* points is a *straight* line. Not a curve, corporal, not a series of angles, not one long meander. The straight line! That is the secret!"

"Yes sir," Hogg said. Meniscus was gratified by the meekness in the corporal's voice. Then Hogg turned from the picture and looked at him, the same bright levity in his eyes. Meniscus was annoyed once more. He looked away and said, "That is all you have."

"All the papers, yes sir," Hogg said.

"Nothing else to be noted, nothing circulating (he mouthed the word contemptuously), nothing circulating among the town gossips."

"Nothing, sir, except that it may snow."

The captain shook his head. "Too far south."

"That's what they say," the corporal said.

"There has never been any snow in Kitabamba. The records show that."

"That's not what the people say, sir. They say it has snowed. Twice in the memory of old men."

"Folktales," Meniscus said. "Our intelligence would mention it; there is nothing on record."

"It looks like snow," the corporal said, adding after a short silence, "sir."

The captain looked at him coldly. "Corporal," he said, "don't talk arrant nonsense."

The corporal looked at Meniscus with strangely mirthful eyes, his large, rather loose mouth set in an indefinite expression.

"That is all, corporal," the captain said.

Hogg straightened his shoulders a bit. "I'm going to lunch now," he said and walked out.

The captain waited for the room to lose Corporal Hogg's pipe smell. Probably smoked it to save his cigarettes for other purposes, Meniscus thought. Of course he could not censure the man for smoking a pipe. Especially since the Old Man smoked one too. But he had never noticed that the Old Man's pipe stank that way. He wondered whether Hogg might affect a pipe—he rejected the thought even as it formed in his mind. Not Hogg. He was too crude a man, despite his bookish learning.

If anything, Hogg might be suspected of disrespect. But Meniscus was not sure. It was no small thing to accuse a man of. Meniscus could not imagine a life in which there was not at least some reverence for the Old Man, in whose service he had been since he was young. He had come in as a private and had risen by perseverance, by courage and stick-to-itiveness, by a certain clear conception of his goals and a decisiveness in his movement toward them that he had never, could never have put into words until the Old Man himself (who was as well-known an orator as a strategist) had let fall those precious words which were now framed on the captain's wall.

Men like Hogg were too cynical. The corporal

would come to no good end. Yet, he did his work well. Meniscus had no complaint on that score. And yet again, there were a lot of things about Hogg that were difficult to forgive. That song, for one. But how to prove that it was Hogg's? Meniscus knew better than to take a false step; he must be sure. But meanwhile the song was gaining in popularity, and the Army was disgraced each time it was sung. Even the urchins were singing it in the streets.

> Chewing gummo, chocoretto,
> Yamamoto was her name;
> All she had was gonorrhea,
> But I loved her just the same.

Captain Meniscus felt like spitting in disgust. It was not true! They were not lecherous carpetbaggers. They were not blackmarketeers. They were men with a mission to perform! And the natives? He had thought of banning the song, but he knew that would only attract more attention to it. Why didn't Hogg use his talents in a different direction? Why didn't he write a song about their mission instead of back-alley rot?

He knew there was no truth in the song. His men were good, clean American boys. Even Hogg, he thought, was guilty in imagination rather than in practice. Meniscus watched them all too closely; his MPs were too efficient to allow things like that. But the agents of a certain power would be glad to have it thought that his men were degenerates, as the song made them out. "*Arigato, sayonara*, Yankee soldier come again." Anger knotted the captain's throat. If he were only sure!

There was a timid knock at the open door and Amakata crept in. Amakata was a little man with crooked teeth and a mournful, embarrassed air. He wrinkled his brown face when he saw the captain, smiling an expectant smile. In he came, ducking his round, short-cropped head, his face expressionless despite the frozen, formal smile. He was dressed in old cavalry breeches; strips of cloth were wrapped around his legs. His feet, in straw sandals, were blue with cold.

"Well," the captain said, "don't stand there."

Amakata understood a bare dozen words of English. He smiled and bowed and began to dust with a dirty rag. Captain Meniscus watched him with growing impatience. Finally he said, "Amakata!"

At the sound of his name Amakata came and stood before the captain's desk. He bowed deeply, his hands touching his knees, then stood quietly before the captain.

"How old are you?" the captain demanded.

Amakata smiled and shrugged, bowed and smiled and looked repentant, as if to say, "I know I am a very stupid person. Pardon me for being so stupid." He did not have to understand what the captain was saying. To appear stupid and humble was his main job, and he knew it to perfection. He smiled and bowed low again.

Meniscus watched him, a chord of cruelty growing within him. Suddenly he shouted, "Don't loll before me like that, you bastard! Straighten up!"

Amakata stiffened into soldierly attention. He understood only the word bastard, but he recognized the tone of voice. Meniscus watched Amakata's painfully rigid form for a long while. Then he began to talk—coldly, evenly.

"You are a fool," the captain said. "Just look at you. Little better than an animal."

Amakata remained in agonized stiffness.

"You'll never get anywhere in life," Meniscus continued, his tone less cold now. "Do you know that? Why, you're almost middle-aged, man. Almost middle-aged. And what have you done? You've wasted your life away."

He leaned back into his chair and put his locked hands over his stomach. "For generations," he went on, "where have you gone? I'll tell you. Nowhere. I've watched you, all of you. You never get to the point. Even when you take a wife, you have to send her a go-between to talk about the weather. You spend all your life, at least ninety-five percent of it, in lost motion."

The captain leaned forward and put an elbow on his desk. "But that is all past," he said softly, almost dreamily. "All that is past. Now you have begun a new life, all of you." Amakata perceived his change in tone, and he relaxed a bit, though he still remained at attention.

Meniscus lowered his voice almost to a whisper. "And then what?" he asked Amakata. "Then what? What when we go away? Won't you go right back to it? To your night soil and your open sewers and your conferences in the right-of-way? You will, won't you? Eh? Won't you?"

Amakata realized that a question was being asked of him and eagerly dipped into his stock of English words. Smiling broadly he nodded and said, "Yes s', yes s'."

"You will, will you!" Meniscus cried. "You will, you dirty bastard!"

Amakata saw that he should have used the other word. He stiffened into exquisite rigidity once more and shook his head. "No s'," he said, "no s'."

Meniscus let him stand in that muscle-straining

stiffness for a few moments. Then he tore a sheet of paper from a pad, picked up a pencil and motioned Amakata nearer. The captain always acted on the assumption that the natives understood more English than they would admit. But this was important; it might very well be epoch-making. He pointed at the Old Man's picture.

Amakata was never surer of what was expected of him. He turned full toward the picture and bowed profoundly, much more profoundly than before the captain. Three times he bowed, while Meniscus watched him with a satisfied smile. Then Amakata turned toward the captain, who beckoned to him to lean over the desk.

"See?" the captain said, making a dot on one end of the page. "This is you. Now..." he made another dot at the other end of the page, "...this is where you are going. See? How do you get there? How is the best way to get there? Do you go to this corner first? To this other corner? Do you go back and forth like this? Do you go around under the paper like this? Of course not." He picked up a ruler and laid it between the two dots. "Like this! This is the way!" He pointed at the inscription on the wall and repeated it, slowly and distinctly.

Amakata was bewildered. There was nothing in his experience to help him guess the captain's meaning. He could not tell how this confusion of curves and angles that the captain had drawn on the paper was related to the portrait of the Supreme Person on the wall. He looked at Meniscus, his mouth open.

"Do you understand?" the captain said. Then, in an unprecedented impulse he repeated the question, brokenly, in Amakata's own tongue.

Amakata pounced greedily on the mispronounced

words. "Yes," he said, also in his own tongue. "Yes, yes, yes!"

Captain Meniscus smiled, then scowled. He ordered Amakata back to his work, and for the next fifteen minutes he badgered him with orders which Amakata had to guess by a gesture or an intonation. The captain made him straighten the same thing again and again, made him wipe the dust off places he had wiped three or four times before. Amakata strained at the captain's every gesture, a horribly anxious expression on his face, hanging on every word of the incomprehensible flow that came from the captain's mouth. He began to sweat. Finally, when Captain Meniscus saw that Amakata's hands were beginning to shake, he was satisfied and let him go.

A short while later Amakata came into the office again, wearing a white jacket and with the captain's lunch upon a tray. Amakata put the tray on the captain's desk and left in a flurry of frantic bows, shutting the door behind him. Meniscus selected the least important of the documents in his "In" baskets and put them beside his tray. As he ate he glanced at them and initialed them.

After a while he became aware of a soft, feathery sound outside his window. It had begun to snow. He stopped, his fork halfway to his mouth, at the sight of the fat flakes falling, falling in a thick cottony shower upon the square outside. The captain let the fork clatter down upon his plate. There was no reason, no precedent for this. It seemed that the weather had willfully set out to contradict him. For a moment the captain pursed his little mouth and glared at the falling snow. Then his features assumed their habitual calm, and he turned back to his work and his lunch.

But he found it hard to concentrate on either. A vague uneasiness seized him. He sat at his desk staring out the window at the snow. Not until Amakata came in with his tea did he resume his meal.

In the outer office there was a sound of running, then a stamping of feet. Corporal Hogg returning from his lunch. Captain Meniscus stopped work long enough to look at his watch and note that Hogg had taken more than an hour, as usual. Then he continued eating and reading, and thinking about the snow outside.

Other feet stamped in the outer office. Captain Meniscus heard the voice of Master Sergeant Fatt saying, "Hi, Lover Boy." Hogg answered in a lower tone, and he and Sergeant Fatt began a conversation that Meniscus could not hear. Fatt was the head of the MP unit, a man whom Meniscus liked and trusted. The captain had often hoped the sergeant would be a good influence on Hogg.

In the outer office Hogg and Fatt were talking in low tones. Hogg was sitting at his desk, fiddling with his typewriter keys, while Fatt, big and beefy, sat sideways on the desk, his large, freckled hand supporting his holster. Fatt thought it his duty to be a friend to Hogg, since both were from Texas. Besides, he felt that he could use the corporal.

"The trouble with you," Fatt was saying, "is that you're interested in nothing but pom-pom."

Hogg looked at him with a playful sort of contempt. "What else is there?" he said.

"For God's sakes, man," Fatt said. "Do you think you'll be here forever?"

"I'll worry about that later. Right now I'll take the girls and the liquor. I get all I want on a carton a week.

Why stick my neck out?"

"Some extra yen won't hurt you," Fatt said. "And there's no risk to it at all."

Hogg looked at him narrowly. "I'll think it over," he said.

Cigarettes brought thirty yen a pack. Thirty yen was two dollars in cash and about fifteen dollars in goods and services. Each man was issued a carton a week, enough to live a high life behind the captain's back. But Sergeant Fatt wanted more than fun. He wanted to make a killing in pearls. One carton of cigarettes could bring thousands and thousands of yen if one man kept selling it and his buddy, an MP, kept confiscating it from the buyers.

"I'll think it over," Hogg said, raising his voice as a sign that he wanted to end the conversation.

"Give it some thought," Fatt answered, also in a louder voice. "I'm doing it because I like you."

The captain had finished his meal. He put the papers he had initialed into an "Out" box. Then, with an angry look at the snow outside, he rose and went to the file cabinet by the wall. As he opened it, he heard the voices in the outer office more clearly. He had discovered, quite by accident months ago, that if he stood in this corner, he could hear almost everything that was said in the outer office. But he never took advantage of his discovery. His sense of honor, coupled with a serene confidence in himself, kept him from eavesdropping, though occasionally he could not help hearing snatches of conversation going on outside. He heard Hogg say, loudly and distinctly, that he would think it over and heard Fatt's reply.

"He's working on Hogg," Meniscus said to himself. "I hope he does the man some good."

Then Hogg said in lower tones, "By the way, aren't you going in to see old Straighten-Up-And-Fly-Right?"

Meniscus moved back to his desk, quickly and noiselessly. Hogg's last words did not anger him. He had known for a long time that Hogg had given him that nickname and that it had stuck, that even his MPs called him that behind his back. He was not pleased at Hogg's impudence, but he did like the name. It had some of the flavor of "Old Rough and Ready." A fit epithet for a leader of men.

There were other names, vague echoes of which had reached his ears, such as "The Anointed" and "God's Little Acher." These Meniscus did not like, and the suspicion that Hogg circulated them behind his back was another cause of his feeling against the corporal. It was through no effort of his, Meniscus thought, that the natives looked upon the Old Man with awe and reverence. And if he, Captain Meniscus, was tinctured in the eyes of the native population by the overflow of this awe, why it made his mission easier.

He called Fatt. Fatt came in as though he were on parade, sharp in his flawless uniform. He marched up to the captain's desk, saluted and came to attention with a click of heels and a light stamp. He gave his name and the reason for his presence. Smiling, Meniscus put him at ease. The sight of Sergeant Fatt, his military bearing, his faultlessness and assurance, made the captain's heart glad. He listened good-humoredly while Fatt reported briefly on the arrests he had made, the patrols he had run in town.

"Very good, sergeant," he said. "Dictate a full report to the corporal."

Fatt saluted and came to attention again, waiting to be dismissed.

Meniscus smiled. "Sergeant," he said, "I've said it before, I will say it again. You will go far in the Army."

"Thank you sir," Fatt said.

"I admire your devotion to the unswerving path of duty," Meniscus said. "Stay on it. Remember, sergeant." Fatt looked up expectantly as Meniscus raised his hand. "Those words, sergeant."

"Yes sir," Fatt said.

Meniscus smiled paternally. "You may go," he said.

Fatt saluted, about-faced and marched out. After he left, the captain sighed. He took off his wristwatch and placed it on the desk, noting the time there was left before 3:19, when the train would arrive. He took out papers from an "In" box, put them neatly in order, taking only those which he knew he could finish by 3:19. He quickly divided the number of pages by the number of minutes until train time and began to work on them, checking the time now and then to make sure he was moving at the right speed.

Every day, with the arrival of the train, a little ritual was enacted at Kitabamba in which Meniscus was the chief actor and the crowd of townspeople both audience and supporting cast. Across the square was the railroad station, and from the doorstep of Meniscus' headquarters (straight as a piece of string stretched between the two points had been able to make it) a low narrow boardwalk ran unerringly to a post on the station platform. The post was marked with a sign which said, "Kitabamba, 27th Military Government Headquarters, Captain Meniscus commanding."

Here, day after day without fail, stopped the coach bearing the courier with the mail from General Headquarters. And at precisely the right moment, Captain Meniscus would start from the door of his own headquarters, just as the train—an express—drew into the station. As he stepped out, the local police force, drawn up for the occasion, saluted and presented their truncheons. The MPs guarding his route at scattered points parallel to the boardwalk stiffened into attention as he passed. Under the station portico, the local band was arrayed, and beyond the police and MP cordon every soul in town stood watching.

With perfect timing, Meniscus would march down the boardwalk, reaching the signpost just as the courier, a white-helmeted lieutenant, sprang from the coach. Like actors in a play, they would meet, precisely at the right moment, meet and salute each other smartly. Two soldiers of Meniscus' command, standing on either side, presented arms. Captain Meniscus and the courier exchanged pouches and saluted again, more smartly if possible. Then the captain about-faced and marched back along the boardwalk, his eyes on the door out of which he had come.

As Meniscus about-faced, the courier would jump back into the train, which pulled out immediately, signaling its departure with one shrill whistle. The whistle was the signal for the band under the station portico to strike up a shaky version of "America" or "Anchors Aweigh" or some other American piece in their repertoire. The military guard stationed around the square presented arms. The uniformed station personnel, native, saluted. To all this, Captain Meniscus seemed oblivious. He looked at none of it, nor at the crowd of gaping natives, sprinkled with a few soldiers off duty. Eyes straight on the door of his own headquarters, he returned on the same straight line, holding in the crook of his arm close to his heart the communications from the Old Man to him and the town of Kitabamba.

Of course, none of those communications ever were from the Old Man himself. But they were in his name, and the natives were convinced that every day at this hour the captain received a personal letter, in which each day his right and authority to rule, regulate and improve the town of Kitabamba were reaffirmed. This alone made the daily ceremony worth the effort. Every day the natives would gather in a great crowd around the edges of the square and in the station to see the captain parade from his office to the station and back again. The village stopped its activities at this hour. Those who had cameras and were bold enough to use them took pictures for their children and their children's children. Farmers from the surrounding countryside, who had come to the village to bring their produce or to buy salt, fish or seaweed paste, stayed beyond their expected visit to see the edifying sight. And Meniscus acted as if the crowd did not exist, even though it was for them that the whole thing was staged. While they watched, he came and went as though he and the courier were the only two persons in the world.

Captain Meniscus finished his allotted work at 3:18, one minute before the deadline he had set for himself. The minute passed but there was no sign of the train. The captain leaned back in his chair and looked out at the station directly across the square. It had stopped snowing. On this last day of such an important year, the crowd was larger than usual in spite of the snow. It was already gathered around the edges of the square, waiting for the train. The band was forming at the station. The captain looked at his watch—3:20. He wondered if his watch could be fast, but he immediately dismissed the thought. Rising, he went toward the window, going near the file cabinet in the corner to look beyond the station for a glimpse of smoke. As he did so, he caught a sound of humming in the outer room. It was Hogg's voice.

He's not singing that thing again! thought Meniscus. He went closer to the wall and made out the tune that Hogg was humming. His face softened. No, it was not the chewing gummo song; it was a march. "Ta-da-DA, ta-DA, ta-DA, DA. Tee-DUM, tee-DUM, tee-DUM, tee-DUMitty, DUM," Hogg sang. It was "The Captain's March." Meniscus smiled.

"The Captain's March." It was going to be the high point of the day's ceremony. For almost a month the band had been practicing the piece, which the rat-faced little bandmaster had composed in Meniscus' honor. Today it would be played in public for the first time as Meniscus marched back to his office with the message from the Old Man. To have a march composed in one's honor was no mean achievement, though he had successfully concealed his pride behind the detached, almost cold attitude with which he had treated the bandmaster. Then there was also Hogg. In spite of himself, the captain felt self-conscious when the natives paid him homage in front of Hogg. Hogg had agreed with the captain that it was quite an honor to have a march named after one. But his eyes seemed to be laughing when he said it. And not long afterwards he managed to let fall a remark about the way native musicians murdered Western music. On another occasion Meniscus had overheard Hogg telling Fatt, "It sounds just like an old radio commercial I once heard in West Texas. Advertising a cough medicine. Just exactly like it!" But Meniscus was not sure what Hogg had been referring to. In any case, it was heartening to hear Hogg now, humming "The Captain's March" to himself with such obvious enjoyment.

Then the captain heard Fatt's voice. "Come on. Sing it, man; sing it."

Hogg snickered. Then he sang, "When it snoooowed in Kitabamba, the MONkeys wrapped their TAILS around the TREES." He stopped. "Let's see. What rhymes with trees? Freeze?"

Fatt said, "How about 'The monkeys' tails did freeze?'"

"Good, very good," Hogg answered with quiet mockery. "But we already have monkeys in the other line."

"Put Meniscus up there."

"Meniscus wrapped his tail around the trees?"

The captain waited to hear no more. He walked quickly to the door and threw it open. Fatt leaped to his feet, his red face turning sickly pale; Hogg looked down at his typewriter. Meniscus stood in the doorway, looking about the room furiously as though he expected to see iniquity in every corner of it. He opened his mouth to speak.

In the distance the train hooted its approach into the cold, snow-washed air. Meniscus snapped his mouth shut with an audible click. Fatt sprang out of attention and rushed outside, blowing his whistle and shouting orders to the guard. The captain followed him to the main door, but not before shooting one last vindictive glance at Hogg.

Outside the square looked unfamiliar in the snow. The boardwalk was half-hidden, a long white lump in the blankness of the square. The smoke of the engine now appeared at a curve on the far end of the yards.

When It Snowed In Kitabamba

Meniscus waited one full minute. Then he straightened his uniform, put his cap at the right angle and walked out. He stopped outside the door, measuring the distance, casting his eye along the boardwalk faintly marked by ridges in the snow. Then, at precisely the right moment, he started walking across the square, directly toward the spot where he would meet the courier, straight as a bullet flying, walking as he had walked this route, this pilgrimage, so many times since he had been made military governor of Kitabamba.

As the captain stepped off, the band at the station gave a preliminary wheeze and then struck up "The Captain's March." Meniscus faltered at this unexpected change in the order of today's events. Then he caught the swing of the march and strode toward the station, his carriage stiff and military, his eyes forward. It was a good march, he thought proudly as he strode along. When it snoooowed—Damn that Hogg! Had him singing it too. This was the end! He must do something about that man. He shook his head to dispel Hogg from his thoughts, and it was at that moment that he slipped.

He had walked straight enough. Perhaps he had merely started too close to one edge of the boardwalk. As he took a longer step than usual in response to the rhythm of the band, his foot came down on the very edge of the walk. On dry boards it would not have mattered, but the wet snow beneath him gave way, and he slipped.

He slipped and went off the edge while the band played, and he fell face down in the snow.

He was up in an instant, disdaining to brush the snow from his face and his clothes, still erect and military, as if nothing had happened, as if this was part of the normal course of things. So he rose to his feet and stepped off again and again he fell. Again he rose and again he slipped and he fell again, again, and again and still again, to the rhythm of the lively march which rang crazily in his ears, "When it snooooowed in Kitabamba, the MONkeys wrapped their TAILS..."

The sharp, piercing shriek of Sergeant Fatt's whistle cut through the insane braying of the band. Fatt bounded across the snow, one hand on his whistle chain, the other cradling his flapping holster. He leaped on the station platform and gave the bandmaster a loud slap on the ear with his whistle hand. The music stopped abruptly and with it also ended Meniscus' efforts to get up and march. He lay across the boardwalk in the middle of the square, his face in the snow, his feet upraised behind him.

So he remained, immersed in a white silence, until he heard the squish of feet as Sergeant Fatt came cutting heavy-treaded through the blankness of the snow. Then Meniscus rose to his hands and knees, shaking the snow off his face, and slowly got to his feet. In the station the train left, with its customary whistle. At this familiar signal the band gave one convulsive wheeze and then squashed itself into silence again. Meniscus shook off Fatt's hand fumbling at his arm and turned to face the crowd, his eyes cold and commanding. He would stare them down. He would dare anyone to laugh. The crowd was one huge, faceless blur. Captain Meniscus put his hand up to his bruised, nearsighted eyes and allowed Sergeant Fatt to lead him away.

Once in his office and wearing another pair of glasses, the captain felt more like himself. Like a part of himself, rather, because he felt as if a great segment of him had been torn out and that he was now but a portion of a man. Not daring to raise his eyes to the wall in front of his desk, he turned to look out the window instead. The crowd was still there, staring at him as he stood at the window looking out at them. It was the same crowd that had watched him every day. He looked out at them angrily, in the way he had wanted to look at them in the square minutes before, staring them down, daring anyone to laugh. But they did not laugh, they did not smile. They just looked at him with sadness in their eyes.

At first, when Meniscus had risen and fallen to the rhythm of the band, the crowd had been amused. They had watched delightedly, with open curious faces, this strange New Year's ceremony of the conqueror. Then they were puzzled, and when Fatt came running to stop the whole thing they understood. They understood and their faces were clouded over with an old and patient sadness that went far beyond Meniscus himself. So now, when the captain showed himself at the window, they looked at him with that same ancient sadness in their eyes. And the captain, seeing their faces and the pity and the fellowship in them, became enraged at the sight. He shouted to the guards outside to drive them away, to beat them, to hit them with their rifle butts.

The guards drove them away, but they did not beat them. They pushed at the crowd with rifles and clubs, calling at them in the flat, impersonal tone policemen sometimes use with crowds, "All right, break it up. *Hayaku. Hayaku.*"

The crowd broke up, leaving the square deserted. Master Sergeant Fatt came out and quietly dismissed the guard. In his office Captain Meniscus still stood at the window, looking at the soiled snow of the square. He muttered a curse, a foul unaccustomed oath that failed to drain any of the moil inside him. His eyes blurred. No, he told himself, fighting back his tears. No. And then he thought how much easier it would have been if they had laughed. But they had not laughed. He kept staring out the window at the dirty snow and at the wallow in the middle of the square, where he had danced his strange dance to the tune of the native band.

He turned as the door opened and Amakata came in, the courier's pouch in one hand and the captain's broken, twisted glasses in the other. Amakata ducked his head quickly, almost perfunctorily, in a bow that almost was a nod. Meniscus pointed to the desk and looked away. Amakata put down the pouch and the glasses and went out again.

The captain touched the broken glasses with the tips of his fingers. Then, out of habit, he opened the mail pouch and let its contents fall out on the desk. Something caught his eye—a letter from the chief of staff. His small-featured face lighted up. Quickly he tore open the envelope and read the letter, not once but twice. It was a commendation for his work in Kitabamba. He could have sworn that the Old Man's signature, over that of the chief of staff's, was in ink and not mimeographed. But that could not be. The Old Man never…He moved toward the windows to see the signature in the light. It was mimeographed. But it didn't matter anyway. Not now.

He heard voices in the outer office and crept to the corner near the file cabinet. Hogg was saying, "Anyway, I think you're a son-of-a-bitch."

Then came Fatt's rumbling chuckle. "What did you

want me to do? Hold him up by his little ankles?"

"You could have blown that damned whistle sooner. It's a hell of a deal, I tell you. The poor bastard!"

"But he looked so goddam funny for a minute there..." Fatt choked back a laugh.

After a pause Hogg said, "Anyway, it serves him right, putting on those silly airs. I guess he doesn't know I'm on to him."

"You sure?"

"Sure I'm sure. He must have changed his name when he left town. I was just a kid, but I remember him. His brothers and sisters too, must have been ten of them. Or fifteen, I never counted them all."

"He'll never make colonel now."

"He'll never make major, for that matter. When this shit hits GHQ he won't be going anywhere. Might be busted, for all we know."

Fatt laughed. "He'd make a good company clerk," he said. Meniscus moved away from the window, trembling.

Hogg and Fatt heard the muffled shot, and when they came into Meniscus' office the little pistol was still in the captain's mouth. His head was among his papers. Hogg grew pale. "Jesus!" said Fatt. "Just look at that!"

They sent Amakata to get more witnesses before they moved the body, and as soon as Amakata was out of the door Fatt opened the desk drawers and began rummaging around.

"Hey!" said Hogg. "What are you doing there?"

"The stores key," Fatt replied. "Ah, here it is!" He displayed it triumphantly. "You can forget about that deal we talked about."

"What am I getting out of this?" Hogg demanded.

"Don't worry," Fatt said, "I'll fix you up."

América Paredes

Captain Meniscus had been the only commissioned officer in Kitabamba, so the detachment remained temporarily in charge of Master Sergeant Fatt until a new commanding officer arrived from headquarters. Meanwhile orders were received by wire to prepare the body for shipment to the Capital on the next day's train. The job fell to Amakata. He had no one to direct him because Sergeant Fatt was busy that night, carrying away several jeeploads of cigarettes, chewing gum, chocolate bars and other supplies from unit stores to the house of a friend. The new officer might arrive the next day, and one of the first things he would do was to carry out an inventory. Corporal Hogg was busy too, celebrating New Year's Eve. From his quarters in the rear of the building came sounds of music, laughter and women's voices.

So Amakata did the job assisted by his wife, a leathery faced old woman in a drab-looking kimono and hair done up in a bun. They laid by a clean uniform, and he undressed and washed the body. Without the uniform and no longer speaking those terrible foreign words, the captain was much the same as other corpses Amakata had seen in the past. As he was about to draw the pink dress trousers over the captain's legs, he stopped and looked toward his wife.

"Come," he said softly. "Look."

She came, holding the shirt she had been unbuttoning, and looked at the captain's hairless shins, barked raw like those of an errant schoolboy. "Poor thing!" she said. "It must have hurt him, with the cold."

Amakata drew the trousers over the captain's legs. "Yes," he said. "Poor thing."

In Corporal Hogg's quarters the geishas were singing "You Are My Sunshine."

Ichiro Kikuchi

My name is Ichiro Kikuchi, and I am alive. Which might not be such a good thing. Being alive, I mean. Being Ichiro Kikuchi is all right. That's my legal name, my Japanese name. The legitimate son of Keigo Kikuchi and María de los Angeles Bermúdez de Kikuchi. My given name means "first born." The funny thing is that I am the only one.

My mother calls me Lupe because she had me baptized with a Mexican name soon after I was born. Juan Guadalupe. Juan for San Juan, the town where she was born, and Guadalupe for Our Lady, the Mother of all Mexicans. My mother had me baptized without letting my father know and my father was angry when he found out. But his anger did not last long, my mother says. He was never angry about anything for very long.

But I am glad my mother named me Guadalupe. It is because of her, the dark Virgin, that I am alive today. You smile, though you yourself are a Mexican, even if you are an American soldier. But it is true. Whether you see it as a miracle of the Virgin's, or whether you think it was just an accident. A lucky break, as you would say. My mother is convinced it was a miracle. My father says nothing because he does not know. And he says very little about anything these days, coughing his lungs out as he is. And it is best that he should die without knowing. Only I, my mother, and now you, know. And one other person, a sergeant in the American Army like you, a sergeant named Melguizo. But he does not want to know.

I'm telling you this because you are my friend. And because I trust you. Because you are a Mexican too, even though you are not a believer. And because you do not know much Japanese. I am sure that even if you would want to, you could not tell others here what I have told you. No, I do not mean to offend you. I know you will keep this to yourself at least until my mother and I can leave this country. When, I do not know.

Then we will be able to go back to our place outside of Cuernavaca, on the road to Acapulco. I often think of it. It is very beautiful, with acres of flowers and fruit trees. It is the way my father used to tell me Japan was, a beautiful country. But that was not the way Japan was when we got here five years ago. And it got much worse soon afterward, as you well know.

Outside Cuernavaca we had a large farm. We still have it. My uncle, my mother's brother, owns a half-interest in it, and he is keeping our interest for us. He has written my mother that we are welcome whenever we choose to go back. But we cannot go just yet.

My uncle and my father owned the farm. My uncle, being native-born, was legal owner of the land. My father put up half the money to buy the land, and he also contributed his knowledge of Japanese farming methods. We raised some fruit, but the richest and most beautiful harvest was the flowers. I thought there was nothing so beautiful as our farm.

But my father would tell me, "Wait till you go to Japan. It is so beautiful that you'll think this farm is a poor place compared to the country of your fathers." After I finished the primary grades, my father got a Japanese lady to teach me the Japanese language, but I learned to say only simple things in it. It was easy to speak, but I just could not learn how to read it. When I entered preparatory school, I studied English instead. My father was disappointed. He said, "Wait till you go to Japan. Then you will find it easy to learn Japanese. But I don't think you will ever know enough *kanji* to read a newspaper even." Those are the Chinese signs, you know. When my father talked like that my mother was very quiet.

A lot of things happened when I reached the age of eighteen. My birthday was celebrated with a big fiesta. Japanese friends and Mexican relatives came all the way from Guanajuato and Jalisco. I had finished public school, and my mother wanted me to become a *licenciado* in something, she did not care in what. So I was thinking about what I would study at the university. And then one day my father comes home from Acapulco with his big surprise. He just came in and told us, "Get ready. We'll be leaving for Japan in three weeks. He had already booked passage for the three of us on a steamer coming from Chile on its way to Yokohama.

"But Kei!" my mother said. "People are fighting over there!"

"The war is far to the south," my father said. "We won't be in any danger."

What if the Americans attacked Japan, my mother

wanted to know. We all knew how angry the Americans were because of all the Japanese victories. But my father was sure that Japan and the United States would never fight each other. It was all propaganda. But what about the university, my mother insisted. We would be gone only for a few months, and when we came back I could go to the university. Unless I fell in love with Japan, as my father hoped I would, and then I would want to stay. My mother looked gloomy.

I didn't fall in love with Japan, but I did stay here as you can see. Japan was a flower garden, my father had told me. When we landed in Yokohama what I saw was an armed camp. From Yokohama we came here to Tokyo, where my father's family is. Barely had we got here when war began with the United States. The neighbors did not like my mother and me very much, and it was even worse when Mexico declared war against Japan a few months later.

I had a difficult time, being only half Japanese and not knowing the language very well. They put me to work on the government radio broadcasting to Spanish America. I was not very good at it; still, it gave me a job to do. Everybody had to have a job. Three years later I was drafted. We had been hearing about the great battles our army and navy were winning, but everybody suspected we were losing. Now they were taking everybody in trousers—old men, schoolboys and people like me. My mother took it very hard, and I was sorry for her. But I felt worse about my father. He said he was very proud of me. He was supposed to feel that way, and I'm sure he was. But he was very sad, and a bit angry. Not at anybody but himself, I think.

Not long after, I was landing in the Philippines,

exactly where I never knew. Our ship was one of the lucky ones; many others were sunk by your airplanes and submarines. My memories about combat, you say? Terror, bombs and artillery shells. Terror, smoke, confusion and retreat. We were not trained. We were given rifles, put on a ship and sent over. Perhaps I am trying to excuse the fact that we surrendered. We had been ordered to fight to the death, but a lot of others were surrendering too.

There were about fifteen of us. Among us was a boy named Yokoyama, Nobuo Yokoyama. He was small and near-sighted and was afraid all the time. We had known each other in Tokyo, and during the fighting he had stayed very close to me. I did my best to take care of him. He called me Elder Brother. And now I tried to set his mind at ease. "You don't have to be afraid anymore, Younger Brother," I told him. "The war is over for us."

We were taken as prisoners of a unit that had seen much fighting, from the looks of them. The man who was in command was talking to another, a sergeant. The sergeant was arguing, it appeared, but finally he saluted and came to where we were. He looked familiar somehow. He picked out a dozen of his own men, and they took us back some fifty meters toward their rear. All the others went ahead. When we stopped, the Americans guarding us took their spades from their packs and dropped them on the ground in front of us. Then they moved back and made signs to us that we should pick them up.

"They are going to put us to work," one of us said. But we soon understood what they wanted. We were ordered to dig a long, narrow trench. There was nothing we could do but obey, but we dug very slowly. Then

Nobuo began to cry. He was digging right next to me, and I could see the tears running down his face. A great rage seized me. "Hurry up!" I shouted. "If we must die, let it be over quickly! And let us die with dignity!" I began to dig as fast as I could, without lookin at Nobuo, for if I looked at him I was sure I would start crying too.

The two top buttons of my shirt had been torn off, and as I dug the chain I wear around my neck with the pendant at the end spilled out. The sergeant came up to me and shouted, "Hey, you! What is that you're wearing?"

I looked up at him, and now that he was close to me I saw why he had looked familiar. He was Mexican. Like you. An American Mexican. So I answered in Spanish, "A medallion. La Virgen de Guadalupe."

"Put down that spade," he said, also in Spanish. "Get out of that hole and come with me."

I was trembling as I climbed out of the hole, trembling and praying, giving thanks to La Guadalupana and to my mother, who had put the medallion around my neck when I was home for the last time. I did not look at Nobuo. All I saw, all I knew, was myself. I was alive, and that was all that mattered. The sergeant led me away, to the rear where I was put in a pen with some other prisoners. Not many of them. We were halfway there when I heard the volleys. I did not look back. I shuddered but I felt happy I was not there, back at the hole. I am a coward, I know. But it was not until later that I felt any regret, any shame.

I heard somebody call the sergeant Melguizo, that's how I know his name. I didn't see him again in the Philippines. It was only recently that I met him at a street corner here in Tokyo.

"¡Melguizo!" I said. "¡Qué gusto de verte!"

He stared at me. "I don't know who you are," he said in English and walked away.

It was the same man, I am not mistaken. I wonder why he pretended not to know me. Why he wouldn't let me thank him. Is he ashamed of what he did for me?

My father does not know. He is the one who should never know about this at all. It was my mother who decided we should not tell him, because he would not understand. "Let him die happy," she said, "happy that he saw you come home. There are so many others who will not be so fortunate." She made me go see Nobuo Yokoyama's parents. "It is painful for parents to know that their son is dead," my mother told me. "But it is worse not to know at all."

So I went to see them and told them Nobuo had died in combat, and that he had been buried in a grave dug by his comrades. And then I broke down and wept. They were moved. They thought I was weeping for Nobuo.

In a way it is easier to deceive my father, and again it is not. He can barely talk, so he does not ask many questions. But I wish he would not look so proud and happy every time he sees me. He still is walking around, though he gets weaker every day. But there still is a lot of life in him, I am sure. He was an air-raid warden during the fire bombings. The section of town just downhill from where we live was set afire before dawn one day. There was a woman with three children, whose husband was in the army. When her house started burning, she shouted to the eldest to follow her, and she took the two younger ones out of the house. But the eldest girl did not come out, and she tried to go after her, but the neighbors held her back.

Then my father went into the burning house and took the girl out. She was dead. The first bomb to land on the house did not explode. It went through the roof and hit the girl while she was in bed. They found that out later. My father got the girl's body out, but he damaged his lungs. Some people say he breathed fire and that his lungs were cooked. Perhaps it was the heat, perhaps the smoke. We don't know. Whatever it was, he's dying. Very slowly, but he's dying.

Just a few months ago, a consul from Mexico came to look after Mexican citizens caught here by the war. He has been very helpful. My mother and I have passports of our own now. Not my father, since he never was a Mexican citizen and is too sick to travel anyway. My uncle in Mexico, my mother's brother, has been very good to us too. As the consul told us, he could have kept all of our farm for himself, and it would have been legal. But he has written us, and the consul too, that he is waiting to welcome us home, and that half of the property still is my mother's and mine.

I suppose I will give up the idea of going to the university. I'll become a farmer just as my father was. But my mother says that she will see to it that I become a *licenciado*. Only God knows what will happen. And the Virgin. I have promised my mother I will go with her to the Virgin's shrine in Tepeyac and give thanks for the miracle that saved my life. But I don't think we should crawl on our knees there. Anyway, we are not there yet. We have not left Japan.

The consul has arranged everything for us, and my uncle has sent us money. But we will not leave until after my father dies. The consul is getting impatient. He would like to get our business out of the way, he says, before he returns to Mexico.

It is a terrible thing for us to be here, waiting for my father to die. Sometimes I wake up in the morning, and the first thing that comes to my mind is, "Perhaps he died during the night."

I get up and go look at him, and I am glad he's still with us. I really am. He was very brave, going into that burning house. My mother says the neighbors called him a hero. But that was before the war ended. There are no heroes now.

Sugamo

From the window, Private J.C. Jones could look down on the messboys playing in the courtyard. He smiled wryly to himself. Watching a crowd of gooks play ball. Christ, what an occupation. The sound of their high laughter and their staccato voices came up to him. Funny little men, playing ball in their old, ill-fitting khaki clothes, throwing a little rubber ball about without a care in the world.

Now one of them missed the ball; it went right between his outstretched hands and hit him on the chin. The ball bounced away, and they all laughed, and it seemed that the man who was hit laughed the most. Private Jones' smile grew hard and superior. How different they are, he thought, nothing like Americans at all. It was their size especially, but it was more than that. They acted so damned happy about everything, always grinning, always so polite. It made them look like children. That was it; they were just like kids. There they were, having a good time. What did they care what happened to them? Or to anybody else? He wondered whether gooks thought very much about things. How could they, grinning all the time? Just kids, he thought, just a race of kids that never grew up. It gave him a cozy, secure feeling, standing up so high above them, looking down at them from a distance and thinking things.

There were steps in the hall outside, and Private Jones turned away from the window. His stomach gave a cold little jump, as when one remembers something very important that one should have remembered ages ago. Two MPs came striding down the hall and stopped before the barred door. One of them was big and beefy; his red face had "cop" written all over it. The other one was half a head shorter; his face was paler, thinner too. About his narrow lips there hovered traces of what might have been a smile.

"Here's the coon," the red-faced MP said.

The thin-faced one took out a ring of keys and unlocked the door. Private Jones watched him intently. The door swung open, and the thin-faced MP said, "Okay, kinky-head, let's go. There's a lot of brass waiting to see you."

Private Jones walked out of his cell, and the MPs stepped up on either side of him. They walked down the hall abreast. When he looked to each side, Private Jones could see over their helmets. White helmets they were, shiny white.

"Button that pocket," Thin Face said. Private Jones felt about on his shirt front until he found the offending button. Lots of brass waiting; the major would be there too. If he could only get a word with the major, then everything would be all right. The major would understand, he was sure of that. The major would know what he was talking about. But only the major would understand, because it was something between him and the major, a sort of secret.

Be back in fifteen minutes. That was what the major said. And now, here he was. But what the hell, the major knew he was a good soldier. Who says colored boys can't fight? the major said. That's why he got the leave. That damned leave. Why didn't he stay in Pusan? But no, the major said he was a good soldier and he deserved a leave.

In the hallway there was a little man with a mop and a pail of water. He was busy mopping the floor, and he did not see them coming. The MPs kept walking straight at him. At the last moment the little man saw them, and he hurried out of their path. But he was not quick enough; Thin Face brushed against him, making him spill water on the floor. They stopped. The man was ducking his head in a furious succession of bows, and Red Face said, "Look sharp there."

The man bowed his head still faster and said, "Thank-you-very-much. Thank-you-very-much."

"Thank who, you silly bastard," said Thin Face, grinning. He threw out with the back of his hand at the bowing head. The little man sucked in his breath and backed away, mop and pail in either hand, ducking and bowing.

"Ain't these gooks stupid," said Thin Face, still grinning.

"Aw, it's all a matter of the words you use," Red Face said. "You gotta know their language."

Thin Face's grin widened. "Been sleeping out lately?" he asked.

"All you gotta do when you want them to do something," Red Face explained, "is to yell A-No-NAY! and they prick up their ears. Then you tell them what you want in plain American. They understand."

"A kick in the pants is just as good," Thin Face

said. "How about you, Sambo? You don't like them either, do you?"

"He sure don't," Red Face said.

Private Jones scowled and looked down at his combat boots.

"Come on," Red Face said, "we can't stand around all day."

They resumed their journey down the hall. No use talking to pinks like these, thought Private Jones. Gooks were better than them, any day. They were okay, the gooks; he liked them. Call them *tomodachi* and they are all for you. If they only wasn't so polite. Orientals are a very polite people, it says in the handbook, the green little handbook with "Far East Duty" on the cover. And the picture of a smiling, happy soldier. Join the Army and see the world, join the Army and get an education, join the Army and wear shoes, you goddam nigger, ever had three squares before? If they only wasn't so polite.

They came into the big room where he had been before. Up against the farther wall hung a big American flag, and right under it was a long shiny desk, and there was the major, sitting between a master sergeant and a lieutenant. He could tell that major from every other major in the United States Army, and nobody was going to tell him it was somebody else. He felt like just hiking straight up there to the desk and saluting and saying, "Major sir, don't you remember me? We were outside Taegu together."

He knew the major would understand because the major knew he was a good soldier. But he knew they wouldn't let him, and he felt sort of shy anyway, in front of so many people, especially when they all had that now-see-here look on their faces. He'd wait awhile, and after they all got through talking, he would ask them again if he could see the major.

Everybody was staring at him, and he passed his hand slyly over his shirt. Nothing out of place, everything was sharp. Nobody was going to say that the QM didn't have sharp soldiers. They told him to sit down, and he sat, the MPs standing behind him, facing the desk where the major and the other officers were. The major sat straight in his chair. His mouth was straight too, and his forehead jutted over his eyes like the eaves of a house. Those eyes were a peculiar sort of grey, Private Jones knew. He couldn't see them at this distance, but he had seen them up close before, and nobody was going to tell him he hadn't.

That time outside Taegu, when the gooks ran all over the boys at the front. The sergeant gave him a grease gun and said, "This is it, boy, this is it."

Talk about being scared. Brave men get scared, the lieutenant said. And then they got the lieutenant, and they got the sergeant too. They would never have got out, except for the major. He showed up all of a sudden, all by himself, with his pockets full of grenades, smiling at them like he was all of them's father coming home from work. Good man, that major. And that evening, before they pulled their tails out of the fire, the major picked him, Private Jewel C. Jones, to carry out his orders. Out of twelve men the major picked him. That major knew he was a good soldier. He said it so himself. Be back in fifteen minutes, the major said. If only the gook hadn't kept saying thank you; that was where all the trouble started. But the major would understand. He had to have a word with the major. He would go up and salute and say, "Major, sir ..."

The little lieutenant with the pursed mouth and

the glasses was talking now. They had sent him from JAG too, and he was almost as bad as the captain. The captain called people lots of names, but what the hell. That was his job. This little lieutenant had nothing in his head, but he was social. There he was again, talking about sharecroppers and Civil War and little red school-houses. Private Jones wished he would shut up and go away. He tried hard to think of something else.

His throat was hot and dry, and he wished he was back at Tokyo Tropical having a beer. They knew how to make beer in this part of the world, and they made it in great big bottles about the size of jugs. The Tokyo Tropical was a nice place to spend your time, and there was that nice little number, Kimiko. There's something about these gals that gets you, he thought. And she liked him too. He was sure she would have been nice to him if the manager hadn't butted in. Maybe he wanted her for himself. Like the day. He went in there and sat down and ordered a beer, and another and another, and no Kimiko. So he had another beer and the manager brought it, and he told the manager:

"Where's Kimiko? You better get Kimiko right away."

The manager smiled and bowed and said, "Kimiko *sewashi-i*."

"What was that?" he said.

"*Sewashi-i de gozaimasu. Sewashi-i.*"

"Washie, washie," he said. "Talk American, man."

"No tickee, no washee," said a GI at the next table, and everybody laughed.

He said, "Listen here, shifty; where is Kimiko."

The manager thought very hard, and then he said, "She. No. Come."

"I know she no come! But why she no come?"

"Isogashi-i."

"Stop jabbering at me!"

The manager took out a little dog-eared dictionary. He started to thumb through it and Private Jones knocked it out of his hand. The manager stooped down and picked up his dictionary. He bowed and smiled as if it hurt him to move the muscles of his face.

"Get out of here," Private Jones said.

"Yes s'," the manager said. "Thank you s'."

Private Jones' scalp crawled. "Do you want a smash in the mouth?" he said.

"No s', no th-thank, no s'."

"Don't thank-you-sir me, you !"

"Yes s', no, thank you s'... no."

He followed the manager through the little tables and the potted palms, the beer bottle in his hand, followed him all the way into the little room where they kept the liquor.

And he stopped at the door. He stopped and looked back at the major, who was looking him straight in the eye, the corner of his mouth twitching just ever so little. The major had a rifle in his hand, checking the working of the bolt, and Private Jones stood at the door with the gook. Be back in fifteen minutes, the major said. So he took the gook out the door and behind the hut. He was a young one, didn't look over fifteen years old, though with these people you couldn't tell. His head was bandaged, and he was chewing on one of the chocolate bars Johnson, the medic, had given him that morning. They went into the ravine behind the hut and walked for a little while. Then he motioned the gook to stop. They stopped and the gook looked at him. To the north of them, somewhere, was

Sugamo

Taegu, and far to the south the faint rumble of battle echoed against the late afternoon sky. Beyond that rumble was headquarters.

"Take him back to headquarters and be back in fifteen minutes," the major had said. "As soon as it's dark we'll make a run for it."

The major knew which man to pick; he had picked a man with brains. None of those other boys back in the hut would have understood. It was a joke really, a joke on the gook, but he didn't know it yet. Then, as Private Jones watched him, the gook knew. He was looking up into Private Jones' face when he suddenly looked down at the grease gun and his eyes popped.

The gook began to talk American. "Thank you," he said. "Thank you, thank you, thank you." He pointed at the gun and shook his head and said, "Thank-you-thank-you-thank-you."

Private Jones moved up closer. He wanted to put the muzzle against his clothes so there wouldn't be much noise. But the gook backed away, and he began to cry. The tears just poured down his grimy face, and all the while he kept saying, "Thank you." Only he was saying it faster now. Then he started to scream, and Private Jones let him have a burst, a little short one which made parts of his cotton shirt jump away in little pieces, like the paper in a firecracker when it goes off. Then he went up and shot him in the head, to make sure there wouldn't be any more noise. His mouth was full of chocolate.

"Get up now," the red-faced MP said, and Private Jones stood up at attention. Somebody started to read aloud.

Well, it finally stopped, and he went back to the major and stood up as straight as he could and saluted and he said, "The prisoner has been delivered, sir."

The major looked him straight in the eye, the corner of his mouth twitching ever so little. "Good, good," he said. "As soon as we get to Pusan, I'll see that you go on leave. You need a rest."

"You are a good soldier," the major said.

But the guy wouldn't keep still, so he hit him over the head with the bottle one more time. Then he hit him again and the bottle broke, so he stomped him and stomped him.

"...until dead," the major behind the desk said.

He stomped him until the MPs came.

Nobody was talking anymore, and one of the MPs reached out and touched Private Jones on the arm. "Let's go," he said. The three of them walked out into the hall.

The little lieutenant from JAG was there, and Private Jones asked him, "Can I talk to the major this time?"

The lieutenant pursed his lips. "I took it upon myself to see the major," he said, "and I got bawled out for my pains. The major says he was never in Taegu; he's never seen you before."

"He called me a damn fool," the lieutenant added, a quaver in his voice, and he hurried down the hall.

"See now what you did," Thin Face said. "The major is mad at him, and all because of you."

Private Jones said, "But I gotta see that major; he's my friend."

Thin Face laughed. "Sure, he's your friend. So he makes you a Christmas present."

"Nice little necktie made out of rope," Red Face said.

"Well, I guess the coon will get the best Christmas dinner of all his born days," Thin Face said. "Best ever."

"Best ever," Red Face said. "Best ever."

The Terribly
High Cost

"But you should have told me," Professor Travis Williamson said, somewhat peevishly. "You should have told me the truth, Peter."

"But Willie," Professor Richards said, "I did not deceive you. I thought you were aware it was a print and not a painting."

"Please don't call me Willie," Professor Williamson said stiffly. "My friends call me Trav. or Travis. Williamson, if you prefer to be formal. But not Willie, please."

The two were having tea in Williamson's faculty office, a neat little room full of books and colorful pictures. The books were mostly on the life and literature of the Southwest. The pictures were reproductions of paintings by Tom Lea. They contrasted with the owner's lack of color. Williamson was a squarish man with a very pale skin, blond eyebrows that were almost invisible, light blue eyes, a bald pate and a vapid face with no distinguishing features. He was living proof that stupidity is no obstacle to the attainment of a Ph.D.

"I'm sorry, W...Travis," Peter Richards said. "For me the name Willie has an aura of adventure, which I think you personify." He was a visiting professor from Indiana, a long-legged, red-haired man with a cavalryman's mustache. This last he stroked with a large, sunburned hand.

Travis Williamson was not mollified. "You said it was a distinguished piece of work, and I took your word for it. I gave it a place of honor in my house. And then I hear of a couple in New York who have one just like it."

"And that upset you."

"I was furious! I banished it to a back room."

"It's a genuine Hiroshige, made from the original wood block. Hiroshige died a century ago, as I'm sure you know. There may be a few other copies in existence, but if so, they all are collector's pieces."

Travis Williamson unbent a little. "I'll have to take another look at it," he said.

"You seemed to like it a great deal just a few weeks ago. Had a lot to say about its artistry."

"It really is well done, I must admit. Where did you find it?"

"I got it from a Japanese friend. It had been in his family for several generations."

Williamson's colorless face lighted up for a moment. "That is very interesting, Peter. Will you have more tea?"

"Yes, please." As Williamson poured, Richards added, "You are very fond of tea. I thought all you Texans loved strong coffee. A pot over the campfire and all that."

"Not all of us are wild and woolly cowboys," Travis Williamson said primly. Then in a burst of confidence, "I come from a pioneer family, you know. My father was a cowboy in West Texas before he became wealthy. He still likes his coffee black and strong. No tea for him."

"He's my kind of man. How is it that you prefer tea?"

"I went to school in the East. Harvard. And I spent some time in Oxford." Williamson's degree was from a Texas university. He had been at Harvard for one disastrous year and had visited Oxford but never was a student there.

"So you lost your Texas ways," Richards said. "What a pity."

"One learns to appreciate the finer things in life, and then one does not want to go back to one's parents' ways."

"Still," Richards said, stroking his mustache, "one never forgets the scenes of one's childhood, when one's sense of values are impressed upon one."

Williamson was silent for a moment. Then he said, "Speaking of value. That Hiroshige print must be a valuable piece of art."

"I suppose so."

"It must have cost you a pretty penny."

"It cost me nothing. It was a gift."

"Oh?"

"A Japanese friend gave it to me. In appreciation for something I did in his favor."

"What kind of service, may I ask?"

"I helped him resolve a terrible dilemma he was facing. Which was the greater burden for him, the cost of living or the cost of dying?"

"You are joking."

"I am not. This friend of mine was one of the janitors in the building where I worked in Tokyo."

"Now I know you're pulling my leg."

"It's true. Let me tell you about it."

As you know if you've read my c.v., Richards continued, I stayed overseas for a couple of years after the fighting was over in the Pacific. My wife ditched me toward the end of the war, and I wanted some time away from relatives and friends to put myself back together. There were civilian jobs aplenty in Tokyo soon after September 1945. I got me a good one with the Civilian Property Custodian, and it was there I came across this man, Kunio Yoshida. He was one of the cleaning crew in the building where I worked, and I don't think I ever noticed him during the first few weeks. They all looked so much alike, shabby and sad-looking, always bowing at every American in sight.

One autumn morning my office felt excessively hot, so I tried to open a window. It stuck. I went to the door to see if I could get some help. This Japanese man was walking by, so I called out to him, "*Anoné!*" What that means depends on whom you ask. Our G.I.s translated it as "Hey, you!" A Britisher I met at a party told me it means, "I say there, old chap!" I suppose the true meaning of the word falls somewhere in between. At all events, when I said "*Anoné!*" the man stopped and bowed. He was slightly built, in his forties it seemed, though with Japanese it's hard to tell. He wore glasses, as most of them do.

"*Anoné!*" I repeated, a bit louder to make sure he understood. "Window no open. *Dekimaska?*"

He came and tried the window but couldn't budge it either.

The Terribly High Cost

"You get *ichi, ni, san* people," I told him. "You fix *hayaku-hayaku*."

He bowed again. "I am extremely sorry for the inconvenience," he said. "The windows in this building never were opened during the war. I shall inform the sergeant in charge. If you will excuse me." He bowed once again and went out, leaving me staring after him. With my mouth closed, I hope.

A few minutes later a big sergeant came rolling into my office with two Japanese workers in tow. "I'm the Jap pusher for this building," he announced. "That little Jap that talks English funny tells me you have problems with your windows."

I said such was the case, so his two carpenters got busy, and soon both my windows were working smoothly. It just happened that by the time the men finished, the steam was shut off, and I had to shut the windows anyway. But I said much obliged to the sergeant and *arigato* to his men. And as soon as they were gone, I looked for the Japanese who "talked English funny."

I found him down the hall, wielding a floor brush. We managed to talk for a few minutes. Then the "Jap-pushing" sergeant showed up, and my janitor friend bent to his task. We did agree to meet after quitting time and so we did. I walked with him to Tokyo station, where he took a train to his part of town. He would not let me drive him home. After that, I made it a point to seek him out and know him better.

Kunio Yoshida had a doctorate in American literature from an Ivy League school, I forget which. His family had been well-to-do, and he was an only son among several sisters, who had married well. As a young man he had spent most of his time abroad, coming back to Japan to stay when his parents decided it was time for him to marry. They got him a suitable wife, and he settled down to teach literature at a Presbyterian school in Tokyo.

After war with the United States broke out, there was no place in Japan for professors of American literature. He was in his forties, with a family, so he was not drafted. He was sent to work in the factories, and since he had little mechanical aptitude, he ended up doing menial jobs. During the war his mother died, and all the family had was destroyed in the Allied fire bombings of the city.

"But why are you still working as a janitor?" I asked him.

"Ah, my friend," he said, "such is the disadvantage of being a professor of literature, at least in present-day Japan. Unless one has other talents, and I never learned to do anything except read, write, and talk about literature."

"There must be something else you could do."

"What else may I do? My father once had powerful friends, but they are now as destitute as we. No. The humble carpenters who repaired your windows the other day make a better living than I."

It was about this time, when he felt he knew me well enough, that he invited me to his home for tea. I picked him up one Sunday afternoon at Tokyo station, and he guided me to his house in one of the outlying districts of Tokyo. It was a depressing place, a desolate scene of burned out buildings dotting large areas where nothing else stood. Here and there were little houses of paper and wood, neat and new. Kunio Yoshida's house stood among the ruins of what must once have been a compound with a courtyard and a garden.

The Terribly High Cost

I had stopped by the commissary before meeting him, so I arrived with a few gifts—some canned goods, candy and cookies, cigarettes. Kunio's wife was slender and smooth-faced as so many of these aging Japanese ladies manage to be. She knelt and bowed in traditional fashion as we took off our shoes in the tiny vestibule. I gave her my visitor's offerings, which she received with many words I did not understand but which I knew expressed gratitude and pleasure. So I said, "Don't mention it." Kunio translated those three words into three or four sentences of Japanese, which I am sure made me sound like the courtliest of men. Kunio then introduced his children, three little boys and a daughter about fifteen years old. Quite a beauty she was.

Not until all these preliminaries were over did Kunio's father enter the room where we were. The old man looked as if he had just stepped out of a painting from the days of the shoguns. His white hair was cut short, though, and he bore himself like a military man in his dark kimono. He stood before us, grim and silent. Kunio introduced us, and he bowed stiffly, from his head and shoulders only. Then he sat down and ignored everyone for the rest of the afternoon.

I ceremoniously declined the ceremonial invitation to stay for supper. We had tea. To my surprise, it was not green tea but the black Lipton's variety, served from a beautiful western-style tea service. Kunio diffidently explained that he had been able to bury a few valuables before the fire bombings began in earnest, among them some paintings and prints and the tea service he had brought with him from a trip to England. After tea and some sweet cookies I had brought, we made some small talk, in which the old man did not participate. Then I excused myself. The old man acknowledged my departure by getting up and bowing in the same curt manner as before.

Kunio followed me outside and apologized for his father. "The war was especially hard on him," he told me. "He lost his wife, my mother, and he has not yet recovered."

"I understand," I answered, and I thought I did.

During the week that followed, I didn't see Kunio, though I had him on my mind. I had spent some time pulling strings on his behalf. The week after that, I happened to see our sergeant, and I asked him about Kunio Yoshida.

"Oh, your Jap friend," he said. "He was gone all last week. He's not here this week. He's out of a job. Period."

It was not until the third week that Kunio showed up. I heard the sergeant shouting at him in the hall, telling him he was fired. As I stepped out, the sergeant said, "And now, get the hell out of here!" He turned and walked away. Kunio began to go past my office on his way out of the building. He saw me standing at the door, hesitated, bowed formally, and was about to pass by. I stopped him.

"Good morning," I said. "Please come into my office." Again he hesitated before walking inside. He looked haggard. I shut the door and gave him a cup of coffee.

"We are violating regulations," he said in a tired voice. "You should not be fraternizing with the natives in this fashion."

"Regulations be damned," I said. "You are in trouble, and I want to know what is the matter."

He sipped his coffee. "Do you know of a place

called Otani?" he asked.

"Yes. A very beautiful place, I hear."

He smiled. "That Sunday you were so kind as to visit my house. A few hours after you left, my father went to Otani."

"I'm very sorry, Kunio," I said. "I'm terribly sorry."

I never visited Otani during the time I was in Japan, Willie. I don't have a taste for the morbid. But I did hear a lot about it as the suicide capital of Japan. It is supposed to be a strikingly beautiful little town on the coast. There is a picturesque cliff high above the rocks at the edge of the water. Before the war, when arranged marriages were the rule, star-crossed lovers used to hold hands and jump to the rocks below. It was up to the city government to have the mess cleaned up and locate the parents of the couple. This involved time and expense, but not many lovers were so inconsiderate of their parents' feelings as to prefer suicide to marriage with the mates their elders had chosen for them. So the city fathers accepted the occasional expense as an inevitable corollary to the fat profits they made from thousands of romantic vacationers who came to enjoy the dangerous scenery but not to jump. There had been suggestions, it is true, that access to the cliffs be blocked by a wire fence or that signs be posted saying, "No jumping, please." But they were vetoed by the practical minded and the lovers of beauty both.

Things changed drastically after the end of the war. If one were to believe the city fathers, there was a steady stream of people coming to Otani to take the jump. And few of those were lovers. So when Kunio told me his father had gone to Otani, I knew what he was talking about. "My friend," he said, still smiling, "fortune has not been kind to me."

"It is a sad thing to lose one's father," I said. "But you still have much to live for."

"Do you think so? If you will allow me to bore you with my problems, I will tell you what my life has been like since I last saw you."

"Please do," I said. So he told me, succinctly and unemotionally, as if he were telling someone else's troubles rather than his own, now and then smiling his crooked, apologetic smile.

For some time Kunio's father had been saying that useless old men like himself had no reason to be alive. He was ill and unable to work, even if there had been something for him to do. He could do nothing to help his son, who could barely provide for his family. He was in the way, an irksome burden. Kunio and his wife would tell him, "No, grandfather, you are not in the way. Your wisdom is a comfort to us. Your grandchildren love you."

"My father was a samurai," he would say. "I should die like a samurai, but how can I do so? First His Majesty's government commands that I give up my swords to the army. Then the Americans bomb my garden. How can I die an honorable death?"

The family would smile behind the old man's back, not believing what he said. Then one Saturday afternoon the local grocer came to see Kunio. The old man had tried to buy rat poison at his store. The grocer told him he was out of poison and later told Kunio about it. Kunio talked to his father. Next day was the Sunday of my visit to the family. The morning after, the old man could not be found. No one knew where he had gone, not even the police. Late that evening a neighbor visited Kunio and told him he had seen his father that morning, boarding a train going south. Early next morning Kunio took the train to Otani.

It was a journey of less than sixty miles, and the old man had been at the Otani cliffs by ten o'clock the previous morning. People had seen him jump. But since he was old and weak, he could not jump out far enough. He landed halfway down on a jutting rock that disemboweled him. It took a team of cliff climbers and workmen a good part of the day to get his body down.

The mayor of Otani was enraged. Still another suicide, and a costly one. Another great expenditure. The town would go broke, he complained to the American colonel in charge of the area. "Find his relatives!" roared the colonel. "Throw them in jail! Make them pay!"

And next morning Kunio Yoshida showed up looking for his father. The mayor did exactly what the American colonel had told him to do. He threw Kunio in jail and demanded he pay all expenses incurred by the town because of his father's suicide. Kunio had some trouble convincing the mayor he could not be in two places at once, incommunicado in an Otani jail and in Tokyo trying to raise the money required of him. So it was not until well into the next week that he was allowed to write his wife.

It took her several days to comply with Kunio's instructions. She sold what she could of the few valuables they had saved during the fire bombings. With the money, along with what she could borrow, she finally set out to Otani to seek the mayor's merciful ear. Meanwhile, back in Tokyo, Kunio's daughter Fumiko had caught the eye of a Nisei corporal, who convinced her he could help her father get a hearing at

MacArthur's headquarters if she would go downtown with him on his jeep. When he brought her back home late that night, she had lost her innocence, as the saying goes. And now her father had lost his job.

"So I do not know what I am going to do, friend Richards," he told me, "now that the sergeant has told me he has employed someone else in my stead." He smiled. "Even suicide is not a viable option for me. I simply cannot afford it."

"But you can!" I cried. "I mean you can afford not to commit suicide. I can help you."

He half-raised a hand. "No, no. I cannot let you spend your money on me."

"I won't, though I could lend you some to tide you over. I'm talking about a job I have lined up for you, teaching in Nippon College."

"Nippon College? Forgive me if I do not believe you."

I must explain, Willie, about Nippon College. Immediately after the war, it was decided that a better educated, more democratic Army would serve the Occupation better. So plans were set in motion that same autumn for a two-year college in Tokyo. Its official name was the Armed Forces College, but everyone was calling it Nippon College long before it registered its first student. The dean was Stephen Webster, a friend and former comrade-in-arms of mine.

One evening we were having a few drinks before dinner in the Dai Ichi Hotel, when he told me about his problems with the man who was to teach sophomore English literature. "He's some West Texas lout called Danny Glenn," he told me. "Doesn't know his English lit from a hole in the ground. Has a bachelor's in English from some country college there, but they must have given him the degree as a gift."

"That bad, eh?"

"He calls Keats, Kates, and Yeats, Yeets; and he thinks 'Kates' had a contemporary named Shrelley. His grammar and diction are atrocious."

"Why don't you get rid of him?"

"For reasons almost too numerous to mention. For one thing, I don't do the hiring and firing. Personnel does. To get them to fire the man, I would have to prove he's grossly incompetent. He sure as hell is, but I would have to submit a written evaluation of his performance in order to prove it. And he hasn't started teaching yet. Or started trying to."

"But surely, if he's that bad..."

"That's not the worst of it by far. He's the nephew of some big-ass politician in Texas. That's how he got the job in the first place."

"Now *that* is a real problem."

"And even if I could surmount all those goddam obstacles, where would I find an adequate replacement within the next six weeks?"

Now that made me happy. "I have just the man you need," I said. "He has an Ivy League doctorate in English and American literature. He speaks flawless English, and he lives right here in Tokyo."

Webster looked at me suspiciously. "Pete," he said, "this is no laughing matter."

"I'm not kidding, Steve. I know such a man."

He brightened. "What's his name?"

"Kunio Yoshida."

"Japanese." He looked gloomy again. "I knew there would be a catch to it."

"But Steve, the man is more than qualified for the job. He should be teaching in some major university."

"In some major university, yes. But not to a bunch

of GIs who just finished fighting a war against Japan."

"Steve, if you just close your eyes when he talks, you would think you're listening to a Boston Brahmin."

"You want the whole class to keep their eyes shut while he lectures? Or perhaps you want him to talk through a bamboo screen."

"That's it!" I said. "That's it!"

"Have him lecture through a screen?"

"No. Through a dummy."

Webster took to the idea immediately. And Danny Glenn was more than happy to have Kunio as his "assistant." The poor devil was aware of his limitations, you could say that much for him. Kunio would do everything but stand before the class and lecture. He would work out the course outline and the reading lists, prepare the lectures and the question-and-answer sessions. Supplying Danny Glenn with answers to the questions, of course. He would grade the essays and the pop quizzes. Besides, he would coach Danny on the pronunciation of names such as Keats, Yeats and Cowper, not to mention other, more ordinary words in the English language. The three of us were happy, so it was agreed I would talk to Kunio the following Monday. And the following Monday Kunio did not show up for work.

But now Kunio had shown up, and he should very well believe he had a job at Nippon College. Of course, I told him, he would not be officially on the faculty. I explained the conditions, and he was not at all offended that he would be doing all the work while the American got most of the pay. After all, the Japanese had lost the war. Furthermore, he would be earning many times the salary he had been getting as a janitor. I lent him a few thousand yen to help him make ends meet until his first payday, and he went to work.

Within a month he was back in my office to repay part of the loan. He looked quite cheerful. Things had been going well for him, very well. He had begun to pay off the debts he had incurred because of his father's suicide. Just as important, his job at the American college teaching American literature to Americans had earned him high respect among his colleagues. The Japanese college where he had taught before the war was resuming classes the following month, and the trustees had begged him to return to his former position. Soon he would be bringing home two paychecks every month. Furthermore, his domestic life was rosier. The Nisei who had led his daughter down the primrose path wanted to marry her.

"I owe it all to you, my friend," he told me as he handed me a brown-paper parcel. "Here is the last thing of true value I have left from happier times, before this lamentable war. Please accept it with my thanks." It was the Hiroshige print I gave you, Willie.

About two months later he came to see me again, bringing the rest of the money I had lent him. He was much better dressed. In fact, he would have looked dapper, except that Japanese tailors just cannot produce a decent man's suit. He didn't look as cheerful, though, as he had been the last time.

"Are things going well with you?" I asked.

"Well. Very well, thank you."

"And your family?"

"All well, except for my daughter Fumiko."

"What's the trouble? Is she ill?"

"That Nisei corporal, do you remember? He went back to his home in Hawaii and left her pregnant."

"I'm terribly sorry," I said. "It must be very hard

on the poor child."

"Oh, she solved her own problem," Kunio said calmly. "She followed my father to Otani."

"How horrible!" I exclaimed. "Please accept my condolences!"

"Thank you," he said. "Still, it could have been worse." He smiled his crooked smile. "At least this time I can afford it."

Getting an Oboe for Joe

I'm a Mexican, but I'm not crazy like Joe. And then there's Pablo López. He's Mexican too, and he may be stupid but he's not crazy by far. That's what I keep telling Moriarty, the mess sergeant, because he keeps talking about you crazy Mexicans this and you crazy Mexicans that. But Joe is a special case, of that there isn't the most minor doubt, as my father likes to say. Any Mexican who would rather blow into an oboe than play on a guitar is not exactly right in the head. And that's what everybody else in camp thinks, the same as me.

When we all got to Kamakura the *gabachos* heard that Joe was a musician, and they wanted to hear "El Rancho Grande." What should be our great surprise, as my father says when he's telling a story, what should be our great surprise when he shows up with that silly contraption of a tube instead of a guitar. ¡Mis dos...pistolas! Was I embarrassed for both of us. And then the songs he plays. They don't have any names, just numbers, and they don't begin or end anywhere. All except that old song that says, "How far am I from the land where I was born." Believe it or not, he can play that song and make it sound beautiful, even on an oboe.

Joe is built like a heavyweight boxer, and that's what you would expect him to be. But no. Besides playing that oboe, he's a baker. And a very good one at that. It's what he did for a living back in Jonesville on the Rio Grande, where he comes from. A man has to make a living, I guess. After all, they don't have oboes in the *mariachi* bands down there.

His name is not Joe, if we are going to say the truth. It's José Evaristo Longoria-Garza de la Garza, as he keeps reminding us. But in the Army they shortened it to Joe Garza. The Army will do things like that. Joe comes from where the Rio Grande runs into the Gulf, and that might explain why he is the way he is. The people around there, my father says, have lived in the same place too long. And they keep marrying each other. That's why some of them are sort of odd. That's what my father says.

My father should know, even if he isn't from there, because he came into the States through Jonesville. My father is from beautiful San Fernando, not the place in Califa but that town deep in Tamaulipas, where all the people are supposed to be one-eyed. The main and only reason is that all they eat is dried beef, which is tough and rubbery. They grab a hunk of it with their teeth and pull and pull, and finally a piece comes off and hits them in the eye. Over and over, all the time. My father has both his eyes, but he squints a lot.

When my father decided he would come to the United States, he came in through Jonesville, as I was saying. I wasn't born yet, which was just my luck. My father's name was Juan Brito y Duero, but the *rinche* at immigration wrote down Juan Picadero, and that's what my father's name became in the States. Perhaps the character had just been to a bullfight across the river in Morelos. Who can tell. At least he could have made it Picaduro, my father likes to say, and he grins and looks at me sideways. He thinks I don't catch on, but after all his son Johnny is a *bato al alba* from San Cuilmas (San Antone to you).

Me and Pablo López didn't meet Joe until we landed in Yokohama from Okinawa. We went straight to Camp Harter, and there's Joe in the headquarters mess, baking French bread Texas-Mexican style and dying to talk Spanish to somebody, anybody. So me and Pablo oblige him. Every night, long after bed-check time, we walk back to camp from Kamakura and stop to talk to Joe in Spanish. He is so grateful he gives us several loaves of bread each time, and cheese and butter and apples and whatever he can lay his hands on. So me and Pablo don't ever have to get up at some ghastly hour of the morning to have breakfast. We have it in our quarters, along with a couple of cans of beer, so long as we get to the I&E offices by eight or so.

Or even nine. Major Schmidt, the man in charge, is not a spit and polish man, you can say that for him. He's a good guy, but he does some stupid things at times. And he's always talking about making bird colonel. But everybody knows he'll never make it because of that time he ordered 21,000 ping pong balls for the camp when he meant to order 21. But that's another story.

Pablo isn't very bright either, you have to say that for him. Who would go into the army just for the hell of it when there's a war on? That's what Pablo did. He was born in Coahuila, though he says his father is from Chihuahua and that the Pablo López who raided Columbus with Villa was his uncle. Anyway, he grew up in San Antone, in the same *barrio* with me, and he was living there on the seventh of December of forty-one. So, does he hightail it for Coahuila? No. He stays and is drafted. He wants to see the world, he says. And he sees plenty of it, all right. Leyte, Mindoro, Los Negros, Mindanao, Okinawa—the whole holiday tour. And me right there with him. Not that I wanted to see the world, but I wasn't born in Coahuila.

Then we get to Tokyo Bay, and Pablo does something smart. He asks me a question. "Say, Picadero," he says, "how do you say *dibujante* in English?"

I think for about a minute and then I tell him, "I don't know. Maybe there's no word in English for that. What's that paper you got there, anyway?"

"I got it from the company clerk," he says. "There are some jobs open at I&E here in Camp Harter. They're starting a newspaper. I don't want to spend the rest of my time in the Army at some post out in the boondocks."

"Just put down that you're good at drawing," I tell him. And I hightail it to the company clerk, since I worked for a newspaper once in San Antone. I was just an office boy, but the company clerk don't have to know that. I tell him I was a crackjack reporter, and he gives me a paper to fill out.

So we both end up at I&E, within walking distance of Kamakura and a short drive to Tokyo. Pablo told them no lies. He can draw anything you ask him to. But me, I don't have a brass monkey's chance in hell once the chips are down. So I tell Major Schmidt how Pablo and me grew up together since we were babies in the cradle. How we saved each other's life in combat innumerous times, enduring unspeakable dangers, how bad it would be for our morale if we were torn apart. The major takes it all in, and for a minute there I think he's going to cry. Then he says, "All right, Sergeant Picadero, you can remain with us, but what *can* you do?"

"I can do many things around the office," I tell him. "I can make that mimeograph machine purr like a baby, for one thing."

So he keeps me anyway, as the office boy, even though I'm a staff sergeant and Pablo, who's only a corporal, is on the newspaper staff. I also get to drive the major around in his jeep. And that's what got me into trouble.

One night me and Pablo are coming back from Kamakura, and we stop by the mess tent to see Joe. But Joe's not around. Moriarty, the mess sergeant, is there. He's a long, thin glass of water. I don't know how he can be around so much food and be so thin. "Picadero," he says, "you gotta help me. Joe isn't reporting for duty."

"Oh," I say, "he gets these spells, you know." Joe gets spells once in a while. He gets homesick for Jonesville, where everybody speaks Spanish. Then he can't work at all. He leaves the kitchen and goes to the barracks, where he takes out his oboe and plays sad music until he feels better. Then he goes back to work. So I tell Moriarty, "He'll be back before long, and he'll work twice as hard. You know that."

"Not this time, Picadero," Moriarty says. "Remember you were here last night about this time? Well, he went to the barracks as soon as you guys left, and he hasn't been back since."

"Not even to eat?" says Pablo, who is thinking of all the stuff Joe gives us every night.

"I've been taking him his meals," Moriarty says, "and he has plenty of beer. But I can't talk him into coming back to work. If he doesn't pretty soon, he'll end up in the stockade."

"Playing his oboe doesn't help this time?" I say.

"That's just it. He can't play the damn thing because it's broke. Last night the oboe was lying on his bunk, and he was feeling so sad he didn't notice it was there. So he sat down on it."

"And since he can't play the oboe," says Pablo, "he keeps getting sadder and sadder."

"You should have been a detective, Pablo," I tell him.

"I've tried to talk some sense into him," Moriarty says, "but he won't listen. I told him if the first sergeant hears about it, he'll have him court-martialed. And you know what he said?"

"What," says Pablo.

"He said, 'Let him try, the mother-loving son-of-a-bitch. He don't know what it's like to tangle with...' And then he let go with that yard-long name of his."

"José Evaristo Longoria-Garza de la Garza," I tell him.

"Right," says Moriarty.

"¡Viva México!" says Pablo in that stupid way of his.

"I need Joe," Moriarty says. "I need him real bad. The major won't eat any bread but the kind Joe makes."

"And Joe needs his oboe," I tell Moriarty right back.

"Well, by God," says Moriarty, "we just got to get an oboe for Joe. You're his friend, Picadero. You gotta help me."

So that's how I come to borrow the major's jeep and drive to Tokyo looking for an oboe for Joe. Getting the jeep was no problem. I go to the I&E office (nobody's around this late), and I get one of the forms to check out a jeep and fill it out. Under destination I put official business, and I sign the major's name. The corporal on night duty at the motor pool just takes a quick look at it and lets me have the jeep. So I take off like a roaring bird. Five minutes to Kamakura and I'm in Tokyo in half an hour more. No oxcarts on the road this time of night, which is good for them and for me too.

Then my real problems begin. It's almost eleven o'-clock, and all the music stores on the Ginza are shut down for the night. Same for the pawn shops. I stop a few people on the street and ask them where I can get an oboe, and the damn fools just fan their hands in front of their noses and say, "Wakara nai." Which means, "I don't know." There's a young one who keeps staring at me, but he doesn't come up close. An older guy, sort of dark looking, grabs me by the arm and tells me, "You come. Me get you some oboe."

"Where's the oboe?" I tell him.

"Me no Jap, me Korean. Me American friend. You take me to America?"

"If you help me find oboe for my friend Joe."

"We go jeepu," he says, and so we do. After a lot of turns in dark streets, suddenly there are lights ahead, and music. Soon we are in a street full of people, men and women and more women and men. I stop the jeep. "What the hell!" I tell him. "This is the whorehouse district!"

"Lots of oboe here," he says, grinning like a Cheeser cat. "Lots of Joe come for oboe here."

I call him all sorts of names, none of them nice, and tell him to get out of the jeep, but he just keeps telling me he's my blood brother and that he knows just the girl for me. So I drive a few blocks in the direction of the Ginza and then push him out of the jeep. And not too soon, either, because another jeep comes down the street just about that time.

There's an MP buck sergeant in it. He stops me, comes up to where I am, and shines a light in my face. "Hey, buddy," he says, "you didn't have that Jap riding with you, did you?"

"I wouldn't dream of it," I tell him. "I know it's against regulations."

"I'm glad you know that," he says. "By the way, isn't that a yellow oak leaf I see on your license plate?"

"Yes," I tell him. "This is Major Schmidt's jeep. I'm his driver and I'm running an errand for him."

"Okay," he says. "Run your errand, but don't pick up any Japs while you're doing it."

He drives away and I let out a great big sigh. This is getting me nowhere, I can see. I'm not going to find an oboe for Joe anywhere in Tokyo. So I decide to give it up and go see my girlfriend Mabel, who works at the Red Cross club across the street from the Imperial Palace. I park the jeep in the alley behind the club, just in case. Mabel is there, handing out coffee and doughnuts to a bunch of GIs. She's a Nisei, one of those who got caught in Japan during the war, but she's one hundred percent American, same as you and me. I look at her fondlingly. Her face is sort of flat, but the rest of her isn't, and she's a lot of fun.

She sees me and comes over. "Hello, Johnny," she says, "what are you doing in town in the middle of the week?"

"I had to come see you, Mabel," I say to her. "I just couldn't stay away for a whole week."

Getting an Oboe for Joe

Mabel laughs. "That's nice, Johnny," she says. "And I believe you."

"Honest," I tell her. "How about a date?"

"I don't get off till one a.m.," she says.

"Good," I say. "I'll pick you up then, and we can go have some fun at the Club Ichiban, the best EM club in town."

"The only EM club in town," Mabel reminds me, "and it closes at twelve."

"Oh, all right," I tell her. "I'll take you home instead."

"The long way?" Mabel wants to know.

"The longer the better," I say, and she laughs. So I go out of the club feeling pretty good. On the way out I see the desk where a Red Cross lady sits most of the time, but this time she's not there. There are some flowers on the desk. I take them along wrapped in my handkerchief. Nothing's too good for Mabel.

I come up to the jeep happy as a hummingbird, when all of a sudden a light is in my face. Up comes my friend, the MP sergeant. "Hi, buddy," he says, "you sure take a long time doing your major's errands. Better tell me more about them."

"It's a long story," I tell him.

"I bet it is. You might also tell me what you're doing in Tokyo in a jeep with a Camp Harter registration number."

"I'm here on an errand of mercy and compassion," I tell him.

"Is it a funeral you're going to? Is that why you're holding those flowers in your hand?"

"Listen," I tell him, "it's the truth. I had to make a quick trip to Tokyo to find an oboe for a guy named Joe. The well-being of Headquarters Company at Camp Harter depends on it."

"Yeah, yeah," he says, not at all pleasant-like. "Let's see your pass."

"My what?"

"Your pass. You're thirty, forty miles from your billet in the middle of the night."

I give him my trip ticket. He looks it over. "Come on, Spanish," he says, "you've been in the army long enough to know what a pass looks like. This is a trip ticket."

"I know," I tell him. "The major sent me on this important mission in such a hurry that both of us forgot about the pass."

"And what may that important mission be?"

"I told you," I tell him. "I'm looking for an oboe, an oboe for a guy named Joe. He doesn't have his oboe to blow on, and if he doesn't get one soon he won't bake the major's favorite bread, and there'll be hell to pay in Headquarters Company."

"Getting an oh-bo for a guy named Joe," he says. "You better come with me to the station and talk to the officer on duty."

"Look," I tell him, "this is important. Why don't you let me finish what I have to do, and we'll straighten things out in the morning."

"Come on, come on," he says. "Just get on your jeep and follow me. I wouldn't be surprised if that trip ticket ain't forged. And maybe those stripes you're wearing don't belong to you either." He goes to his jeep, and then he turns around and grins back at me. "And even if the stripes are on the up-and-up," he says, "I bet you won't be wearing them for long." That's the way buck sergeants feel about a staff. Any day of the week.

I sit in my jeep while he drives by and gets ahead

of me, and meanwhile I'm figuring out the strategic points of the situation. I'm in trouble as deep as I can get, so why not get in deeper a little more. So I follow the MP jeep for a bit. Then I turn out my lights, scoot into a dark alley, and away I go like Buck Rogers. I know exactly where I'm going, to the Dai Ichi Hotel parking lot. That's where the majors and colonels stay when they're in Tokyo. Major Schmidt's jeep will be right at home in there.

I get lucky and don't run into anything driving without lights, except for one handcart that I knock over in an alley. So I ease the jeep into the parking lot, in between a lot of other jeeps like it, and I'm home free. Well, not exactly, but if I can stay low until morning that MP and his buddies will be off-duty. I can come for the jeep and hightail it back to good old Camp Harter. But I can't hang around the Dai Ichi parking lot. There's too much light, and security must check the place once in a while. So I start walking. The MPs won't be looking for me on foot. If I stay out of the busy streets I'll be okay. I walk along the dark side of the streets, feeling sorry for myself. No date with Mabel, no oboe for Joe. The only bright light in the night is the thought of that MP riding up and down the streets looking for me.

I go along, thinking very bad thoughts about José Evaristo Longoria-Garza de la Garza, when all of a sudden somebody behind me says, "Pardon me, sir." I nearly jump out of my socks, but it's just a young Japanese man dressed like a student that looks like I've seen him somewhere before, and I soon find out. He was on the Ginza when I met that Korean.

He comes up and says in English just as good as you and me, "Aren't you the American who was inquiring after an oboe?" Or something along that order.

"Yes," I tell him.

"I know where you can get one," he says.

"Lead me to it, *tomodachi*," I tell him.

"It's not here," he tells me. "We must take the elevated to the next station."

"That's the fly in the vaseline," I tell him. "For very special reasons I cannot go up to the station, namely because there's too much light."

"I understand," he says. "It is past curfew. But I think I know how you can take the train with me."

"How?" I tell him. "Can you make me invisible?"

"For all practical purposes," he says. "Come with me, please, to the house of my friend I have been visiting. By the way, my name is Hiroshi."

"Johnny Picadero," I say. "Delighted."

Hiroshi calls at the door of the nearest house, and we are let in. There are a lot of Japanese people in there, of all sorts and sizes. Hiroshi starts talking and the older men shake their heads up and down and say, "Hai! Hai!"

"Fine!" Hiroshi tells me. "They will do it."

"Do what?" I say.

"They will lend you a kimono. My friend's father is just your size."

I've never been so glad I'm not a big guy. Quick as a flash I take off my cap and combat boots. I roll up the legs of my pants higher than my knee and get into the kimono. One of the girls pulls at the tips of my socks so I can spread out my big toes and put on a pair of zoris. I stand up and everybody is going aah-aah and talking very fast.

"They are talking about you," Hiroshi tells me. "You look very Japanese."

Getting an Oboe for Joe

"That's good," I tell him.

"The girls say you look like the Emperor," he says. I'm not sure that's so good, but I say thanks just the same.

Not even my friend Pablo would know me in that kimono. We get on the train and nobody looks at me twice. We get off at the next station and walk to the house of Hiroshi's friend, Mr. Harada. Harada used to be a banker, a very fat banker, he says, but now he's very thin and doesn't have a bank anymore. This he tells me through Hiroshi because Harada doesn't talk much English. He does know a little bit, enough to say, "America! Nice country! Beefsteak! Ice cream! Buttah!" Hiroshi tells him about the oboe. Harada bows to me and says, "Hai! Hai!" And he goes out.

Soon he comes back with a dusty old oboe. I'm up in the clouds, I'm so happy. "Tell him how much he wants for it," I say to Hiroshi.

"It's a present for you," Hiroshi tells me, and Harada bows and smiles.

"Tell him I'll bring him presents too. Chocolate. Cigarettes."

Now it's Harada who is up in the clouds, he's so happy. So we all sit down on the floor and have some tea. And just then we hear the trampling of boots everywhere, and MPs come into the house from all around.

"Just like Gregorio Cortez," I say to myself. "So many of them just to catch one Mexican!"

But they don't even look at me twice. They're looking inside the closets and everywhere, and one of them keeps saying to Harada, "Cigaretto! Chocoretto! Where is it!"

Then Hiroshi speaks up in his best English. "Gentlemen," he says, "this is a respectable residence. There are no black market goods here."

The MP who's talking to Harada has captain's bars on his collar. He looks at Hiroshi in great surprise and then says, "I do believe you're right." And out he goes. A second later you can hear him yelling in the next room. "Moses, you fool! You'll answer to the colonel for this!"

"But sir," says a voice I'm sure I've heard before, "I got reliable information, very reliable information, sir."

"You idiot!" says the captain. "Go in there and apologize to the man of the house! Then round up the rest of the men and get them out of here. I'll see you back at the station!" And out he stomps.

"Jee-hee-zus!" says the voice I'm sure I've heard before. And who should walk in but my old friend the MP sergeant. I sort of die inside, but Moses just takes a quick look at me and goes to old Harada, and he says, "We sorry! Gomen nasai! Mistake! You know? Miss-take!"

Hiroshi talks to Harada and Harada talks to Hiroshi, and then Hiroshi talks to Moses, "He says everything is all right. No harm has been done."

"Good," says Moses. "I was sure you'd see it that way." Then he looks at me again and says, "Haven't I seen you somewhere before?"

I fan my hand in front of my nose and say "Wakara nai." Which means, "I don't understand."

Moses stops staring at my face and looks at my feet. "Are those GI socks you're wearing?" he says. And before I can put my mind in gear, I have looked down at my socks, stupid fool that I am.

"Aha!" says Moses. "The smart operator in the major's jeep." And before he's finished saying all of that, I'm out of there like a shot, holding up my skirts with one hand and the oboe for Joe in the other. It's not easy jumping and running like that, especially when you have nothing but socks in your feet, but I manage. Except there's a small army of MPs outside, and Moses is blowing his whistle and yelling, "Head him off! Head him off!"

That they do, but not until I dodge them around a few houses. Then they're in front of me and in back of me, so what can I do but jump through the paper door of somebody's house. The MPs are right behind me, and others are coming in through the back. But once they're inside they don't pay me much mind.

There's a big party going on in there, with all sorts of people besides the native element. A Chinese or two, or maybe they're Koreans. Two civilian whites and a couple of our guys in uniform, a lieutenant and a sergeant. And behind me, Moses is bawling his head off, "Hold it, all of you! Hold it!" He and the other MPs all have their forty-fives in hand.

Moses pushes me aside and tells the lieutenant, "You're under arrest, sir! All of you!" The lieutenant and all the rest just sit there on the floor, around some little tables where they have been drinking sake and smoking something that is not tobacco, for sure.

From another room an MP calls out, "You oughta take a look at what we got here, sarge. This is no regular black market stuff. Drugs, I betcha."

And Moses calls back, "I knew it all along!" The big phony.

Well, after that there is a lot of frisking and shaking down and snapping on of handcuffs, while I just stand around holding the oboe for Joe. Moses is as happy as a jayhawk. He comes by me, and he gives me a smirk and he says, "Well, Spanish, won't the captain be proud of me. This is a big, big haul, and I did it all by myself. I'm looking at extra stripes. Staff, or tech perhaps." He leers at me. "And you'll be the icing on the cake, boy."

"Big deal," I tell him. "Listen, Shylock Holmes, you never would've got these guys except I led you to them. And that's the first thing I'm gonna tell your captain when you haul me in."

He looks at me sort of funny and tells me, "You wouldn't do that."

"Try me," I tell him back. "But I don't have to if we make a deal. I can tell him I was working for you, undercover, and that's why I'm wearing this kimono."

Moses thinks it over for a second or two and then he says, "Nah, I don't like the idea." Then he says, "Spanish, you're up the crick without a paddle, and you know it. Out of uniform. Caught in an off-limits house. Stealing an officer's jeep. Resisting arrest. Why, you'll be in the stockade forever, private."

"I have my side of the story," I say.

"Look," Moses says, "I'm a good-hearted sort of guy. I know how you got into this jam trying to get that oh-bo thing you got there. Tell you what I'm gonna do."

"What," I say.

"I'm gonna tell you to get the hell out of here and go back to Camp Harter."

"I'll pray tonight they make you a master sergeant," I say.

"Yeah," Moses tells me. "It's almost daylight." Then he says, "Tell me one thing. Where did you hide the jeep?"

Getting an Oboe for Joe

"In the Dai Ichi parking lot," I tell him.

"Get out of here," he says, "before I change my mind."

"I hope they make you a general," I tell him and get out fast.

The sun is out by the time I get back to Camp Harter, and I am feeling sleepy, hungry and all-around bad. My only chance is to talk Major Schmidt out of giving me the whole works. Most of the time I can talk him out of almost anthing, but this time I'm not so sure. I may not end up in the stockade, but I can lose my stripes. I can also lose my job and end up doing latrine duty. But I have the oboe for Joe, and that makes me feel better. I turn the jeep over to one of the mechanics, and Jacobs, the motor-pool sergeant, comes out of his hut.

"A good mawning to you, Picadeero," he tells me. "Major Schmidt is asking about you."

"I know," I say.

"Better get your tail over there fast if you know what's good for you," he says.

"I'm on my way," I tell him. But first I want to take the oboe to Joe. After that, we'll let the sparks burn holes in my huarches, as my father likes to say.

I go to Joe's quarters, and he's not there, but a second later here he comes with a towel around his neck. "Where you been?" I asked him.

"Taking a shower, Picadero," he says, "as any fool can see. It gets pretty hot working all night around those ovens, you know."

"You're back at work?" I say, sounding as stupid as I feel. "What about your oboe, for God's sake?"

"Oh, it's all right," he tells me. "I only broke the reed when I sat down on it. Then I remembered I have a spare one, so I changed it. Works fine. Want to hear me play it?"

"No, thanks," I tell him, "many, many thanks. Here I've been going through hell and firewater to get you another oboe, which I have here in my good right hand, and you don't need an oboe after all."

"Let's see it," he says, so I give it to him. He takes a look at it and tosses it on his bunk. "That's not an oboe, *pendejo*," he tells me. "That's a clarinet."

"José Evaristo Longoria-Garza de la Garza," I say to him, "give thanks to God that they have a rule in this man's army, about hanging people that kill other people. Otherwise, your life would be endangered."

He grins at me. "You wouldn't do that, would you?" he says. "After all, you're my buddy. And I'm bigger than you, besides."

"You got a point there," I tell him.

"Can I help it if you can't tell an oboe from a clarinet?" he says. "By the way, the major's looking for you."

"I know, I know," I tell him. "I'm going to see him now."

"By the way," he says, "I gave Pablo plenty of good French bread Mexican style last night. So you can have a nice breakfast."

"In the stockade, for sure," I say.

"Maybe not," he says. "Pablo went over to talk to the major so he won't court-martial you."

"Pablo?" I say in great distress. "Jesus, Mary and Joseph! With that stupid ox speaking up for me, I'll get twenty years to life."

So I hurry down to I&E, knowing that all is lost, as Porfirio Díaz said when he took that boat to France. At least, that's what my father says. I walk into the major's office and salute. "Sergeant Picadero reporting, sir," I say. "About that missing jeep, sir. I hope you will let me explain, sir."

"There's no need for that, sergeant," he says. "Corporal Lo-oh-pez has been here, and he gave me all the particulars in the case."

"But, major, sir," I tell him, "Pablo López is a good man, but he sometimes gets his facts backward. Perhaps I can straighten things out."

"No need, no need," he says. "Ah," he says dreamily, "loyalty, initiative, self-sacrifice. These are the eternal verities in a soldier's life. Corporal Lo-oh-pez has made it all clear to me."

"But, major, sir," I say.

"No need to be modest, sergeant," he says, holding up his hand. "I understand the loyalty you people have for each other. And how you have the same feelings for this man's army. I admire you for it, sergeant. For what you did for your buddy and what you did for Headquarters Mess."

"Thank you," I say, "thank you, sir."

"I think thanks are due also to your friend, Lo-oh-pez, who made it all clear to me. He's a very intelligent man. I'm sending his name in for promotion."

"Pablo López? A buck sergeant?"

"I knew you would be happy to hear about it," the major tells me.

"I'm all enchantment," I tell him.

"Only one thing," he says. "Next time you want to borrow my jeep on a mission of mercy, you tell me first."

"Speech fails me," I tell him, "in the face of your generosity."

"One thing more before you go, Picadero," he says. "Corporal Lo-oh-pez does not have a corner on the smarts around here. You're a pretty sharp cookie yourself. If you'd just stop clowning around and speak straight English, you could do very well for yourself."

I don't think I talk crooked English, but all I say is, "Yes sir."

"In fact," he says, "I've been keeping an eye on you. I'm sure you could go far in this man's army. You're good officer material."

Officer material? ¡Mis dos...pistolas! Why don't he just call me by my mother and let it go at that!

The American Dish

Here I am, all dressed up in ribbons at the Fina La Negra café, when out of the rain walks this character in the beret. And me in Santa Rosa with the best of intentions in mind, mainly and only to see my old friend Pablo and let him know Johnny Picadero is finally home from the wars.

It's a little late to be home from the wars, I must admit, but I'm never one to do things in a hurry. Grain by grain the chicken fills her crop, as my father likes to say. So when the shooting stops, I sign up for another four years with my Uncle Samuel. Home can wait, I say to myself, and so can the girls in Milam Park.

But what should be my great surprise, as my father is fond of saying, what should be my great surprise when I do return to old San Cuilmas this summer. I walk into a bar and one barmaid says to another barmaid, looking all the time at all the ribbons on my shirt, "What's that, Susie?"

Susie, who used to be Jesusa Mata before the war, answers back, "Why it's a soldier, Josie. You know, a soldier. They've got lots of them over in Fort Sam."

"Oh," says Josie, "here I'm thinking it's perhaps a

205

Christmas tree."

So I walk out of there and take the next train for south of the border, where maybe they have not forgotten yet there ever was a war. Not Pablo at least, because he also was in this war we had.

Pablo let them put him in the Army when the war began because he wanted to see the world. He's never been very bright. But after visiting the Philippines and Okinawa, he had enough sightseeing. Soon after we hit Japan he went home, all the way to Coahuila where he was born. Not me. The best part of a war is what comes after. If you win, that is. So I stay and live the good life in Occupied Japan until they send me home.

I get off the train at Santa Rosa, in the United States of Mexico, wearing my snappiest suit of tropical worsteds, complete with decorations. You should have seen the girls when I walk down the street. Even a gendarme at the corner gives me a salute, thinking I'm a general. Nevertheless, with this and that and the other, night finds me over a beer with my friend Pablo at Pedro Morales' café, Fina La Negra.

You've heard of Fina La Negra. She sings over the radio from Mexico, D.F. Pedro Morales loves music more than any other man who owns a restaurant, to be sure. In fact, I would say he loves music more than any other man who lives in the northern part of Mexico. That is why he named his café after Fina La Negra. And that is why Pablo is always welcome around his place, because Pablo plays three chords on the guitar, and that is why we are drinking beer at the Fina La Negra, because Pedro Morales is setting them up, since Pablo would never buy me a beer, mainly and only because Pablo is always broke.

The American Dish

I'm telling Pedro Morales about the old days, when me and Pablo fought all the way across the Pacific and what a pretty figure I cut in Tokyo with the girls. Pedro Morales shuts off his radio set and listens to everything like a gentleman, but Pablo keeps making stupid remarks. Pablo was never very bright, even when he was in the American Army. It begins to rain, and Pedro Morales goes to the kitchen and closes the windows. Then this character walks in, shaking the raindrops from his boots and khakis.

"One of those *gachupines* from the next village down," Pablo whispers at me as the character sits at a table across the room. "Catch the funny little hat he's wearing."

"That, my friend," I say to Pablo, "is a beret. I knew a Frenchman in Japan once who wore one. That is he wore it part of the time, when he didn't dress up like a geisha girl."

"You're the biggest liar I have ever known," Pablo tells me in a friendly sort of way. "Out of one fat *gachupín* you make up Frenchmen and geisha girls."

"Okay," I say to Pablo, "keep your *gachupín* for all I care." *Gachupín*, by the way, is an affectionate pet name by which they call Spaniards down Mexico way.

Pedro Morales shuffles out from the back, tying on a clean apron at the same time, whereupon the Spaniard says like this, "*Buenas noches*," which means good evening. He has a deep, thick voice, like a man from the north of Spain.

"*Buenas noches, señor*," says Pedro Morales. "What is your pleasure tonight?"

"Chili Con Carne," says the Spaniard. "Big bowl."

"*Chile con carne?*" says Pedro Morales. "And how would you like the meat, *señor?*"

"The meat?" says the Spaniard in great surprise. He takes off an eyeglass he wears in just one of his eyes and thinks a moment. Then he says, "Oh, anyway you like."

"Aha!" I tell Pablo softly as Pedro Morales goes back into the kitchen. "A fellow wanderer, or my name is not Johnny Picadero."

"Your name is not Johnny Picadero," says Pablo. "It's Juan."

Nevertheless, I walk over to the table of the character in the beret and smile my best smile. Then I say in English, "Welcome to the fair land of Mexico. It's nice to meet a fellow American so far away from home."

The character puts on his eyeglass, gives me a dirty look and then he says, "I do not understand." He says it in Spanish.

This offends me. Now, if my mother says, "I do not understand" or if my father says "I do not understand" or if my oldest brother who was also born in Mexico says "I do not understand" I think nothing of it, mainly and only because when I speak English they do not understand. But what would Miss Burlinghame in English 7B think if somebody tells her Americans cannot understand English? She would be scandalized.

But I am a gentleman. I smile again and say in correct and faultless diction, "Pleased to meet you, I'm sure. Picadero is the name, Johnny Picadero, San Antone." At the same time I stick out my good right hand.

But the character does not see my hand. He pushes back his chair and says in Spanish, "Curse you!" More or less, but a little stronger. Then he gets up and walks out of the café.

The American Dish

"You're a fine one," says Pablo when I come back to our table. "Eleven o'clock and that Spaniard was Pedro Morales' third customer."

"That is no Spaniard," I tell Pablo, "that is mainly and only an American tourist, just like me. But he is not a very polite fellow, I must say."

"American tourist? Him?" says Pablo. "How do you get the way you get, Johnny Picadero?"

"Listen," I say, "when a fellow walks in and orders Chili Con Carne, what first comes into your mind if you've got one?"

"That he's hungry. What's wrong with a fellow wanting something to eat?"

"Pablo," I say, "do you know what Chili Con Carne is?"

"Sure," says Pablo, "meat with *chiles*."

"You're wrong," I tell Pablo patiently. "Listen well, so you may educate your poor, ignorant Indian self. In the United States of North America, they take their left-over meat and grind it up real fine. Then they cook this mess with lots of red peppers. This kills all the taste, which is just as well. Then they put this stuff in bowls and call it Chili Con Carne, a genuine Mexican dish."

"Now I remember!" yells Pablo. "It was in Little Rock, Ark. And it made me so mad I got three months in the guard house. Mexican food? The dirty fakers! Is that being good neighbors, I ask you."

"Take it easy, Pablo," I say. "There's no sense in getting all hot about it now."

"I see," says Pablo thoughtfully. "Chili Con Carne is not Mexican. It's an American dish, so if a Spaniard comes and asks for Chili Con Carne, that means he's not a Spaniard because if he is a Spaniard, Chili Con Carne will mean meat and *chiles* to him and not a special dish, and that naturally means the character in the beret is not a Spaniard at all but an American."

"Pablo," I say, "sometimes I'm almost sure you're not dumb."

"You're no genius yourself," says Pablo, "if you know what I mean."

"Where is Señor Garcés?" asks Pedro Morales, coming out of the kitchen with a plate.

"How do you know his name is Garcés?" says Pablo, quick like a district attorney.

"He was here this morning for breakfast," Pedro Morales says. "He lays his identification card on the table, and I got a good look at it while I was serving him."

"Identification card?" I say. "Do you mean a Mexican card?"

Pedro Morales moves his head up and down, meaning yes. "He plays the piano very nice," says Pedro Morales. "He told me all about it."

"That's funny," I say to myself out loud. "A tourist will try to pass himself off as a Mexican or a Spaniard just to try out his Spanish. But he won't go to the trouble of faking an identification card. Why does this red-faced…"

"I get it!" yells Pablo, so loud I jump in my seat.

"Get what?" says Pedro Morales and me as well, together at the same time.

Pablo calms down and a foxy look comes into his eye. "It all adds up," he says, trying to look like Charles Boyer in the movie about the thin man. "Listen, what if I tell you this *gachupín* in the funny hat offered me twenty pesos to guide him on a trip into the mountains?"

"Did you take the money?" says Pedro Morales.

"Naw," says Pablo. "Who wants to go wandering

around in the mountains? But why would a foreigner go around acting mysterious and trying to fool people he's a Spaniard? For all we know he isn't a *gringo* either. For all we know he's..."

"A spy!" says Pedro Morales.

"Correct," says Pablo. "It all comes to me when Johnny Picadero says the word 'red.'" He gets up out of his chair and grabs my arm with his big satchel of a hand. "Come on," he says to me, "we got work to do."

Before I can draw a deep breath we are out in the street. The rain has stopped falling and Pablo and me stop for a drumhead council of war.

"He'll go to La Valenciana, Antonino's hotel," Pablo says. "Everybody knows Antonino is a communist. He gets magazines from the United States with red all around the cover."

I stop to think this over and Pablo adds, "Besides, it's the only hotel in town."

So we hotfoot it to La Valenciana without meeting anyone on the way. Who we do meet is María Ester. We meet her inside of the hotel. She is standing behind the counter where they give out the keys, and she looks not bad at all. But Pablo is ahead of me, giving her his big-ox smile, so I gather that she is his girl, so I lay off, mainly and only because I don't try to make the girls of my friends and also because Pablo is so much bigger than me.

"María Ester," Pablo says, "I love you. When can I play the guitar again for you to sing?" María Ester giggles. "She thinks she can sing and I kid her along," Pablo tells me in his broken English. I lean over and take a personal look at María Ester, and I don't care if she can't talk even. In fact, this business of chasing spies begins to look much better. Perhaps she has a sister.

We ask María Ester about Garcés and she says, "Oh yes, I know him. He's upstairs with Antonino right now."

But she does not like the idea at all of letting us take a peek at what they might be doing without letting them know about it. She says no, that it's wrong and she wants to go to Heaven when she dies.

"Listen, María Ester," I tell her, "do you love Pablo?"

"Of course I love Pablo," she tells me, giving me what they call in Mexico a falling of the eyes.

"Don't you want to marry him?" I say to her.

"Of course," she says with a little squeal.

"Hey, listen," says Pablo, "what's all this talk about getting married?"

"Don't pay attention to him," I say. "He's just shy."

María Ester gives Pablo a dirty look and then turns around and gives me the warmest look I can stand without melting into tallow. "I won't pay any attention to him," she says. "I'd rather listen to you."

So I start telling her all about how a woman has to obey her husband to lead a very happy home life and how this business about democracy in the home is just a foolish Yankee fad. I paint such a beautiful picture of home life for Pablo and María Ester that even Pablo gets a dreamy look around the eyes, and María Ester is heaving her bosom up and down so I'm afraid the next moment she will bust her blouse.

It ends up that María Ester gives us the key to room number seven on the upper floor, saying in the meanwhile that it is in room number five that Antonino is and that there is a door between the two rooms and that the door has a nice, large keyhole that just about fits the eye.

Pablo and me hotfoot it like a mouse up the stairs

and into room number seven. We scarcely close the door when I'm over on the other side of the room peeking through the keyhole. What I see gives me the terrific nervous shake of my young life. María Ester is right. Garcés is in there, Antonino is in there. But other characters are in there besides. In fact, the room is full of characters. Besides Garcés there are three or four other funnies like him dressed in khaki and boots and berets. To top the climax, there is also another character, one tall, dark-faced individual dressed up in a Mexican cowboy suit.

I let Pablo take a peek and he gets pale underneath his skin. "Holy twenty thousand virgins," Pablo says, lapsing into the vernacular, "that's Juan Terán of the constabulary. He's the meanest man in northern Mexico, besides being the best shot in the same general area."

"What of it?" I say, mainly to give courage to Pablo, and I take the keyhole away from him so he can recover his morale. The characters are talking in English, and it is something terrible to hear. They all have accents. One of them turns around and calls Garcés Mr. Rugoff.

"Rugoff!" I whisper to myself.

They are talking about shooting some Mexican Indians and Rugoff is very angry about it. "Why don't you wait?" he says. "Why don't you wait since you know there's a bunch of stupid Mexican police nearby and that you'll get into trouble maybe?"

Another of the foreigners jerks a thumb at Juan Terán and says, "We have this lout in the monkey suit with us. We'll be all right."

When he sees they are talking about him, Juan Terán hitches up his pants and smiles with pride. I deduct that Juan Terán of the constabulary may be a wonderful pistol shot but he will never get a passing grade from Miss Burlinghame in English 7B.

They talk for a little while longer, and Rugoff is laying down the law about another bunch of people they have to take care of before tomorrow night. Juan Terán keeps patting his forty-five and smiling.

"What about United States?" says one character.

"We sabotaged *them* plenty," says Rugoff. "This is one time they won't be number one."

Antonino has been listening to all of this and saying nothing, but now he springs up and looks around. Then he walks quickly over to the door going out into the hall, and he throws it open. Crouching over where the keyhole was a moment before is a girl, a very blonde and pretty girl. Since the skirt she's wearing is not the New Look style, it goes up where she crouches and I can see that it isn't only her face that is nice.

Antonino grabs her wrist and jerks her inside, and he shuts the door again. "This," he tells Rugoff, "is Miss Ross of United States." They all look Miss Ross over from head to toenails, and I'm doing the same thing through the keyhole, only these characters keep getting in my way.

"We'll have to keep her with us for the present," Rugoff says, "at least until this job is over."

Miss Ross acts in a way that makes me very proud of her. She draws up that figure of hers straight as a dice and looks Rugoff in the face. Then she turns around and gives him her back. And a very pretty back, at that.

"We'd better get under way," says one of Rugoff's friends and companions.

Rugoff turns around to Antonino and says, "Antonino, go down pretty soon and check on the car and see that it's ready so we can travel."

I grab Pablo by the arm and rustle him out of room number seven. "Where are we going?" Pablo whispers as we come out into the hall.

"Into action," I say.

"Action?" Pablo tells me with great surprise. "Listen, Johnny Picadero, I don't want to go into action. Besides I don't like it. And why should I, just because Chili Con Carne is an American dish? For all I know the Spaniards eat the stuff, and Rugoff is a Spaniard making believe he is a spy."

I give Pablo a long and dirty look, but I'm not seeing his stupid face. I am seeing Miss Ross. "Listen, Pablo," I say, "you got us both into this and we're not getting out just when the fun is starting. I wouldn't be surprised if you got cold feet because you saw that forty-five Juan Terán is wearing in his waist."

"I wouldn't be surprised either," says Pablo.

"Pablo," I say, "this is our fight. It's your fight, it's my fight, it's Miss Ross's fight. Pablo," I say, and Miss Ross's figure dances in front of my eyes like colored lights, "Pablo, have you ever heard of Continental Solidarity?"

"No," says Pablo.

"Well, come along anyway," I say, and we rush down quietly to the lobby.

The plan of attack has already formed in my mind, and it's simple beyond approach. Antonino's automobile, an ancient model A, is sitting out in front of the hotel. All we have to do is break a few wires and Rugoff can't leave town until we call the police.

María Ester is still in the lobby when we come down. She yawns and says, "Holy Mother, it's almost four o'clock in the morning. Did you tell Antonino to hurry down so I can go home? And why are you looking so sad, Pablo, life of my life?"

To all of this we do not answer, but merely go through the lobby and into the street. The hood is clamped down on the model A with baling wire, and it takes several minutes before I can get it up and put my good right hand inside. I have barely done so when a big voice says right in my ears, "Sort of early for mechanical work, no?"

I turn around and there is Antonino beside me, with Pablo behind him looking helpless. I have not seen this Antonino close up before. He is bigger than Pablo, and that means he is huge. "Hi, Tripa," I say, just to be friendly.

Antonino turns around to Pablo and says, "Tell your friend my name is not Tripa."

"Oh, Tripa isn't a real name," I say, since Pablo cannot talk at the present moment. "It's just something we use in San Cuilmas to denote an affectionate pet name."

Antonino turns around to Pablo again and says, "Tell your friend I don't like affectionate pet names."

There is nothing more to say, so when Antonino turns around to talk to Pablo I hit him. I hit him in the stomach as hard as I can. Antonino turns around and handles me around the Adams apple with his big fingers. He starts squeezing, and I kick him in the shins and try to yell. Things start getting dark, and there is a big roaring in my ears like the Nigeria Falls when the next thing I know I'm standing on my knees, coughing and catching my breath. Over me is María Ester with a heavy nightstick in her hands, and Antonino is stretched out all along the road beside me. There's blood on his head and on the night-stick too, and María Ester is looking up at the starry sky and praying as fast as she can talk, which is very fast if one should tell the truth. She is asking one and all in Heaven to please not let Antonino die so she won't have to go to Hell.

Pablo wobbles up to María Ester and takes the nightstick out of her hands. I don't get mad at Pablo for not helping me, because I can see from his looks that Antonino has been knocking him around with one hand while he massages my Adams apple with the other. Also, for the moment I can't talk at all.

"He isn't dead," Pablo tells María Ester. "You couldn't kill him if you tried all day long with no rest periods in between. We got to tie him up before he comes to."

María Ester runs inside and comes out with some wire and an old dish rag and tells us she hears foot-steps upstairs and that maybe Rugoff and his gang are coming down in a hurry. I tell Pablo as best as I can speak to drag Antonino into the brush and tie and gag him, and so he does with the help of María Ester.

Before I can get my hands inside the model A again, out of the front door comes Rugoff and the rest. I have barely time to step back into the brush next to the car when they come up. I give a blessing to the fact that my skin isn't so very light, in fact, because the brush comes up to my neck only. It covers my sun-tan uniform, luckily, but not my face. I wonder what will happen to me if Rugoff catches me now when I can't even scream for help because my throat hurts so much, but I think I'll be all right as long as I keep my mouth shut.

Rugoff, Juan Terán and three other characters

have Miss Ross between them. They look around for
Antonino. Miss Ross is standing with her back to me,
so close that I can reach through the branches and
touch her if I want to. But I don't want to, at least not
at the present time.

The characters can't find Antonino and one of
them is going to light a flashlight. I nearly faint until
Rugoff tells him not to do it because people will see it.
They see that the hood is up, and one of them says he
guesses Antonino is putting water in the radiator. Rugoff says to hell with the water and get the hood down
and let's go.

They get the hood down and get in the model A
and they drive away. Miss Ross does not seem to want
to drive away, but Juan Terán uses a bit of persua-
sion, mainly putting his arm around her waist and
lifting her into the automobile while she kicks at him.
This makes me very mad, and I make a mental note of
it in case I should catch up with Juan Terán someday
when I become a whiz with the forty-five automatic.

After they are gone, Pablo and María Ester come
out of the brush, where it seems they took a long time
tying Antonino up. María Ester is crying and saying
over and over, "What will I do now? What will I do?"

"She's right," Pablo says. "She'll lose her job, and
we'll both be personas non gratas in this town for the
rest of our lives. And all because you say that Chili
Con Carne is an American dish. Maybe those characters are spies and maybe they aren't, but now they are
gone. All we got left is Antonino, and he's going to be a
very angry individual when somebody comes along
and unties him."

"If only I can follow them," I say, mainly to myself.

"If only my aunt had wheels," says Pablo, thinking

he's a wit, "then she would be a bicycle."

"You got it!" I say to Pablo. "You got it!"

"What's it?" he says, suspicious all of a sudden.

"That's all right, Pablo," I tell him. "What I want you to do is nothing brave. You will not get hurt. All I want you to do is run and get help while I follow those characters that are kidnapping defenseless women and threatening the Continental Solidarity."

"How?" says Pablo.

"On the bicycle I saw a little while ago behind the counter where they give out the keys."

"You can't use that bicycle," says María Ester. "It belongs to Antonio."

"I'll pay him rent," I tell her. "Don't worry." And I wheel the machine out on the road.

"Where will I go for help?" Pablo asks me in that stupid way of his.

"To your aunt's house!" I answer back. "The one with wheels." And I pedal away, just to show him that Johnny Picadero always has the last word.

I start pumping the feet as fast as I can after the model A, which is nowhere to be seen. As I pedal I try to think up some sort of plan. Here I am, not even a little knife with me, and all those characters armed to the teeth, I am sure. The truth of the whole matter is that if it wasn't for Miss Ross I would not be in very much of a hurry to catch them at all. But every time I see Miss Ross in the apple of my mind's eye, I pedal a little faster. And when I think of Juan Terán's arm going around her as it did when he put her in the car, I pedal faster by far, to say the least.

Up in the sky it starts getting sickly looking, so I know it will be dawn very soon. And here I am, chasing after a bunch of tough characters, all because as

Pablo says, Chili Con Carne is an American dish. My only consolation is that Pablo by this time is at the police station and the gendarmes will be along in about five minutes or ten. I see a little red light and I stop quicker than you can say Jack Robertson. The model A is stopped a hundred yards ahead, and I kiss my good right hand for doing the job after all.

I park the bicycle behind some bushes and study the land before advancing. The road runs along a hillside, which is long and sloping and has a lot of big boulders between the timberline and the road. I decide on camouflage, and for camouflage on a night like this there is nothing better than the skin my mother gave me, since it is several shades darker than my clothes.

So I take off my overseas cap and pants and shirt, and my shoes and also a white T-shirt I'm wearing. That leaves me in socks and shorts, both of which are olive drab. So garbed and clutching a good-sized rock which I pick up just for luck, I approach the model A silenter than a Chappie patrol coming up on a foxhole at midnight, all the time praying beneath my breath, just for luck.

Then here comes all this noise of running feet, and Miss Ross dashes out of the dark and hits me so hard she almost knocks me down. This stops her and gives Juan Terán, who is right behind her, a chance to catch up. Their shadows come together and then Miss Ross says, "Stop it! You're hurting me!"

"Shut up!" says Juan Terán. Then he squeezes her to himself and Miss Ross makes a choking sound. Juan Terán moves his head away from her face and starts to laugh, which he never finishes doing because that is the moment I hit him over the head with my rock. Juan Terán lets go of Miss Ross and reaches for his forty-five, not realizing I've already got my hand over it. He's got a pretty thick head, and it takes several applications of the rock before he relaxes, and I lay him down on the ground. The next thing I do is expropriate his pistol and cartridge belt. This makes me feel better, to be sure, but I still wish Pablo and the gendarmes would show up around the bend of the road.

"Are you all right, Miss Ross?" I ask.

"Who are you and how do you know my name?" she tells me.

"Johnny is the name," I say. "Johnny Picadero, United States Army. Pleased, I'm sure."

"The pleasure is mine," says Miss Ross with a little laugh that makes me shiver all over.

Somebody starts calling from the model A, and I take Juan Terán's forty-five out of the holster. "Let me put a bullet through this character's head," I say to Miss Ross, "and then we'll see what we can do for the boys in the flivver."

Miss Ross almost shouts at me. "You'll do nothing of the sort! That is murder!" Then more softly she says, "Don't get into any trouble on my account. Please."

"Trouble?" I answer back. "What is this we're in now?"

And by way of showing how mad I am I heave a shot in the general direction of the model A, where all the characters are calling to Juan Terán to come back with the girl and quit acting like a Latin lover.

The forty-five gives out a big boom. There is a crash of breaking glass, from which I deduct that I have hit the windshield. Then there is a howl and everybody in the car yells at once. One of the characters with the heavy accent says over and over again, "Mr. Rugoff has been killed! They have killed Mr. Rugoff!" This makes me feel better than the time I short-sheeted Big Sam Dunkelberg at Jefferson Barracks and his feet went right through the linen.

But Miss Ross turns to me as mad as she can be. "You…you murderer!" she shouts at me.

This is more than I can stand from anybody, even Miss Ross. I stand up square beside her and start to give her a piece of my mind, but I don't get very far because as I open my mouth there is a very familiar noise from the general direction of the model A, and here comes this bullet and cuts the air between us with a very nasty sound.

"Hit the ground!" I tell Miss Ross, dragging her down with me. From the model A the fire becomes intense and bullets are kicking the dirt all around us.

"Rifles!" I yell in Miss Ross's ears. "Thirty-thirties!"

"But how can they… " she begins to say.

"They sure can," I say back to her and my lips barely touch her hair just then. "They won't stop at anything to get what they want. That boulder over there. Can you see it?"

"Yes," she says, and the next thing I am hearing in the dark is sounds as she crawls along on her belly. I follow her with more practice and finesse, and we stop behind the boulder, where I tell her, "Even with all those fellows shooting, I am wishing it was daylight right now."

"Why?" she asks unsuspiciously.

"Just so I could have seen you," I tell her, "crawling along on your belly ahead of me."

Miss Ross sucks in her breath and I think that perhaps I am being rude. "You're no gentleman!" she says. "If I could see where your face is I'd slap it." At the same time she brushes against my bare shoulder and gives a half-scream. "Oh!" she says.

Somewhat incensed, I say to her like this, "I got a decent and proper pair of underpants on. But you're right, I am no gentleman. However, I won't intrude my presence on you, Miss Ross. You stay here and I will find a boulder of my own from which I can send a few of these characters out of this continent and out of this world, even though my efforts be not appreciated by one and all."

"But Johnny," she says, and it sounds real nice the way she says it, "Johnny, you just can't, you mustn't…"

"Don't worry about me," I say. "Anything for the Continental Solidarity. That's my motto." So saying I make a rush from behind that boulder, and after a short run I slide for dear life behind another boulder. The slide is over some gravel, which takes a lot of skin off my belly. This makes me so mad I heave several shots in the general direction of the model A. Rugoff's boys answer with their thirty-thirties, and the air is alive with lead. I sit behind my boulder and curse my good friend Pablo, who has time now to call out all the police in the north part of Mexico.

After a while the shooting slows down, and I get a chance to answer with a few shots of my own. I don't get any results anymore. The only consolation I get is hearing Rugoff groaning. He should die very soon, I say to myself, in great satisfaction.

Then, to my great horror, as my father likes to say, to my great horror I notice that it is getting light. The next thing I know I can see over to the next boulder, where Miss Ross is crouching to keep out of the line of fire. She is all doubled up behind this rock, and she is pretty to watch. But just then she turns around and sees me in nothing but my shorts, and she puts her hand over her mouth and shakes with laughing, which does not make me feel good at all.

"All right," I shout at her. "Laugh! Laugh!"

She doesn't answer because just then we hear the sound of a truck coming up the road. Sure enough, a truck full of soldiers comes around the bend, and ahead of it there is a jeep. There is a man that looks like a general beside the driver, and sitting in the back is my friend Pablo, armed with a big machete. They all climb down when they see us, and the soldiers go ahead toward the model A. Pablo pulls me up from the ground and hugs me.

"Where have you been?" I ask him.

Pablo grins like a big ox. "To my aunt's house, just like you told me."

I bounce Juan Terán's gun up and down in my hand. "Pablo," I say, "don't forget what it is that I have here in my hand right now."

Pablo grins again. "Honest," he says. "My aunt lives down the road in the next village. That's where the troops are. When you tell me to go for the police I think about Juan Terán, who is a policeman too, and I think I'd better get the army instead. I have to wake up the general, though, and he's a very heavy sleeper."

"Give me my pants," I say coldly.

"Here comes the general now," says Pablo as I'm putting on my pants. The general comes up, looking very military in his pot belly. "This is the American soldier, *mi general*," Pablo says.

The general looks me over and I stand up at attention. I salute him and he salutes right back. Then I point up the road to the model A and say to him like this, "Arrest those men, I beg of you."

"On what charge?" he says, just as a matter of form.

"Spying for an enemy country," I say. "Shooting tribal aborigines within the borders of Mexico, carrying deadly weapons and making use of them."

"Good, good," the general says. I can see his mind's eye and it is full of pictures of firing squads.

The soldiers come up with the prisoners. And there, big as life, is Rugoff himself. He has his hands up in the air like all of them, his face is cut and bloody but he is nowhere dead. One does not have to be a fool to see that Rugoff is plenty mad.

"Did you collect all their weapons?" the general tells the squad leader.

The squad leader is a young lieutenant. He salutes and looks embarrassed. "We couldn't find any weapons," he says. "Only these." He takes from one of the soldiers a couple of .22 caliber rifles, the little single-shot kind.

This makes me mad. "There were a half-dozen rifles shooting at Miss Ross and me," I say. "Thirty-thirties. Take another look, lieutenant, and you'll find them. None of this pea-shooter stuff, I beg of you."

The lieutenant looks embarrassed all over again. "They had nothing but the little ones," he says. "That is all except for a couple of boxes of cartridges." He gives me a look and says, "Twenty-two. Short."

The general says, "By the way, where is this Miss Ross I have been hearing about?"

I look around and Miss Ross is nowhere to be seen. She has just disappeared from the face of the earth, and I notice that so has my bicycle which I borrowed from Antonino. The general looks at me, and I can see he's still thinking of firing squads, only maybe he's done some changes in the personnel. "Maybe Miss Ross has gone where the thirty-thirties that were shooting at you went," the general tells me gently.

Rugoff speaks up then and says, "General, sir, if you will let me put my hands down for a moment and rest my poor wounded body maybe I can explain."

"You can put your hands down," the general says. "You can all put your hands down."

Rugoff does not put his hands down. He puts them to his head instead and sways back and forth, saying all the time, "General, sir, as protector of law and order and dispenser of justice in this fair land, I come to you with my complaints, hoping you will do me justice. To your question as to whether Miss Ross is real, I answer yes. This rascal did not invent her as he invented the thirty-thirties and so many other things for his mean and miserable ends. However, Miss Ross, his partner in crime, has escaped and is probably making her way to the border by now, satisfied she has made a laughing stock out of you."

The general lets out a roar like a small bull. "Nobody makes a fool out of me!" he says.

Now I am sure about the firing squads. However, even with that, I cannot help admiring Rugoff for his beautiful command of the Spanish language. And while I stand there with my mouth open, admiring his style of speech, Rugoff is using the time to make some very serious remarks about my person. He tells the general how he is a big movie director from Hollywood and that these other characters in the boots with him are his assistant directors. Miss Ross, he says, works with a rival company that is trying to muscle him out of his business.

The business Miss Ross is trying to muscle him

out of consists of taking pictures of Mexican Indian tribes doing strange, secret tribal dances for a big movie extravaganza. Miss Ross, for her own evil purposes, has hired this young thug to do him harm.

By this young thug he means me, and it makes me very mad, but before I can say anything Rugoff is talking again, telling the general how I attacked them and beat them up and shot at them. All they have is a couple of toy rifles to shoot rabbits with. He asks the general to throw me in prison at the very least, if he doesn't shoot me soon, which is what I deserve. The general looks at the lieutenant and the lieutenant looks at the soldiers and the soldiers look at me.

All of sudden I realize I still have Juan Terán's pistol in my hand, and I drop it fast. Before the soldiers make up their minds whether to grab me or not, my friend Pablo butts in bringing me my shirt and cap. "Here you are, Picadero," Pablo says in great sorrow. "You may be a criminal, but you were once my buddy. I hate to see you executed out of uniform."

I grab my shirt out of his hands and put it on in a hurry. The soldiers get an eyeful of all my ribbons on my chest and they don't know just what to do then. The general and the lieutenant meanwhile have taken a look, and the general stops frowning. He comes up and points at my chest with his saber. "Where did you get that?" he asks.

"It's a long story," I tell him.

"What is that ribbon for?" the general insists.

"That's the Silver Star," I tell him. "I got that in the Philippines for saving the life of my commanding general."

"Word of honor?" says the general.

"Word of honor," I tell him back. "The enemy had

broken through on our left flank," I begin. And I don't stop until I tell the general for fifteen minutes how I got my Silver Star, and all the while he doesn't know it really is a ribbon you get for being in a battle with thousands of other soldiers and that's all.

The general wants to know what all the other ribbons mean, and things are going along fine, but then Juan Terán has to spoil it all. He comes up with his hands over his head, where there are several big bumps, as all can plainly see. When he sees me he puts two and two together, and he makes a grab for me. I make a strategic retreat while the soldiers hold Juan Terán. He keeps yelling for his pistol so he can shoot me. He tears loose from the soldiers and rushes after me, and it is all I can do to keep the soldiers between him and me. As it is, it takes some fast moving on my part.

On one of my turns around the soldiers, who should I bump into but Miss Ross, looking as fresh and pretty as ever, although a little breathless. "Miss Ross!" I say, so happy that I forget Juan Terán. He catches up with me when I stop, but he takes one look at Miss Ross and he stops too. The general also takes a look at Miss Ross, and there are no firing squads in his eyes.

"Are you Miss Ross?" the general says.

"Yes," says Miss Ross, "I am Miss Ross."

A little man with a very thin and dark face steps out from behind Miss Ross. He is wearing a beret and boots, but he has no eyeglass like Rugoff. "And this," says Miss Ross, pointing to the little man, "is Mr. Schwartz of United States Films."

"Ha!" says Mr. Schwartz.

"United States Films, of which Mr. Schwartz is president," says Miss Ross, "has exclusive rights from the Mexican government to film the tribal dances of the Culomula Indians."

"Ha!" says Mr. Schwartz.

"These men," says Miss Ross, pointing to Rugoff and company, "are criminals. They run a fly-by-night movie company. They beat up two of our cameramen to keep them from their work. They kidnapped Mr. Schwartz's secretary, namely me."

"Ha!" says Mr. Schwartz.

Miss Ross points at Juan Terán. "They bribed this policeman to help them so they could illegally film dances when the Mexican government only gave permission to United States Films. Furthermore, this policeman so forgets himself as to makes passes at my person, which might have succeeded except for the timely and heroic intervention of Mr. Picadero here, who fought valiantly in defense of my honor."

"Ha! Ha!" say Mr. Schwartz and the general, so close together it sounds like they're laughing on the cooperative plan.

The general gives Rugoff and his buddies a dirty look and tells the lieutenant, "Put them in the truck." Then he turns to Juan Terán and says very sadly, "So you were taking bribes. How could you?" Juan Terán does not answer, so the general says, "How much? How much were you getting?"

Juan Terán tells him, "I"m not saying."

"Take him away!" says the general. "And give him plenty of room!"

"Come on! Move!" says the lieutenant. Juan Terán starts walking in the general direction of the truck, but very, very slow. "Faster! Faster!" says the lieutenant. But Juan Terán walks slower than ever, staying as close to the lieutenant as he can till he climbs into the truck. He's nobody's fool, that Juan Terán.

The general shakes his head sadly. "What a pity," he says, "what a pity." And he turns on his heels and walks away.

"With your imagination you would do well in Hollywood," says Mr. Schwartz to me back at the hotel, after the soldiers pick up Antonino and take him away. "If you ever decide to do so, look me up."

"Maybe I will," I say, looking at Miss Ross. She gives me a great big smile.

"Ha!" says Mr. Schwartz and he walks away, leaving us alone.

"Miss Ross," I say, "will you be very busy tonight?"

"No," she says, "and don't call me Miss Ross. Call me Beulah."

"Beulah," I tell her, "perhaps we can go for a walk under the stars tonight, and discuss Continental Solidarity."

"I think it's a good night for a movie," she says. She's nobody's fool either.

Just after supper that evening I'm all dressed up in fresh suntans as I come out of Pablo's house, where I'm staying. Pablo is sitting on the front doorstep. "Where you going, Johnny Picadero?" he says.

"To a movie," I tell him.

"With Miss Chili Con Carne?" he says.

"What do you mean Miss Chili Con Carne!" I ask in anger.

Pablo winks and gets out of the way so I can go by. "Sure," he says, "the American dish."

He thinks he's smart, that Pablo. Little does he know that María Ester has been down to the church, talking to the priest.